PRAISE FOR *THE ANIMALS IN THAT COUNTRY*

NAMED A "BEST BOOK OF THE YEAR" IN:

THE SUNDAY TIMES	*ABC*
SLATE	*THE SATURDAY PAPER*
THE GUARDIAN AUSTRALIA	*THE AGE/SYDNEY MORNING HERALD*
THE AUSTRALIAN	*BROADSHEET*

"McKay has a PhD in literary animal studies, and there is some stunning nature writing here ... Her writing about people, meanwhile, is filthy, fresh, and funny; this is prose on high alert, hackles up and teeth bared in every sentence. The novel becomes both a stirring attempt to inhabit other consciousnesses and a wry demonstration of the limits of our own language and empathy."
THE GUARDIAN

"What is so exciting about McKay's novel is the way she refuses both anthropocentrism and the philosophical position that non-human animals are inevitably alien to us ... [A]nother of the novel's strengths is that its thought experiment is conducted without sentimentality, though it is always characterised by humour and warmth ... *The Animals in That Country* will be the wildest ride you take all year."
THE SATURDAY PAPER

"Sly, sardonic ... takes Dr Dolittle's dream about talking to the animals, turns it into 'zooflu', and infects Australia with it."
THE SUNDAY TIMES

"A standout debut novel of 2020 ... Original, hugely entertaining, and superbly crafted, this is one heck of a road-trip novel, whose timing and insights into human behaviour in a crisis could not be more prescient."
READINGS MONTHLY

"An incredible achievement in storytelling, and absolutely worth your time ... one of the best Australian novels of the year."
BOOKTOPIA

"A wildly inventive dystopian adventure ... Both a hell of a ride and a revealing thought experiment about our place in the natural world."
SLATE

"As we grapple with a worldwide pandemic, Australian author McKay's novel is incredibly timely and feels all the more real for it ... filled with humour, optimism, and grace: a wild ride worth taking. An eye-opening glimpse into a world that's turned upside down and eventually becomes its own version of whole."
BOOKLIST

"McKay is a master at building tension through sparse, abrupt language that mirrors Jean's decades of alcohol abuse, and the excellent world-building is enhanced by the exquisite chemistry between Jean and her canine companion Sue. Visceral and discombobulating yet tender."
BOOKS+PUBLISHING

"What a pertinent time to be reading *The Animals in That Country* ... the responses and lockdown efforts of the government and authorities in this novel mirror the scenario unfolding around the coronavirus pandemic ... The writing is vibrant, energetic, and refreshing, and the narrative leaps off the page. Jean is an unexpected and unforgettable main protagonist. She's gutsy, raw, degenerate, and believable ... [A] wild, engaging ride."
THE AUSTRALIAN

"This is an absorbing and affecting book, and one to which I'm able to pay the highest compliment: that, in the days after finishing it, the world felt different to me, its animals not speaking but not silent either."
AUSTRALIAN BOOK REVIEW

"The genius stroke of *The Animals in That Country* is the preternatural 'body talk' of its animals ... an affecting book, one that gets remarkably close to the unknowable wildness of animal sentience."
THE AGE

"You know when you finish a book and you know that book will occupy your mind for a long time? *The Animals in That Country* is one of those. I haven't read a book like it and I don't think I will again ... The speech is almost poetic, full of metaphors and stunted syntax that (initially) confounds those hearing it ... This book is simultaneously laugh-out-loud funny and soul-crushingly depressing, in a way I can only describe as reminiscent of *Waiting for Godot*."
GOOD READING

"A wild and original ride of a read."
NEW IDEA

"Laura Jean McKay, an expert in animal communication, has her animals speaking in hallucinogenic haikus—it's disturbing but compelling, and somehow totally believable. I loved every bizarre, unexpected moment."
HERALD SUN

"Eerily prescient ... *The Animals in That Country* offers a timely take on the fraught ways animals feature in our lives, and how devastating it would be if we heard what they had to say."
ARTSHUB

"McKay has written a searing dystopian critique of our relationship with the natural world ... Through poetic projections of what the animals might say if they could, McKay highlights our limited capacity to communicate with language, and our human-centric view of the natural order ... Earthy, visceral, at-times obscene, and all-too-real, *The Animals in That Country* is nevertheless compelling and oddly buoying ... McKay is a masterful storyteller, and her talent truly shines in this quest for family and belonging."
PRIMER

"This is a game-changing, life-changing novel, the kind that comes along right when you need it, and compels you to listen to its terrifying poetry. Compulsively readable and yet also pushing the boundaries of what is possible in terms of language and narrative, this is a brilliant and disturbing book that will make you rethink everything you thought you understood about non-human animal sentience and agency. I don't think any reader can ever forget a voice like Sue the dingo's—wise and obscene in equal measure. A triumph."
CERIDWEN DOVEY, AUTHOR OF *ONLY THE ANIMALS*

"Engrossing, subversive, and surprisingly profound, *The Animals in That Country* does something only the best fiction can do: it has the power to skew the reader's perspective on the world. This story will stay with me for a long time, and its protagonist, Jean Bennett, will be with me even longer."
J.P. POMARE, AUTHOR OF *CALL ME EVIE*

"Deliriously strange, blackly hilarious, and completely exhilarating, *The Animals in That Country* is a wonderful debut from a genuinely original and exciting new voice."
JAMES BRADLEY, AUTHOR OF *GHOST SPECIES*

"Funny, original, and heartbreakingly timely. A love letter to family, communication, and 'battlers' everywhere—both human and non-human."
R.W.R. MCDONALD, AUTHOR OF *THE NANCYS*

"A taut exploration of loneliness and devotion, *The Animals in That Country* is rich with raw heartache and strange, carnal poetry."
SUE RAINSFORD, AUTHOR OF *FOLLOW ME TO GROUND*

"In this warm, wild, and irreverent debut, Laura Jean McKay takes us into the minds of animals to reveal the complexity of their lives. *The Animals in That Country* avoids the trap of anthropomorphism, showing instead the absurd, intense, and shifting bonds between humans and animals."
MIREILLE JUCHAU, AUTHOR OF *THE WORLD WITHOUT US*

"An imaginative tour de force—assured, compelling, and utterly original, this book will change how you see the world. Laura Jean McKay's powers are in full evidence here: her singular gift for empathy, enviable storytelling chops, and deftly elegant language will shift your frame of reference and leave you altered, in the best of ways. A unique and important work that explores the bond between humans and animals—and indeed throws the whole dividing line between us into doubt."
MEG MUNDELL, AUTHOR OF *THE TRESPASSERS*

"Weird, wonderful and strangely moving. I will be thinking about this strange book, about Jean and Sue, for a long, long time."
ELOISE GRILLS, AUTHOR OF *BIG BEAUTIFUL FEMALE THEORY*

"McKay is a master of voice-driven narrative. I never thought a substance-abusing grandmother was just who I needed to take me on an apocalyptic road trip—and that long after I gulped the book down, I'd be haunted by the words of a dingo called Sue."
SOFIJA STEFANOVIC, AUTHOR OF *MISS EX-YUGOSLAVIA*

Laura Jean McKay is the author of *The Animals in That Country* (Scribe 2020) — winner of The Arthur C. Clarke Award, The Victorian Prize for Literature, the ABIA Small Publishers Adult Book of the Year, and co-winner of the Aurealis Award for Best Science Fiction Novel 2021. Laura was the recipient of a New Zealand Society of Authors Waitangi Day Literary Honour in 2022. She is also the author of *Holiday in Cambodia* (Black Inc., 2013) and a lecturer in Creative Writing.

THE ANIMALS IN THAT COUNTRY

LAURA JEAN MCKAY

SCRIBE
Melbourne • London

Scribe Publications

18–20 Edward St, Brunswick, Victoria 3056, Australia
2 John St, Clerkenwell, London, WC1N 2ES, United Kingdom
3754 Pleasant Ave, Suite 100, Minneapolis, Minnesota 55409, USA

First published by Scribe 2020
This edition published 2022

Some lines and phrases in this book were published in other forms as poems
and short stories in *The North American Review*, *four*, and Grieve Anthology.
The Acknowledgement of Country on p. (xi) was adapted from text found
at the Australian Centre for International Justice: https://acij.org.au/about-
us/acknowledgement-of-country/. Quote on p. (xv) from Helen Garner's
'Red Dog: A Mutiny', first published in *The Monthly* (May 2012), used
with the kind permission of Helen Garner. Quote on p. (xv) from Margaret
Atwood's 'The Animals in That Country' reproduced with permission
of Curtis Brown Group Ltd, London, on behalf of Margaret Atwood.
Copyright © Margaret Atwood 1968.

Typeset in Garamond Premier by the publishers

Printed and bound in the UK by CPI Group (UK) Ltd, Croydon CR0 4YY

Scribe is committed to the sustainable use of natural resources and the
use of paper products made responsibly from those resources.

978 1 957363 16 5 (US edition)
978 1 922585 13 4 (Australian edition)
978 1 913348 85 4 (UK edition)
978 1 925693 92 8 (ebook)

Catalogue records for this book are available from the National Library of
Australia and the British Library.

scribepublications.com
scribepublications.com.au
scribepublications.co.uk

This book was written on the traditional lands of the Wurundjeri people and the Wathaurong people of the Kulin nation, as well as on the traditional lands of the Kungarakan people and the traditional lands of the Larrakia people. The author acknowledges the Traditional Owners and custodians of the lands on which she works, and pays respects to Indigenous Elders past, present, and emerging. Sovereignty has never been ceded. It always was and always will be Aboriginal land. The author recognises the past atrocities against Aboriginal and Torres Strait Islander peoples of this land and that Australia was founded on the genocide and dispossession of First Nations people. The author acknowledges that colonial structures and policies remain in place today and recognises the ongoing struggles of First Nations people in dismantling those structures. The struggle to seek justice, to remember and address this nation's past, is ongoing and is a necessary requirement for individual and collective healing.

The author supports the Uluru Statement from the Heart to achieve justice, recognition, and respect for First Nations people and a referendum to enshrine a First Nations Voice in the Constitution. The author gratefully accepts the invitation contained in the Statement to walk together with Aboriginal and Torres Strait Islander peoples in a movement for a better future.

For grandparents, especially my Ma and Nana.
And for animals — all of us.

In this country the animals
have the faces of
animals.

Margaret Atwood, "The Animals in That Country"

But I'm afraid that somewhere in his wild dog's heart, he secretly
despises me.

Helen Garner, "Red Dog: A Mutiny"

I can see the wild in her. She looks and acts like any dog. Plays, wags, stares into my eyes with her baby browns; does chasey, catch, begs for biscuits. Then the dusk comes and she lifts her neck and howls the saddest song in all the world, and there's that wild. Dingo, owl, night thing — that sound is a warning. Loneliest you'll hear. Wraps around your face, your sleep, your dreams. She's saying:

'Hey, *hey*. There's something coming.'

The rangers here are always telling me, don't talk like that. They say how dingoes are just establishing territory, checking on their pack. Dingo admin. But stand on the hot road that runs from the gift shop to the enclosures, and listen to the dingo in her cage call out to the packs on the other side of the fence. Tell me that's not special. Tell me she doesn't know something about the world that you and me haven't ever thought of.

ONE

Everyone wants to see the wild ones. Dingoes, crocodiles, stingrays, maybe a snake. That's what they ask for when they come to the Park. We've got wallaroos with striped faces and fat bums. We've got quolls and sugar gliders crouched in dark tree hollows. We've got a bird-of-prey show we do in the morning, before the kids get screamy and the dads get yelly. We've got water birds and a lizard that'll eat out of your hand. End of the day? Tourists just want to stare into the eye of a four-metre croc, hold a blonde python, then sit on the zoo train with the breeze in their faces while I chug them on down to the back of the Park, to where we keep the dingoes.

'Afternoon, ladies and gents, I'm Jean Bennett and I'm a guide here at the Park. Look to your left there and you'll see a little house in the bush. See those twigs? Blue plastic? Bowerbird made that to attract his sweetheart. Thinking of getting him to do up my place.'

Most days you'll find me driving the zoo train — sturdy old girl that runs on electrics. A few years back they talked about replacing us guides with an automated driver. A plastic man who sits in the driver's booth, moulded in the same ice-cream colours as the seats. Did a survey and nine out of ten visitors said they liked the real guides better — one even mentioned me. Management had to stick that in their pipes and smoke it.

3

At the dingo enclosure, I ease the train to a stop and turn on the radio. The tourists pile out and stretch their legs like it's the end of a road trip. Newsreader's talking about those poor suckers down south, where I'm from. Barely winter and they've already got the same flu, won't respond to antibiotics or anything. I remember that. Being sick, and sick to death of the rain and the cold.

From where I sit up here in the driver's carriage with my knees in the late sun, I can see the dingoes before the tourists do. At first, it looks like there's nothing in there. Just the fenced-in enclosure of low, scraggly trees, rocks, and piles of dirt. Then, movement. The tan earth grows, takes shape. The dingoes are long and the colour of sand. Manila folders. Their length buckles out at the ribs and then rises high — almost as broad as a greyhound but prettier. Long, curved legs and a feather-duster tail. A springiness. A mustiness. Dust and hair. The tourists edge forward. I've got three paper bags jammed in the glove box next to the medical supply kit. One has my sandwiches — I've got low blood pressure now. One sloshes. One has dog biscuits. The tourists practically skip over to the dingo enclosure with those biscuits.

'Dingoes!' they holler. 'Look, Jason! Dingoes!'

The dingoes bunch back by the fence, alarmed. We're not supposed to call them dogs. Not *Canis familiaris*, your normal domestic dog, but *Canis lupus dingo*: made out of wolf. All the info signs say they're more like cats. Tree-climbers. Hyper-agile fur-police. A whisper to us is normal talk to them, and they can hear a thing coming before the thing even knows it's on its way. Then, one of the tourists throws a biscuit and it's business time. Half of the chow ends up in the moat for the fish, half in the dingoes' bellies. Those tourists love feeding the dingoes, and the dingoes love getting fed. Mister, the big male, grinds his paws into the dirt and dips his head low, keeping his rear and tail high: the play position. Those tourists should be flattered. They laugh and say, 'Who's a good boy?' Kids nag Dad for a dingo pup until Dad looks like he might go drown himself in the moat. The other dingo boy, Buddy, springs up a sheer boulder and moves down the other side

4

like he's yellow water trickling downstream. The tourists lean in. A woman lifts her baby high to see. This is noted with alarm. Everything is. Dingoes aren't love-drugged or bored like your golden retriever. You can't pop them in a backyard and expect them to be there when you get home from work. They'll jump clean over your fence, be out ripping up chickens, finding a pack before you can blink.

The heat peaks late in the day. It won't rain for another four months and then it won't stop. They're still going on about that superflu on the radio. The sniffle and fever only lasts half a day with this one, but after that it's visions of pink elephants for they don't know how long. I turn it off. Fish flick through the lily pond, and the mozzies replace the tiny nipping midge bugs that give you great itchy welts on your arms and legs. The dingoes start parading about, prancing up the rocks like the rangers taught them and play-fighting as if it was the last battle on earth — dingo against dingo, canines to the death. Those three aren't even wild — half camp-mutt-kelpie-cross, half dingo and living the soft life. We found them cuddled like beans under a bit of tin. When the little female, Sue, opened her eyes to the world for the first time, there I was. She's a sleek and beautiful thing and hardly feral. Gets cuddles and chow every morning from the rangers, but I'm the one she looks for every day. They're one-person animals.

Even though these three are mixed, their colouring is dingo and they put on a good enough performance. Last year we brought in a male from another zoo — big, pure-bred dingo, a woolly-headed thing — hoping Sue would fall in love and we could spawn little show-star pups from them. She bit that male on the nose.

The tourists are bent over the rail like they're at the greatest event on this earth. A row of sweat-cracks. I take my moment. Pull out the hipflask from my paper bag and have a nip, just enough to coat my tongue. Then I get on the mic.

'That's right, ladies and gents, you're at the Park dingo enclosure. Dingoes only came here about 6,000 years ago. Might seem a long time ago to you and me, but people and animals have been here for a lot longer than that, haven't they. The ...' I check the little post-it note the logistics guy, Glen, has stuck on the dash. 'The Kungarakan people are the traditional owners here.'

The boy dingoes are hamming it up. Skulking low between the boulders, then scaling the tallest rock with long, low hops.

'You can see the two males there. One's saying: "Give me that chow, you mongrel."' The tourists titter. The vodka swills and burns in my gut. 'And then the other one says: "Hey, I'm no mongrel. I'm purebred." "You might have pure bread, but I got the last dog bickie!"'

Right on cue, big boy Mister shoves forward and gets the last of the chow, then takes off up the rocks to eat it alone. You wouldn't read about it. The tourists clap and push each other. Doesn't matter if they're fatsos from the other side of the world or greenies from up the city: they all like a show. I flick on the mic again.

'But you know who really runs things around here, ladies and gents? A woman, of course! Here's sweet Sue.' The tourists crane their necks as I look for her. Usually spot her right away even if she's in hiding, because we see one another, me and Sue.

'How many dingoes can you count in there, kids?'

'Two,' shouts one boy with a haircut like I don't know what his parents were thinking.

'Count again, kids. There's three dogs, right?'

The boy shakes his head. 'There's two.'

'Three. I see three,' says a girl. She might be my granddaughter in a couple of years. All hair and eyes and limbs. She makes me smile.

'What's three doing, sweetheart?'

The girl takes a breath of enormous importance. 'He's stuck. He's stuck. His —'

6

'His foot is stuck in the fence,' the boy shouts.

I climb down from the zoo train and go over. The two males are still rooting for biscuits, tails high, eyes on the crowd. Sue is over by the fence. The long luxurious scruff on the back of her neck, the white blaze on the caramel chest, white socks of her feet. She eyes me and moves forward, but she's pulled up short. I run back to the train and radio in, but the tourists are uneasy, and the sky is threatening dusk, and meanwhile Sue over there with her foot in a fence, no water or nothing.

Once upon a time I could hitch my leg over a barrier and get in to just about anywhere. Now, with all the tourists watching, I drag my old limbs over like I'm hauling two pig shanks up a hill. Slip down the sharp bank to the moat. The water comes up higher than I thought, fills my pants with lilies and gunk and soaks the paper bag in my pocket. The males start yapping and whining. An information booth above the pond says dingoes can't bark, they only howl, which is a fat load of bull when you're in there with them. Over by the rocks, Mister starts *woof woof*-ing and Buddy, who has never done anything without Mister doing it first, takes up yapping too. I don't look at the boys, though. My eyes are all for beautiful Sue. She sees me coming and tries to make a break for it. The sound of the fence twanging and her foot all tangled. Behind me, the tourists gasp and wave. One kid asks if I'm going to die. Has a point. Sue can be quiet and low on the nights when I take her for a walk because she's on my terms, out of her territory. Those evenings she dances for the lead, leans into me while we walk, like, 'Don't leave me! Don't leave me out here!' Now I'm in *her* space.

Dingoes wear their fur like feelings: all sleek and shiny when they're relaxed, a thick bank of heckle when they get wound up. Sue is wound up. Her fur so spiked it's like an echidna has taken up residence on her neck. She looks bigger, meaner — rough patches and teeth behind it all. Her foot is caught up in some wire that's been used to repair the fence but the wire has snared her knobbed heel, not dug in like I feared. Still no ranger in sight. All the tourists quiet now, watching me in the pit.

'Hello, Sue,' I say. 'Sweet, sweet Sue. They made a song about you, didn't they? I don't know the words. Here we go, Sue.' I toss her a few of the less soggy biscuits from my pocket. She pretends not to sniff them, keeps one eye on me, but her nose betrays her. 'Hello, Sue.' I keep my arms down — you have to do that. Arms up is dingo fighting language. Arms down and talking gently and scattering the kibble and saying, 'Hello, Sue. You're a sweet Sue' is: you're-safe-with-me. I edge closer. She bucks and the whole fence rattles. I'm sure she'll break away but the wire holds fast. Back in the crowd, the girl who looks just like Kimberly is staring down with moon eyes. She lifts her hand in a tiny thumbs up.

I take a breath, walk into Sue's space. I'm at the fence and pulling on that wire before either of us can shit ourselves. Don't think she can believe it. When I've nearly got her free, I give the wire a good sharp tug, and she turns and grabs my hand with her teeth. Her oversized fangs, yellow as her pelt, slice clean into my flesh. Canines don't need to bite hard to do damage. She's so fast that at first I don't feel it. Just the blow of being bitten. My little Sue: chomping on my hand. Then she's gone. I can't even feel the bite. Can't see where she went either. Is she limping or bleeding? She scrambles through the scrub for a while then appears, triumphant, on a rock on the other side of the enclosure — not hurt or nothing.

The tourists roar, and I feel it in my hand. A couple of the men — all brave and buff now — jump the fence to help the old girl out of the moat. I swear they almost carry me back to the zoo train. I'm a football hero, a crowd surfer. Once I get over myself, I find a bandage in the glove box kit and play the wound down. *I'm fine, thanks, ladies and gents, it's just a scratch, I can still drive.* The little girl is sitting up behind the driver's carriage.

'What did she say?' she asks. 'The dingo. What did she say to you?'

The whole lot of them is listening, so I get the mic out. Make my voice high and feathery, like a wild dog tail. 'She said, "Jeanie-girl: you're my best friend".'

They love that.

Back at the gift shop and café, Andy cranes his neck out of the Guide Manager's office and moves it this way and that like a snake-necked turtle. I waggle the paper bag of vodka at him. He widens his eyes: *not now*. Angela is in there with him. I change direction toward the staff toilets, just cleaned by Mona for the crowd that will stay on for the Thursday night shows. Didn't mind the cleaning job when it was mine, but Mona's better. Wash out the cut in the spotless sink and leave the bandage off so it can dry a bit. It's deep but not that deep, just a warning bite — Dingo Sue's way of saying, 'You're in my face, bitch'. What a thug. I grin at myself in the mirror, but I look thrown. My makeup has sweated off and my hair looks like it's been put on sideways. What was blonde this morning is now grey. Sweat patches under my arms. When I get out, Angela is waiting for me.

'Quick chat.'

She's got a beautiful figure, our Ange — even in her Park khakis — and you can see where Kimberly gets her hair: thick and brown, with a life of its own. All I can ever see of my boy Lee in Kim is her dark eyes, eyelashes you'd die for, and a pointy German nose from my ex's side of the family. God knows what attracted Ange to my son. Angela has degrees, a rich dad, ambitions. Lee was ten years too young for her and dressed like something dragged out of a hippie road show. Devilish handsome, though, like his mum. Ange was still a ranger when he came along jangling his bells. She had a sea eagle on her wrist and a gleam in her eye that turned out to be Kimberly.

Except for putting up a life-sized poster of a wedgetail eagle, Angela hasn't changed her office from that of her predecessor — a dopey young guy with a wandering crotch. There's two nice enough easy chairs by the window, and a little table for coffee, but Ange is

9

serious. I have to sit across from her at the desk. She gets her phone out.

'What's this?'

I peer into the thing. It's playing a video. The two male dingoes mucking about in the enclosure just like they did today, then it pans across. One of the tourists shuffles and blocks the bit where Sue has a go at my hand.

'That's me!'

'Yes, that's you. And they tagged the Park. What the hell, Jean?'

'Poor little Sue —'

'There are procedures in place, Jean. Rangers work with the animals. You're a guide. You haven't got your certificates, and you're not trained to handle them. What if she bit you?'

I keep my sore hand hidden. 'Nah. I've got a way with the dogs.'

'They're not dogs, and it's not good enough, Jean. This is actually serious. Did you see the news?'

'That flu.'

'I'm talking about the break-ins.'

I shrug.

'You need to be across it,' she says. 'These eco-terrorists ... or maybe they're animal liberationists, I don't know ...'

'Animal libs.' I nod at her. 'Greenies.'

'*Someone* is breaking into zoos and releasing animals down south.'

'Yeah? Sucks to be south.'

'Well, it affects us. The board'll lock us down by tomorrow if they get nervous. You in the dingo pit is the last thing we need. If it was anyone else —'

'Sue wouldn't let anyone else near her. It's me she loves.' I test my hand, flexing it under the desk. It doesn't hurt too much. Ange should be halfway through a speech about animals being incapable of love, but she's just staring up at her wedgetail poster. 'You're worried they'll close the Park for good.'

She turns back to her computer and clicks her mouse a few times.

'No. I don't know. I'm in a teleconference half of tomorrow about the releases. In the meantime, I need to give you a warning, to show the staff I mean it.'

'Alright, Ange.' She's so stiff and upright and official. Nails to the quick. Back when she worked with birds of prey, she had flight in her eyes. Eagle maiden with a leather glove, straight out of some medieval fantasy book. Look into those big browns now and there's just a bunch of paper clips and a digital calendar. Sometimes she gets so wound up I think she'll burst. I remember being thirty-five. You still think you've got a life ahead of you, then forty hits and your skin goes south and you're fucked. She doesn't know the half of it. I get up to go.

'Sit down, I haven't finished. I hear you've been doing the voices again.'

That'll be the rangers dobbing me in. Vanessa. Or Liu. Those toff-nosed hags won't say a peep to me, but they've got mouths on them.

'The tourists love it. So do the beasties —'

'It's against everything we stand for at the Park. Respect, accurate information —'

'Exploitation.' Idiot.

'What?'

'Just kidding. But I've read the manual, Ange —'

'Well, read it again. It's not Disney, here. It's not *The Lion King*. You know what it says in the manual?' I open my mouth, shut it again. 'It says people who anthropomorphise tend not to read cues, and people who don't read cues are dangerous. Dangerous to themselves, dangerous to the animals, and dangerous to visitors. I don't want danger here. I don't want to hear that you've been putting everyone and everything at risk.'

She waves me out. I stop by the eagle poster. 'You bringing Kim over tonight?'

She nods sharply, but her face softens a bit. It's Thursday. Kimberly always stays at mine on a Thursday. Ange goes up the city for a business masterclass, then does what single ladies do these days: hangs out with other women doing exercise, changing profile pics, and going to expensive bars. In my time you just went to a pub, got shitfaced, picked up. Never caught her with anyone, no matter how early I drop by the next day.

'Hey, Ange? I was wondering about my application. For the ranger job. You said —'

'Really, Jean? Really?'

I duck out. Rather get bitten by sweet Sue than face Angela, some days.

Out in the gift-shop courtyard, some of the rangers and guides are having an early dinner, alongside the tourists. The chip fryer broke down last week, but they've got it going again and the smell is terrific. My stomach groans. The rangers avoid my eye, but one of the tourists remembers me, calls out, 'It's the dingo lady! Hey, dingo lady, can we have a photo?' Andy pokes his head out and calls me into his office before I have the chance to pose. I go to lean in his doorway.

'Shut it. Jeez.'

I do and pull the hip flask from my pocket. We have a nip. The vodka is cheap. I prefer the sweet stuff — sherry, rum — but voddy is good for work. The Guide Manager's office is tiny, with high open windows. It houses a massive straw-coloured python called Blondie in a too-small cage. She's our showgirl, and when she's not wrapped around the neck of some tourist getting her photo taken, she lives a sad, safe life by Andy's desk. Reckon she's the only actual animal Andy sees most days. I watch her as Andy takes another shot. Will her to lift her diamond-shaped serpent head, but she doesn't.

Sufficiently boozed, Andy grimaces at me. 'Exciting day?'

'Woof. You could sell tickets.' I show him my hand.

'You got bit?' His voice is apologetic, like he's done the damage. He rummages through his drawers, but only turns out a ratty Band-Aid you wouldn't put near anyone. 'You got all your shots, right?'

I nod. 'She's a funny girl, that Sue. Hard to read. You don't know what she'll do.'

'You're not her keeper, Jean.'

'Thanks, I've already been read the riot. Anyway, you'd do the same.'

Andy grins. We both know he wouldn't. A group of rangers pass the office, their voices floating up through the windows.

'What's wrong with it, though? I don't see why the guides can't do animal work if they want it.' That's Casey. New girl, real sweetheart.

A laugh. Liu? Vanessa? 'They're not ... you'll learn. They're un-qualified. Jean can't even get her Cert Three Captive Animals. Angela only keeps her on because she looks after Kimberly. She's a grandma, for shitsake, not a ranger.'

They pass. I've twisted the flask lid so tight I can't get it unstuck.

Andy plucks at my brown guide shirt. 'You'll get your certificate, Jean. Give it another go.'

Too busy with the flask to answer. It gives. I take a slug and pass the dregs to Andy. Outside in the petting zoo, one of the wallaroo joeys hisses at another. Andy looks at the clock, winces.

'Fucking hell, Andy, why do you work here?'

He drains the flask. 'Perks.'

'You want me to feed them?'

'They like you. They don't like me.'

'You've just got to show them who's boss, mate. Don't treat them like they'll rip off your face. Talk to them. Didn't they teach you that in Cert Three?'

I grab for the bucket of special mix for the joeys, made up fresh this morning by the volunteers in the food store. Corn, apple, sweet potato, and pellets, with some vitamins and worming fluid sprinkled through. The bucket swings, makes me stumble a little. My gaze falls on Blondie. Her serpent's eye trained on me now, her regard for me simple: if I feed her, she might not try to eat my arm. Animals are straight up like that. It's people you have to watch out for.

TWO

I keep myself busy. Fridays, I take one of the only things my ex left me with for a spin up the highway for my weekly shop. Classic Holden HR sedan in royal blue, white top, only a bit of rust. Tammy Wynette in the tape player, howling about divorce. I pick up food and a couple of bottles too — some beers for my fridge, a cask of wine, whatever spirit is on sale, and a bottle of vodka, regardless the price. That's my big purchase. That and smokes. The newsagents sell cheap chop-chop under the counter, so if the vodka is expensive, I get a plastic bag of weedy-looking tobacco and spend the week coughing up a lung. Every now and then a special comes my way and so does a packet of menthol fresh. I'd smoke the whole pack in the parking lot, given the chance.

Any booze left by Thursday night when I have Kimberly gets put in the locking cupboard, and the air freshener comes out. I light a bit of incense that reminds me of Lee and, woof, the place cleans up nicely. I do too. It might be me going out instead of Angela. My hair is washed and blow-dried. Beaded top, bright slacks. The bite on my hand looking red so I rub in some antiseptic and put a cloth Band-Aid over the top — better late than never. I pop fish sticks in the oven, carrots and potatoes on the boil, tomato sauce on the table, and lay three plates out on the plastic cloth. The sun paints the park orange. Sue and the other dingoes call in the night. I want to howl along with them.

—

It's dark by the time Angela's car pulls up at my flat. I'm number three in a row of ranger units, neat as ribs on the edge of the Park. Ange carries Kimberly up the little path. The girl is already in her pyjamas, half asleep on her mum's shoulder and clutching Hello Bear. Me and my ex, Graham, gave her that teddy when she was born, not knowing the damned bear would have glow-in-the-dark peepers — it was creepy enough when there were two eyes, let alone just one like now. Angela lowers Kim to the couch then goes for a kiss on my cheek. I can hear her sniffing, checking for booze and smokes but it's Kimberly's night: I'm clean.

'Stay for some grub?' I've got the fish fingers and vegetables over on the table. The three plates. Ange would probably prefer a salad.

She glances out the door to her car. 'I'm late for class.'

'Boxing? No, swing dancing.'

I sit down, wave to a seat. Angela stays in the doorway.

'We're trying a new one. Pole dancing.'

My laugh comes out a cough. 'Pole dancing?'

'It's a form of exercise.'

'You're not going to meet a nice fella at pole dancing, Ange.'

She folds her arms. 'Which isn't your concern, is it?'

I shake my head. Pole dancing. 'I'd love for you to meet someone. Be happy.'

'You meet someone. I'm going to class.'

I follow her out the door. 'I've had my time. I'm happy as I am.'

Angela snorts and mutters, *yeah, right*, under her breath like she used to. She was a sassy bitch before she was with Lee.

As she's backing out, I jog after the car. 'Sorry about today, Ange.' She shrugs. 'But I want you to know I put in good work on my application for ranger. I typed it up and got Andy to check it. If I could be a ranger —'

'I'll look at it next week.'

'It's just that the others are saying you keep me on because of

Kimberly. But that can't be right, can it? I've got skills.'

She gives me a look you might offer a kicked dog. Gets the car into gear. Her bumper sticker reads, 'Ethical investments = global improvements'. Poor girl.

Back in the flat, Kimberly is awake and sitting up at the table with my ancient orange Dolphin torch, tucking into the whole serving dish of food. There's tomato sauce down her pyjama top. I pull it off her and sit down opposite to watch her eat.

'Walam in orner,' she tells me through a ball of mashed fish and saucy carrots.

'Beg yours?'

She swallows and pats the torch with a slimy hand. 'Wallamina was in the corner again. I turned her around.'

'You're a good little ranger.' I steal a fish finger.

'What happened to your hand, Granny?'

'Hungry kid bit me.' Take another fish finger. She squeals and hoards her grub. Shuffling starts up in the backyard at the ruckus. All the flats in the row back onto a section of the Park that's not used for show. That bush block has more rock-rats, wallabies, snakes, and birds in it than you'll ever see behind glass. Don't try to grow a garden. Those seeds'll be eaten before you can put them in the ground. I keep a few cages out the back for the animals I've rescued from around the place. Angela turns a blind eye long as they're quiet. Wallamina Wallaby's mum got hit by a car, and she must have been clunked on the head, too, because she's got funny ways: keeps getting caught in the corner of the backyard and not being able to turn around. I'm impatient — Kimberly is better with her, charming that crazy wallaby around the right way. There's a crow too — arrived one day in the backyard with a fucked-up beak that's coming good. Kimberly named her Princess Pie, and she acts the part, bouncing up and down when I come out with seed, making baby noises. She'll never grow up. She'll always be my silly baby crow. Then there's a little Arnhem rock-rat called Rocky. Hides in the corner of his cage most of the time, eyes shining.

Kimberly picks up the plate and licks the last of the sauce off, and I let her.

'Want to watch the news after your dinner?'

She laughs with red teeth. 'No.'

'You want to read a serious book, then. Wash the dishes. Talk about maths and sewing.'

'No!'

'I know, you can tell me everything about grade one.'

'Granny.'

'I've told you all my ideas.'

She wriggles on her chair.

'Alright, alright, you finish up there and wash your hands and teeth, and I might find us something else to do.'

The animal sanctuary is our big project. Sometimes we sit up too late on a school night, and I don't know how Kimberly doesn't fall asleep in class the next day. We mock up our ideas in a giant scrapbook — I collect magazines from the op shop and doctor's room, for the trees and buildings. We cut out animals from the Park brochures and from print-outs of the hundreds of pictures we take of Sue, or we draw them ourselves. Kimberly is especially good at that. Ever since she started school, she knows things, and quick. One Thursday, she could suddenly draw a wallaby — and that's hard. Next week, she knew all about the sorts of trees that should grow here. One day, she comes along saying we shouldn't have any cats because they eat the native animals. We had to talk about that for a while, decide on a separate mini sanctuary for cats.

'Granny, how are you going to pay?'

'What's that, my lovey?' I'm cutting out a difficult lizard with spikes and humps, my whole body focused on my hands not shaking.

'How are you going to pay for it?'

I look up. 'Are you doing budgets or something at school?'

She frowns. 'How to pay for things.'

'I think you might be ready, then.'

When she gets enthusiastic about something her eyes twinkle. I pull out the striped exercise book, where I keep my figures.

'You see this, Kim? This is where I write down everything I buy.' Not true. 'You can see here what I spend and what I save. Not enough, right? But I have a plan.'

'What is it?'

'Your mum's going to give me a better job as a ranger so I can work with animals all the time. Then I'll save more money and one day, when you're old enough to run it with me, I'll quit and we'll open the sanctuary.'

'We'll call it "Come to Kim and Granny's Animal Place".'

'We will. No animal turned away.'

A barking owl flaps over the row, yapping through the night sky. After a moment, the captive one they keep out the back of the nocturnal enclosure calls back. *Woof, woof.* Kim climbs onto my lap and sticks her thumb in her mouth.

'What's he saying?' she asks around it.

'Well, he's saying, "Have you seen some mice around here?"'

'What's the other one saying?'

'The other one's saying: "Yep, I ate them." "Drats," says the first one. "No, not rats, mice!"'

The nights can go on forever, but there's always something to listen to at the row — one of the young rangers next door fighting with their boyfriend, shooting on the TV, the creatures sliding around outside. Guides and support staff don't usually live on the Park estate. That sweet subsidised housing is for rangers, logistics, and the maintenance guys. It's also the honour I get for being Granny. All the units in the row look the same, except some have a second bedroom squashed next to the first. Mine is single as me. Walk up the short path to the front door and, hey diddly, you're in the lounge room. The dining bit beyond looks through a glass sliding door to the yard, the kitchen a nook around the corner. Then there's the bedroom with the en suite bathroom — a light that extracts as well. I've got a portable evaporative air cooler in the living area I can drag into my bedroom on a bad night when I'm lying there, sweating with heat and worrying that Rocky the rock-rat will get eaten. Make a noise outside the row, drag something along in the wind, and I'm out there with my ex's old unlicensed Colt. I keep it in the fridge. If it still works, it probably wouldn't do much more than scare the shit out of me and the animals.

I always want to wake Kimberly up to hear the creatures that only come out after she goes to bed. The wild rock-rats gnaw something outside the kitchen window. The wallabies edge forward with their short front legs. The owls, and sometimes, but not often, a magpie goose with its sobbing laugh. Sugar gliders crab at their enemies, the sound in their throats like gravel being shaken in a plastic container. Insects scream past. Can I hear pythons slithering over my roof, hunting the rock-rats that either didn't get caught or have such big families they're always replaced? Can I tell where the grubs and centipedes burrow into the ground? Can I hear the naughty cats on their velvet paws, sliding through the undergrowth, stalking the pythons that stalk the rats? It's like the old woman who swallowed the fly out there. Through it all tonight, the dingoes keep howling. They don't normally do that. Dingoes are dawn and dusk callers. I go to the window for a cheeky fag and listen to those ancient voices. Something's up. Maybe it's a good thing, like love or money. Maybe it's death. Fire. You don't have to ask them to know it's serious. Just imagine Sue's pursed lips and her courage, standing out there on the exposed rocks, calling it in. Makes me want to keep the ones I love close. Call Lee. Call my shithead ex. Lock the doors and hold on to Angela and Kim. Make them all safe with Granny Jean.

I don't like walking Kimberly up to the school in the mornings at the best of times. She's like a toothpick in checks, with a mop stuck on her head. The school is made of Besser blocks that could fall and crush her. She could get eaten up by one of the pythons that slide into the cool concrete play yard. If Kimberly stayed at home with me, I could teach her from books, and she'd get learning from life. Angela gets a particular colour up at the mention of homeschool. Red and green at the same time — a nasty look.

'Do you want to go to school today?' I ask Kim.

'Yeah.'

'Yeah?'

'We got an excursion to the crocodile park.'

'That'd be alright, I guess.'

'Crocodiles are reptiles. They're dinosaurs.' Kimberly's mouth is full of mashed Coco Pops. When we get outside the row, the two curlew birds that have been screaming bloody murder all morning fall quiet and watch us with their otherworldly eyes, edging away on backward legs. Kimberly isn't scared of crocodiles, but a murder bird is sent up from hell to creep the bejesus out of her of a morning.

'What are they saying?' she whispers, clutching at my hand with her hot little paw.

'They're saying ...' I clear my throat. *Hell, fire, guts and blood. Fuck the police.* A bird looking like that can't be saying anything nice. 'You really want to go to school today?' I ask again.

'The crocs.'

'It's my day off. What'll I do?'

This stumps her. She's never considered it. She's only six years old.

—

After I drop Kim off, I go back to the row to sit at the table with my mobile phone. Wait. Don't even have a smoke. I stare at the screen and realise it's not working. Give it a quick test with the home phone — it rings. The curlews start screaming, and it feels like they're killing me. My breath hurts. I need to pee, take the phone to the loo, pissing against the side of the bowl in case she calls and I can't hear it. I stand with the phone in the middle of the living room until it's slippery with my sweat. Turn on the evaporative, get the TV going on mute, perch on the couch. Whichever way I sit, my body hurts. I just know that Angela is dead and I'll have to look after Kimberly until she's grown up. The curlews give another bloody scream. I fling open the door. Back in the kitchen, the phone rings.

'All good?'

'Yep. She's at school.'

'Okay, have a good day.'

'You too. Ange —'

She hangs up.

It's ten in the morning and my hands are shaking. I can't get the damned cupboard door unlocked. I need to pee again, and I do, a tiny bit, just as the lock gives. The first bottle is cooking sherry, only a finger full. The burn washes my teeth and flames down my throat. It takes everything to stop before I drink too much. Too much, and I can't drive to the shops for more. Too much, and I'll get done by the cops and lose my licence again, and I can't exactly ask Angela to drive me to the bottle-o in her campervan. I've done some hard things. Watching Graham take off down the road and never come back is hard. Seeing my baby boy make all my mistakes and worse is hard. Dingo Sue up there in her enclosure with nowhere to run is hard. Sitting all alone on the floor of the kitchen, no one to talk to until tomorrow and not drinking that finger of sherry in the bottle is hardest. But I roll a smoke and suck it back and when I breathe out, it's better.

The big sexy engine of my Holden swallows the other sounds. My blood buzzes just enough to get me up the highway. 'Stand by Your Man' so fast on my wonky tape player it sounds like Tammy is on the good stuff. The man at the bottle shop is the old guy who hasn't worked there in months. When I put my beers and voddy on the counter, he sneaks a mini bottle of 'mudslide' for my nightcap and gives me a discount on a pack of menthol fresh.

'I could kiss your cheeks,' I say and, bless him, he blushes. On the way back I'm high, like I'm living the high life. Got my bottles and smokes, and someone left a magazine on a bench outside the super-market that looks to have some good pictures for the scrapbook. I roll down the window and light a menthol fresh. Wind comes through in hot blasts. The tape squeaks to its end and the radio cuts in. They're talking *blah blah*, then they start talking about animals.

'While releases of pets, farm, and laboratory animals across the south are being investigated for possible eco-terror connection,' says the announcer — a bit fuzzy, I tune her in — 'in many cases it is the owners and managers themselves who have let these animals go.' My ex is down south. Last I heard, my boy Lee was down there too, chas-ing dolphin migration and girls. Going around convincing people to let their cats and dogs go is exactly the sort of stunt he would pull. 'Some of the animals have been captured, but others have been hurt or killed and many are still missing.'

'Woof.' I turn it off, suck back. Another hot dry-season day with a wind.

Back home I knock down the rest of the sherry, slug the mudslide, then turn on the TV again. It's all over the news too — those people down south letting poor old Fluffy go. Cows wandering pie-eyed all over the roads. Some messed-up macaque monkeys, half shaven, refusing to be caught. Those newsreaders go over it a billion times, then BREAKING comes over the screen.

'Superflu has reached epidemic stage in only five days.'

I crank the volume. 'So, who died?' Feel my way to the fridge for a beer. 'Those soft-cock southerners.' I can say that, I'm from the south myself. People in cold-weather clothes milling like idiots in front of the camera. I see my ex, that big swarthy shape. It isn't him, of course. The news report is about the cities, and he tucked his tail back down to the country to take up with some teacher or nurse or something. I ring him anyway.

'Hello —'

'You don't sound too sick there, Graham Bennett. I was hoping —'

'You've called Graham Bennett and Amy Olivia. We're not home at the minute so just leave a message.'

I leave a message alright. I lay down the whole beer in the course of it and tell him I hope he dies of sick. What sort of name is Amy Olivia? Crack open the vodka and make a few other calls too. No one is ever home anymore. I leave long messages, explain about myself and the world. Try to get some internet knowledge but I've used up my data again. The TV news flashes between the flu and the animals. Fever-y people lined up outside the hospitals. CCTV footage of others breaking into the zoos and farms. Elephants and zebras. Pigs and chickens. That gets me going. I drag my guide shirt on and pour some vodka into my hip flask. It slops all over my fingers. You could set fire to my life. I'm pumped. Ange told me to get across it, and I'm all over it. The news keeps saying the same thing again and again — the animals, the flu, everywhere.

It's a bit of a slog up into the Park on foot. By the time I get to the car park, I'm woozy as shit. The heat is turned up full, the sun a fried egg above. I'm thirsty, nip under a pandanus tree for a shot of the vodka. The leaves stretch upwards, dead fingers for the sky. The heat of the booze doesn't help. I'm revived but in no hurry to get back out under that sun. A black, orange-footed bush fowl scratches the ground in the little bank of scrub by the car park — dashing low. A deep, dumpy body covered in black feathers with a green sheen. Little crest on its head. The bush fowl calls, *eh oh eh eh oh! eh eh eh eh oh!*

'Uh oh, uh oh, I've lost my keys. Better scratch around for them, aye?' This is my best bush turkey voice — a bit high, a bit busy. Some tourists come past, gaze in.

'She's lost her keys,' I tell them. 'She's saying, "Uh oh, uh oh. Lost my keys. Fucking luck." Sorry.' There's a little boy with them. Looks like he wants nothing more than to escape and hang out with me and the bush turkey. His mum and dad grab the boy like I might eat him, swing him away. The bush fowl leaves too.

'Get to work, Jean Bennett,' I mutter to myself. 'Bloody hell.'

The Guide Manager's office is locked and Angela's office empty. I see them all in the glass meeting room: guides, rangers, office staff, management. Put my hands to the door and lock eyes with Andy. He's sitting at the table where everyone's hunched over some document. Goes all rabbit in the headlights, waving me away. Fuck Andy. I go to push the heavy door but my guide shirt is buttoned up crooked. Forgot to put a bra on. The tiger tattoo on my left boob is crouched, ready to leap over to the other one. Stop halfway trying to fix it and stare down at the maze of buttons. There's no way unless the whole meeting room is ready to cop a flash of boob. Then I spot Ange. She's tearing at those nails with her teeth — going to rip a hole right through her hand next time someone so much as squeaks. For once that person isn't going to be me. I duck away before she notices, stumble off back down the road, parched as anything. After a while, Andy pulls up beside me in a Park ute. Pumps the aircon and puts on the country music station. Back at the row, he puts a brick of ice in the evaporative cooler, changes the dressing on my bitten hand and even puts me to bed. Pours us both whiskey and finds some sleeping pills in my bathroom. I take them all.

'Sometimes I think you *want* Angela to know what a booze hound you are,' Andy tells me.

I strike out at him. Miss. 'I can do whatever I want.'

'Yeah, but do it at home. What if Kim saw you?'

Stupid me starts crying. Andy shakes his head. 'Come on, drink up.'

I drink up. I drink up. I drink up.

This time, it's Andy's problem. We're on the floor of the lounge room, underpants around our ankles, doing not much. We've had a couple of misses and a couple of hits — both times when we've been too sober to appreciate it. Andy is as old as me and he was raised on vagina, but he prefers his men. Has this young guy up in the city now who works on the rigs and fawns over him when he's in town.

'You drank too much, you dickhead.' I'm shitfaced. The pills make the world marshmallow.

'Not that.' He struggles from under me.

'What, then?'

'You've got to stop calling. You've got to stop calling me up at nights.' It's true. I do call him. 'I'm not your husband. You can't leave messages like that. You don't say nice things. He doesn't like it.'

'Jealous.'

'You think?'

'Probably not.' I turn over, present my rump to him. I can see under the kitchen table and out the window into the yard, where Wallamina Wallaby is fixated on a log, trying to get over or around it. 'Come on.' I glance back at Andy. His forehead wrinkled and confused as his dick. 'You're too upset to fuck?'

He shrugs.

'You're a bag of gold. Even Wallamina out there can fuck, and she's half gone in the head.'

It's mean, but we laugh at the wallaby a bit, and it feels strange and good. Wallamina doesn't know. She stares at that log long after we've turned back to drinking.

'Here we go, here we go.' Andy flops in the lounge chair with a sarong across his balls and moves his thumb over his phone. I'm decent enough to pull up my undies and put my guide shirt back on. Cover the tiger on my tit. The news on the muted TV shows army guys and empty farms and stockyards. Beasts out where they shouldn't be, roaming all over the roads, getting into everything. Andy wipes his nose on his hand. 'Listen,' he tells me. 'It says here the people who let the animals out have all had that flu.' He blinks at me. We're sobering up. I pull the last two beers from the fridge-cum-safe. I keep a wad of rainy-day cash alongside the empty revolver in a cooler bag on the very top shelf. Andy keeps reading. 'Says here the normal flu symptoms — your blocked nose, your fever — last a few hours, day at most —'

'I know all this.'

'But once they're gone, you see things. Visual, auditory, olfactory, gustatory. What's that?'

I hand him a cold one. 'I don't know. Look it up.'

'Anyway, it says ...' He shifts to rearrange himself and I look over his body. Hairy and stringy, skin stretched over his big belly. Once, Kimberly made a papier-mâché pig at school by layering gluey newspaper over a balloon. I saw the other kid's creations — lumpy things. Kimberly had sculpted hers smooth and very round, like Andy's gut. He clicks his fingers to get my attention. 'It *says* it wasn't terrorism. Everyone who did it is just hallucinating.'

'Hallucinating what?' Andy doesn't answer. 'What's it say about the cure?'

'Nothing.'

'Has anyone died from it?'

'No.'

'How long's the trip last?'

Andy's phone starts pinging. He waves it at me. 'My man.'

'What's he want?'

'Dick pic.'

'Can your phone take a photo of something that small?'

Now that the booze is gone, I'm sick of him. His big body on my couch. Arsehole wiping over the cushions. I open the glass door to the backyard to get some air. The animals clamour at the screen. Wallamina kicks and the crow bounces, flapping his good wing. The baby rock-rat sleeps on.

'He doesn't really want a dick pic,' Andy calls, apologetic. He thinks *I'm* jealous. I hide my grin in my shoulder. 'He's only coming back this weekend because of the outbreak. They want all the riggers back on land. Something about whales — I don't get it.' He goes back to his phone. The weekend, the weekend, the endless bloody weekend. I work weekends, but only the days. Ange and Kim on endless 'play dates' in the city. The hot little flat. I've almost run out of booze for the week. It's all swilling around in Andy's stomach — impossible to get at — and he doesn't even seem that pissed. I tell him to get out. He doesn't move fast enough. I throw my keys, a boot, an empty can. The animals startle away from the door. Andy is more pissed than I thought. He can't drive. He pulls his pants over his bare bum and stumbles off down the road to hitch a lift up the highway. Maybe he'll get hit, or kidnapped and killed. I don't give a shit. On the TV, the Prime Minister sits there like a lump of mashed potato, saying, 'To maintain order, increase security, and provide essential services to families and ordinary citizens who are affected.'

The light claws at the sky, loses its grip. I get out the scrapbook and the budget book. Look at them both. Kimberly is so good at colouring now she can stay between the lines. She got so mad one time when I used the wrong colour for a hooded parrot's breast.

'That's wrong, Granny. Wrong. You've done it all wrong.'

I stare at the page. I have done it all wrong. A hooded parrot has a turquoise breast and I made it dark green. I rip it out, then realise there's a picture of the cattery on the other side that me and Kim spent three nights on. It's a double-page spread, with a bit for the cats to sleep in, a bit for their feed, plus a play centre, with scratching posts, balls of wool, and paper bags for them to sit in. Cats like that. Now I've fucked it up. There must be 700 rolls of clear sticky tape in this flat, but I can only find thick grey gaffer tape. Only when it sits, bubbled and wonky, through the middle of the cattery do I realise I should have taped it on the other side with the parrot, to give the cattery a clean line. I pull it off. A layer of the paper comes away and the play centre is ripped in half.

THREE

I'm up before dawn, my head like the monster in an alien movie
— skin ripped back, slimy teeth protruding, and when I open my
mouth, another monster comes out. The bite that Sue gave me is
making itself known in angry red. The antiseptic smells like booze.
Everything smells like booze. If I drank some, I'd feel alright. The
bottle feels cool next to the heat coming off me. Barely have it
in me to push that little tinkle of whiskey back into the locking
cupboard and drag myself away. Me and Andy had quite a party.
There are beer bottles and ciggie butts on almost everything.
Kimberly's box of Coco Pops upturned on the couch. Andy's giant
underpants take up half the floor. I drink my instant and take a
can of open baked beans from the fridge and finish it. Peel open a
tin of cat food and retch as it slops out into a dish for Princess Pie
and Rocky. This is a treat for them — usually they get grubs and
seeds and whatever else I can scab from the food store. Wallamina
likes to be hand fed, and she always looks down at the handfuls of
special mix I shove in her bowl, like, 'Are you fucking kidding me?'
My guide shirt stinks. I like to put on extra makeup for the weekend shifts so we can all feel special. Today it's more like grouting.
There are holes in me.

When I can stand without wobbling, I walk. The row behind

me a dusty dream. I started out in one of the bigger houses hidden in the dense jungles of the Park, where Angela and Kimberly live now. Sometimes on a really hot or busy day, or if I've had one too many, I forget I don't live there anymore. My feet walk me right up into the Park grounds where I lived with Graham, and Lee when he came home, in a house that looked over the bushy rear of the dingo enclosure. Back then, Graham did the Park's maintenance and I had a cleaning job doing the toilets, the café, the gift shop, and all the offices. Used to read the manager's emails for a laugh. I know exactly how much shit the Park was in before our Ange took over. It was a good life after being on the road so long. Me and Graham grew a bit of sneaky marijuana in the roof of the house. He could fix anything that didn't have a heart, and our Lee dropped out of high school and went up to the city to play bongo drums and pick up backpackers. He'd come down to the Park on the weekends and test his charms out on the rangers — until he got Angela in trouble and it all went balls up. We battled it out until Kimberly was born, then Graham fucked off back down south and Lee followed him. Me back in the workforce as a guide and moved out to the row. Ange, a single parent with a good head on her shoulders. We do alright.

The estate is quieter than usual today: no Park vans zooming around, no busloads of weekend tourists following their guts and their guides from one enclosure to another. Birds call the morning in, but the heat is already closing its fingers over the north. I move slowly up that lush, bamboo-edged driveway, the air around my legs like bath water, and don't see another soul. The office building looks dead, a single bare bulb throwing a ghostly glow over the door. Up in the trees, leaves rattle like bones. Birdlife shivers and hoots, the dawn chorus louder and louder, but when the sun bursts over the canopy everything goes quiet. No waft of second breakfast cooked up by the sweethearts in the café. No Mona popping new toilet rolls in the bathroom dispensers. The lights are off, the gift shop locked and empty. I gasp water from the fountain in the courtyard and try the offices. Andy hasn't shown up yet. His door is unlocked, Blondie the snake in her cage, the desk empty. When I move to leave, Blondie makes a snarling noise. Never heard that before. Get up closer to see Andy's foot sticking out from under the desk. Shame job. He must've stayed the night, snoring like a lawnmower. Voices from the meeting room up the corridor. Yesterday rushes at me. I have trouble swallowing it back down. Steady myself on the doorjamb and tap, ladylike, on the glass door. The management team — Angela, Glen — glance up from the table. Some of the office staff are there and the finance guy, Trent — I call him Trench because you just want to dig a trench and bury yourself when you see him coming. Ange doesn't shout or throw anything so I push the door a crack. They look worse off than me. Angela's hair is a dust storm. Sweat stains in her pits. Trench has loosened his tie for once and the buttons on his shirt are undone — not a good look. Glen's beautiful eyes are down by his chin. Glen's from out East, where his family have been for tens of thousands of years. Andy said he did a talk on it with pictures. Round rocks on the whitest sand Andy ever saw. Mangroves poking their long fingers into the sea. Carpet snakes making spirals on themselves. Now he's here, at a table strewn with documents, coffee cups, and chip packets from the vending machine in the courtyard.

'You been at it all night?'

'What is it, Jean?'

'I'm after the keys. Want to get into the cleaning cupboard and give the zoo trains a good going over before eight.'

They all stare. I feel woozy as shit. Grip a chair back.

Trench manages a half smile. 'Do you even know what's happening? The whole place has shut down —'

'Is that the correct way to disseminate information?' Ange snaps at him.

He taps his pen. 'Just saying.'

She turns to me. 'I should have called you, Jean. They've confirmed that we can't open this weekend and maybe into next week, while they assess the situation. We've got poisonous and dangerous stock. The crocodile. Some of the staff have chosen to go home, and some are staying with friends. I should have called. I just ...'

I move some saliva around my dry mouth. Don't even know where my phone is. 'What situation?'

'The break-ins. Zooflu.'

'What's that?'

Trench starts chuckling in earnest. I might spew on myself.

'You better find somewhere to stay, Jean,' says Glen. 'Where's your son live now? You got some friends up in the city? They're predicting a week, I'd say more likely two or three.'

'The hell I'm leaving.' I slam my hand on a thick pile of papers — make my point. One of the documents sticks to my sweaty palm. 'This is where I *live*. I don't get sick. I'm tough as shit. And what about Kimberly?'

'What about her?'

'She needs me. We need each other. We're fucking family.' I shake my hand, can't get that piece of paper off. Got sticky coffee on it or something. Trench snorts at this, and the office ladies have a laugh. The whole point of this exercise, I remember now, was to be normal and sober and act the part. I peel the paper off and shove it in my pocket.

Angela is biting her nails. 'Half my staff is gone and the other half is glued to the internet.' Peers at me. 'I need to know whether I've got you. Kimberly needs to know.'

'You've got me. You've got me one hundred per cent. Where is she?'

Angela nods at the meeting table. 'She's sleeping under there. Leave her. Go home, get up to date, keep your phone charged, *please,* and I'll call you. When she's up.'

'I'll keep my phone on all the time, Ange. I won't even call anyone else. I'll —'

'Jean. Just ... Can you just hold still for half a second?'

—

I can do that. I can do that. I clean my place while I watch the news. Anything left in the bottles goes down the sink. Rat out all my hiding places and pour out the lot. The news gets me hooked — pictures of pink-eyed southerners staring at animals. Horses, cows, pet rabbits. Those people look nuts, crying out their conjunctivitis eyes, laughing sometimes, hiding in their houses — poor old Snowy left outside in the rain, scratching at the door but they won't let the animals back in. Breaks your heart. Abandoned pets everywhere. Suicides.

'People topping themselves over a dog?' I ask that TV. Go to change my stinky clothes and find that piece of paper mangled in my pocket. Nothing useful, just 'Zoanthropathy: preliminary report' in bold.

I go out the back to show it to Rocky rock-rat.

'What do you think of this, hey?'

Rocky glares at me from his cage in the yard. The thanks I get for rescuing him from 'the sanctuary'. You'd never know it if you were a tourist, but there's pretty much a second zoo's worth of animals kept behind the food store, out of the public eye. It's more like death row. All those furry, feathered, and scaly inmates waiting for their fate. Too many rock-rats. People find them in their houses or half splattered on the road and bring them in. If it's rare or an uninjured baby, it might make it out of death row alive to be put on exhibition. If it's common as muck, we ask around the other zoos to see if it's wanted. If it's too sick, or old and broken and not good enough to show, we put it down in the little gas chamber. Sounds bad but it's just the business — costs a lot to keep the mob-loads of wallabies, pythons, ducks, and lizards people bring in every other day. That's not all. We breed mice as live-stock too, in the rooms just off the food store. Lab mice. They live a funny life of breeding and dying so we can feed the birds of prey and the snakes. At least they live and die for something.

A wind kicks up the dust at the road edge. My cheap-arse phone plan kicks over with the new month so I'm back on the socials. The whole country's lit up with the animals and the flu. It's the antivaxxers. It's the government. *PLEASE be a RESPONSIBLE pet owner and keep your dogs and cats LOCKED up for their own protection. Has anyone had trouble getting garlic?* Some city chick is all up herself about livestock, reckons they pollute the water and our food, making us weak. Can't ignore that.

'You southerners,' I type my reply to Anna Smith, 'with your cheese and your lattes. Where do you think the milk comes from?'

'I drink soy milk, thanks.'

'Thanks for nothing,' I write back. 'Soy is what caused this problem.' I read that in a forum post — too much soy production giving us extra boobs, making us susceptible to superflu. Can't find who said it now. In the meantime other people get on there like soy is their best friend.

'Don't need conspiracy theorists like you in times like this.'

'Check your facts and your privilege.'

'Go back to scrapbooking, dear.'

'At least,' I type, 'I'm not a fucking bitch.' That shuts them up. Head to another thread to see how they're using ticks as military bio-weapons, but I'm blocked for violation of this, that, and the other. So much for free speech. Find that Anna on another site and go at her again.

'Maybe if you ate the things you're supposed to eat we wouldn't be having this problem,' I tell her.

'Uh, the flu isn't from eating, it's a virus (don't know why I'm bothering tbh).'

'What's with all the cow shit, then?' I write back. Then, 'Ha ha. Cow shit. You heard of zooflu?'

'I'm doing a degree in bio-chem so um yes. It's zoanthropathy.'

She posts a link to a page for scientists. Then blocks me again, the snowflake.

'Zoanthropathy,' the link says, '(from Greek: *zóo*, "animal", *anthroponis*, "human", *pathy*, "disorder"), commonly known as "zooflu", is an H7N7 subtype of influenza A virus, a genus of orthomyxovirus, the viruses responsible for influenza. It is spread through saliva.'

'Bloody Andy.'

'The strain known as zoanthropathy affects cognition in humans, and it is believed that enhanced communication between humans and nonhuman animals is possible. Zoanthropathy is hosted and spread by humans.'

I scroll back. *Enhanced communication between humans and nonhuman animals.* What the actual.

'The disease is very high in morbidity and very low in mortality. Infected humans appear able to communicate (encode) and translate (decode) previously unrecognisable non-verbal communications via major senses such as sight, smell, taste, touch, and sound with nonhuman animals. Zooflu is also referred to as "talking animal disease".'

'Talking. Animal. Disease.' Try to share the hell out of that but I'm pretty much banned from the internet. Talking to myself.

Car outside the row. Ange is at the door to drop Kim off. My girl runs inside and tries to get the cartoons on the telly, but there's news on every channel. She throws herself into my brown couch cushions and wails.

'She's been like that since she woke up,' says Ange. Lowers her voice. 'School's been cancelled next week.'

'It has not! We're feeding the chickens on Monday and it has not!' Kim screams into the cushions until she has no more angry. Watches me through a gap in her damp hair while I get out an old DVD of *The Lion King*. Keep one eye on Ange in case she sniffs out the booze I chucked down the drain. She doesn't seem to notice. Talks the whole time I set up the movie.

'We've got a food supply truck coming in tonight, and not enough people to do the feeding. I've got enough on my plate with the staff and the birds of prey —'

I look up from the player. 'I could do the feed, Ange. Throw some kibble and bones over the fence to the dingoes and that.' She narrows her eyes. 'I wouldn't even have to go inside the enclosures.'

'This wouldn't be a permanent thing, Jean. Just until we're allowed to open again. The dingoes, the whiprays, and the mice.'

'That's what I was thinking. I can do the feed on death row too, if you want.'

'Please call it "the sanctuary".'

'Sure. Kim can help me out if she's off school. We can be partners, Kimbo, how about that?' Kimberly pretends not to hear me. 'Any more updates on this disease?' I ask Ange. 'Zoanthropathy, right? Zooflu?'

Ange glances at Kim. 'What do you know about it?' Not telling my granddaughter useful shit from the internet is one of Angela's hard and fast rules. I grab the crumpled bit of paper instead. 'From the meeting. Something about animals. This flu. They're connected, aren't they.'

Now it's Angela's turn to play deaf. She gets a phone call and has an excuse to take off. I join Kim on the couch. The Lion King has just been born. Kimberly mouths silently along to the song — cheeks ruined from all the crying.

When the song is finished, she asks, 'Are you a ranger now, Granny?'

'Guess I am. We both are. We're in charge of all the dogs, the rays. And now it seems like people can talk to them for real.'

She wriggles closer to me without taking her eyes off the telly. 'We already talk to them.'

In the movie, the animals are chatting away to each other, arguing and dishing out wisdoms.

'Granny. I said *we* already talk to them.'

I flatten the bit of paper out on my lap. Zoanthropathy.

'I know what we'll do, we'll call your daddy. He lives down south, doesn't he? Maybe he can tell us what's going on down there.'

'He forgot my birthday.'

'That'd be Lee.' I find my phone on the floor of the bathroom and dial Lee. It rings and rings, then his soft voice comes through.

'Namaste,' he says. 'It sucks that I've missed you, but I'll get in touch soon as I'm back on the grid.'

'Hi darl, it's Mum and ... come on, Kim.' She shakes her head, blushing. 'Well, it's us and we're up here at the Park, all shut in. Hoping you're okay, with the flu and everything. Darl, if you could get back to me. You know, about the animals. Okay, love you. Bye. Say bye, Kim?' She covers her face. I gather her up in my arms and rock her. My bitten hand smarts when I hold her close.

'What would you say if you could talk to animals?'

'I can, I already told you.' She tries to wriggle from my grip. I hold her tight.

'If they could really, properly talk back.'

She giggles, goes heavy in my arms like when she was months old and milk drunk. 'I'd say ... I'd say, "Hello, are you my friend?"'

'"Hello, are you my friend?" Well, I've got a secret for you, Miss Kimberly Russo.'

She digs her sharp little nails into my skin. 'What is it?'

'This flu means people can talk to animals.'

Her head shoots up. 'I want the flu, Granny. Don't you?'

'Grown-ups don't wish they had diseases, and neither should you.'

'But don't you?'

Outside, Wallamina and Princess Pie are nose and beak to the sliding door, trying to press their way through. Eyes shining.

''Course I bloody do.'

FOUR

Flu galloping up the country toward us. People down south letting those animals loose or killing them. Me, Kim, Ange, and the staff that haven't left are tucked up in the Park, fit as fiddles, surrounded by animals with nothing but a chirp and a snarl between them. Ange and the managers aren't saying shit about the talking part of the disease, but everyone else is. Everyone's whispering. Half the logistics staff get the fear and piss off. You expect it from the wusses in the office and some of the rangers, but I'm surprised when the cleaners and the hard nuts who cook in the café untie their aprons and pull off their hair nets.

'I'm not hanging around here,' Mona tells me, 'for some crummy crocodile to start talking.' She hangs her bingo wing out the window of her little car. 'I've got grandkids home from school with better things to say than that lot. You should pack up too.'

'Got my family here.'

'Ange?' She harrumphs. 'You take care, Jean.'

The gate opens and closes with more cars leaving and only the food trucks coming in, carrying supplies for the animals and some for us leftover staff to cook at the café. They lock the gates and put the 'Park closed' sign out. Chains on everything, perimeter fence electrified all the way around. That fence has only ever been turned on a handful of times for escapes. Can't do much about an octopus or a snake — they get out more times than anyone would like to know — but there's nothing like an electrified fence to stop a rogue dingo or kangaroo. The fence gives off a whine high as tinnitus. We go around shaking our heads.

The phones start ringing and don't stop. Angela has her ear stuck to her mobile twenty-four seven — talking to the government, the media, the other parks. Turn on the telly or the radio and there's Angela, all calm, saying, *no, we're not opening, no, we don't know anything about a spotted quoll talking, our job is protecting endangered species.* Makes me proud to hear her say that. She must want to talk to those animals much as anyone but there's a job to do. Me and Kimberly have responsibilities now. It's our scrapbook sanctuary come to life. *Come to Kim and Granny's Animal Place.* Our job is to feed the whiprays, the dingoes, the mice being bred in the food store, and the animals on death row. Glen has ordered pouches of proper tobacco with the food and doesn't know when there'll be more. We all ration. I could have stretched mine to seven days but don't last five. See someone standing outside an enclosure sucking back smoke these days and you leave them to it — that might be their last fag for the day. My face so tight in withdrawal you could play me like a guitar, but I wouldn't sound so good.

By the weekend, none of the volunteers are showing up so we have to prep the chow for the animals ourselves. Feeding charts on the wall of the massive storeroom. It's edged with big fridges and freezers, surgery off to one side, mouse breeding centre and gassing room off to the other. I've forgotten my glasses so Kim gets to practise her reading. Takes a while. One bucket of dog kibble for the dingoes with three greasy bones from the fridge on top; one bucket of little fish with some handfuls of worms for the whiprays. It says yabbies too, but we can't find them in the Styrofoam boxes lined up neat as coffins in the fridge.

'The rays can go on a diet,' I tell Kim. She's frowning over the words for the mouse food so we get that ready too: one scoop of special mix looks like fancy muesli, some lab blocks to give them their mousey vitamins, and some food scraps being kept cool in the fridge — apple, carrot, bits of bread. I score us a couple of ranger shirts and an extra walkie-talkie from the store, and we swagger around like we're all that.

'Ranger Kim, Ranger Kim, we need some kibble over here stat.'

'Roger, Ranger Granny.'

I don't feel like a fag or a drink so much when I've got a pail of feed in my grip. We head out into the heat, along the short bush track to the café station. Kimberly tries to grab my free hand, but the bite Sue gave me is getting worse — the skin around it bloated like a dead thing in the sun.

I pop Kimberly up behind the driver's seat in the first row of the old zoo train, where she sits holding the buckets of feed like they're the nuclear codes. It all seems lush from the train until we get a closer look down those tracks. Bins spewing — raided by wild animals, and the rubbish dragged off into the bush. No one has been out with the blower to clear the pandanus leaves. A gate with a 'Keep closed' sign hangs open — fuck knows what got out in the night. You think a wildlife park is for animals, but a park without the people in it is like a pool without water. The roads too wide, the signs too bossy, the toilet blocks dark and empty. The gift shop is closed up too. Over the fence, the school still plays its pop song bell but with no kiddies to obey it. Strains of music drift through the trees like mist. Kim cranes her neck at the sound. Her and the animals — little freaks that respond to bells and food. We pass Casey, Liu, and Doug, run off their feet with the rest of the enclosures. They share exhausted grins with us and nod, ranger to ranger. Even Andy is getting his feet dirty in the wallaroo section, scattering feed with one hand and arguing with his fella on his phone with the other, saying how he can't come home, he's got a job to do. That young guy must be spitting chips in the city. Not so keen on Andy being Crocodile Dundee now.

I get on the mic, let it call out through the forest and along the empty roads.

'Good morning, ladies and ... well, just one little lady here.' Kimberly drags her eyes from the school to smile and wave. 'Did you know that the Park has the largest collection of native species in the north?' I clock Kimberly, she's nodding her head — she knows everything. The dingoes start up again with their godforsaken sound. My voice joins them. 'You can discover the creatures of the creeks and seas, the birds and mammals of the trees, and the beasts of the grasslands, all in the one park.' We jump down from the train and head up the paths toward the freshwater whiprays. They look like flaps of rubber in the shallow, muddy pools. Usually, school groups tromp through here a billion times a week to feed them. Now, in the softly howling quiet, Kimberly has the place to herself. She lowers the fish into the water, palms up, so the whiprays can ripple in and eat them with their underneath mouths. They're fish, but their black eyes watch you through the tops of their heads — kind, soft as dogs. Labradors of the river.

Kim stares at them, eyes black and gentle too. 'What do you think they're saying?'

I make my voice deep and goofy for them. '"Fanx. Fanx, you guys. You got more fish?"'

Kimberly gives a half smile. Tells them, 'We got no more fish,' but her heart's not in it.

The closer we get to the dingo enclosure, the louder the howls — hollow through the brush. Only midday and they're already calling. They know something's up. I stop the train and we swing our buckets down the sandy path between the trees to the side gate, light green through the sunshade of leaves. The dingo family prances along the fence. They're used to being fed through this gate by a young woman who's probably back in the city. Now it's me and Kim out the front in our ranger shirts. The dogs' bodies are electric. I hurl a defrosted bone into the enclosure. They pounce and wrestle with it, as though it's still alive. Sue gets the bone to herself and carries it with sprightly steps to the other side of the yard. The boys know not to mess with her once she's got her way. She can see us watching. Her tail wags at the attention. She attacks her bone with extra vigour — she's been taught to show off. We go to move away, and she looks at us with her pale, ancient amber eyes. I want to think of a funny voice to make Kimberly laugh, but I'm lost in Sue's peepers. Swirling, empty. Full as marbles.

Back at the food store, we grab the mouse chow and head into the rooms at the rear. Stinks to high heaven in there — a wet, wheaten stench. Plagues of mice propped up on their fat arses, staring from a dozen straw-filled cages. Their noses go off like little motors. They tweet. Some of the cages have babies — small pink slug-like things that wriggle around a big mama mouse. Kimberly thinks they're cute. I think about how their free cousins get into my kitchen and eat my bread.

'They're so pretty, aren't they, Granny?'

'They're pretty fat.'

'That's the mum one. What's a lady mouse called? Its proper name?'

'I don't know. Sheila?'

We open the cages, give them their pellets and scraps — the mums and dads and babies, the teenagers, who always look like they've had their heads in the water dish. Most of them will be gassed soon, fed to our show creatures. Their beady red eyes take us in when we put more straw in their cages. Their white whiskers twitch like the clappers.

Angela is frowning at me before I even reach the storeroom, but when I give her the thumbs up, her face melts a little. All the animals got fed in record time because me and Kimbo are such a crack team. Ange has ranger Doug check our feeding records anyway, to make sure none of the animals cark it in the night. Apart from feeding those fat mice too much, it's all good. We're practically certified rangers now.

'I'm all over it, Ange,' I tell her. 'Leave it to me.'

She asks if I'll look after Kim again tonight. There's not much food in my fridge so we go over to Angela's house to lush out on the big couch. When Kim falls asleep there, I check out Ange's liquor situation. She's got fancy bourbon and gin. I touch the cool glass bottles but don't open them even for a sniff. I'm a new woman now. Go for some chilly white wine — just a glass or two. Doze off on the couch next to Kim and wake when Ange gets in.

'I'll go,' I croak at her.

'No, it's okay. You can stay.' She never lets me stay. 'I'll get you a blanket.'

So me and Kimberly stay snuggled up on the couch and in the morning, before Ange is even up, we eat toast with honey on the deck — there's no butter or marg. I've washed our ranger shirts — we can practically watch them dry in the sun. Up in the trees the birdlife glistens, shivers, hoots a dawn chorus. We make up voices for them and have them hurl insults until they get so loud we can't hear each other.

Kimberly is just belting out with, 'At least my tail doesn't look like a zombie did a wee on it!' when all the birds go quiet at once. Show over. Behind us, Angela bursts out laughing. Kimberly sticks her thumb in her mouth with embarrassment.

'This is a bit like when you used to live in the big house,' says Ange, coming to sit on one of the rickety outdoor chairs. 'Before I was pregnant. You used to make those epic breakfasts on the barbecue.' I grunt. It was Graham who cooked them. Can practically taste the bacon.

'Lee was still around too,' I say. Now it's Angela's turn to grunt. 'You were a beautiful-looking couple.'

43

'Well. Something good came out of it.' She grabs Kimberly and cuddles her — all that hair making them one big bush.

Ange goes out to check on the Park, and me and Kimberly make up a fresh batch of honey toast and watch TV. On any other Monday morning, I would have gathered up the little backyard bandits — Wallamina, Princess Pie, and Rocky too — and taken them along to the old folks' home forty minutes south of the Park. My ancient mum is in there. She lies on a gurney by the window in the hall and calls out to anyone passing for a 'cup of tea and a piece of cake'. So old she's gone reptile — like a snake. No hearing, just the vibration of passers-by to rely on. Once, I was giving her hand a pat goodbye when she grabbed my shirt.

'They know all about it,' she told me. 'Every single one of the bloody bugger bastards.'

That made me smile. Old god-botherer like my mum running her mouth off. Root vegetables and piss, all the dears trying to get a glass of apple juice to their mouths. Show up with my animals one week and there'll two less people than before, or two new ones. Karen, the head carer, ripping a name tag off a door like she's pulling a Band-Aid. I'm always surprised to find Mum still there on her gurney. The old girls that are left — mostly women by that age — are used to the high turnover. When your friends are dropping off left, right, and centre, you learn to make new ones quick smart. I think that's why they like the animals — they're young, full of life, and if Rocky rock-rat carked it, I could probably replace him and they wouldn't know the difference. Those ladies handle the animals like furs or floppy toys, eyes swimming in their faces, trying to see the hairy creatures I've brought. The animals respond by lolling around, weirdly calm in the crêpe-paper hands. Wallamina Wallaby doesn't bite or scratch, Princess Pie crow doesn't shit on the lap rugs, Rocky wakes up for once and blinks all cute at the adoring faces, nibbles some wriggling grubs that I place on the shaky outstretched palms. Some of the Park staff like rescuing snakes in their spare time. Some like tagging and monitoring crocodiles. Hunting down some poor, half-extinct tree frog. For me, it's passing a soft thing into the hand of another soft thing. Watching them stare at each other through whatever mists old people and animals see the world.

The news on Angela's telly looks like a crazy movie. Horses skittering up the streets. People bashing on hospital doors. A politician getting in the shit for saying we'll have to start eating our pets. Farmers topping themselves. I think of Graham down there on that farm with his teacher-nurse Amy Olivia and his cows.

'Here at the Centre for Infectious Diseases there are thousands of reports of enhanced communication between humans and animals.'

Me and Kimberly high-five.

'... but the Health Minister advises this is unconfirmed and emphasises the need to keep calm and stay indoors. The Prime Minister's "cover and calm" campaign will launch tomorrow. Air and shipping ports have been temporarily closed, leaving tens of thousands stranded. Meanwhile foreign gunships are stationed in close neighbouring waters, to prevent the infected escaping via boats.'

I get out my poor old phone. It lights up in surprise at Angela's connection. The news is the same as on the telly. The airports. The gunships like sharks on the horizon. I'm still blocked from the socials, but one of the forums has let me back in with ideas about where this disease comes from. Chemtrails. Vaccinations. Fluoride. Vegans again. I try telling Kim some of this. She's glued to the news because the Prime Minister is speaking. Classic Kimberly. She's the only person I know who actually likes the PM. Thinks he has a face like a koala. 'Can we play "cover and calm" now?' she asks. 'Like he said?'

Ange comes back in the afternoon and doesn't mind that her lounge room has been taken apart and remade into a couch-pillow fort.

'The system is in place,' she says. 'The fences are on, rosters for feeding allocated — we lost a long-necked turtle overnight but I think

45

he was on his way out anyway. We've decided to release the birds of prey — they're survivors, they'll be fine to hunt for themselves for a few weeks. We might even be able to catch them again after. For the rest, we've got people and animal rations that'll last into next month. None of us is sick ... Our system's working.'

I peer between the pillows. 'They said the animals are talking. Or people can talk to animals. On the news.'

She points at me. 'I don't want you giving Kimberly ideas.'

'It was on the news,' Kim confirms from deep in the fort.

'Alright, Kimbo.' I crawl out. 'Time to put on our ranger shirts. Get stuck in to the afternoon feed.'

Angela narrows her eyes. 'You're happy about all this. You *want* to be able to talk to them. Remember your priorities, Jean.'

I remember to keep my big mouth shut. Go off swinging Kimberly's hand, figuring this zooflu could be the best thing ever happened to me.

On dusk, me and Kimberly pick up Angela in the zoo train and glide down to the café station. I give a toot that makes Ange frown the way she does when she's trying not to laugh. No one can work out how to turn off the automatic goodbye message that plays over the loud-speakers in the café courtyard, so every damned person who staggers in triggers Andy's cheery recorded voice. 'Thank you for visiting the Park. We hope you had a wild day!' The management team has decided we should eat dinners together, so we can ration the food.

'Hey, Ange, it's better here without all those tourists, right?'

'The tourists are what keep this place going.'

'But it's better, right?'

That makes her real-smile. A shadow passes overhead. One of the released sea eagles glides through the sun. An 'oh' escapes Ange. Bird woman. If she could strap Kim on her back she'd be up there too. Find out what's in that feathery brain.

—

The skeleton staff have brought in their better halves and their kids, who mill around in the café like it's their first day of camp. Kim eyes the other children and they eye her, each clinging to a parent. Glen stands by the bain-marie with his brow scrunched, counting out the rations so no one has an extra frozen pea they shouldn't. Trench looks pleased with himself. His wife — a miniature woman who needs some carbs in her life — has finally joined him. Casey and Liu are there — best friends and worst enemies at the same time. Poor Doug is the only guy under forty left and both women are after him, even though tall and dopey are about the only things Doug's got going. The office staff, Tania and Elsa, are from Sweden or somewhere — they can't go home. Andy is behind the bain-marie in a butcher's apron, dishing out the last of the frozen chips with something that looks like curry. The information screen behind him is usually lit up with ads for the Park and zoo train times. Now it shows a map of areas of the country down with flu, red for infection. The south red, the centre red, half the north red. Only the northwest and northeast coasts and the islands off them are brown and green. I feel scorched. Try to hold on to that feeling of driving the zoo train, ranger shirt on, Ange and Kim grinning behind me and the wind in our hair, but I've hit the bottom of my tobacco pouch and I feel the hard landing. The lights buzz bright insect drones. There's a flattened cigarette butt by one of the bins, with a quarter left. My blood itches for it. A bald, burly young man I've never seen before rushes out of the café kitchen before I can grab the stub. Puts his giant foot on my find. He's clutching a white bucket and a big, dead bush fowl. Its orange legs curl like dead spiders, clutching the air above the man's fingers, black feathers marbled.

'Who are you when you're at home?'

'I'm Andy's partner. Keith.' He shoots a doe-eyed look over at Andy, who's got the face of someone who knows the two people he's fucking are talking about him. 'But I'm not one to sit around,' he goes on. 'I've got extensive experience. Armed forces. Navy. I work in oil now.' I fold my arms: so Keith is a bit of a dickhead. No surprises there. 'On the rigs your whole life is in shifts. You get disciplined. But I was navy already so I —'

'What's with the bird?'

Keith juggles the bucket into the same hand as the dead bird. 'First duty is to feed everyone.'

'With the wildlife?'

'We've run out of chicken. Andy's always saying I'm great at making a meal out of nothing. Give me a can of tomatoes and a lighter. But there's not much here. I learned to hunt in the armed forces. Anyway, a bit of bush meat isn't going to be missed.'

The recorded message blurts over the courtyard. 'Thank you for visiting the Park. We hope you had a wild day!'

Andy's young fella starts to look nervous. 'Boss won't mind. Will she?'

Angela is off talking to the rangers. Her face a frowny roadmap again.

'Why don't you go show her?' I'm kind of joking, but the stupid shit grins and takes off toward her clutching the bird. I roll my sleeves, cackling to myself, and get in beside Andy to dish out chips, rice, and dark-yellow gruel into plastic disposable bowls.

'Your boyfriend's good-looking,' I tell Andy. He grunts. A bit pleased. 'Dumb as dog doo, though.' We look outside to see Angela biting young Keith's head off. She points at the bird, then at him, back at the bird.

'Hell.' Andy throws down his tongs. Then they're all out there, Andy between them, pushing Keith back inside, saying *sorry, Ange, sorry*.

'... Are you crazy? I told you not to tell her things,' Andy says as they go past into the kitchen, that poor dead bird still hanging upside down.

'We need some more chips out here,' I call. Andy comes back out like a little storm cloud. 'We need more chips.'

48

'Shut up, Jean. He's doing it.'

'You heard any of the staff talking to animals yet?'

'All I can hear is you. Still talking.'

Me and Andy serve the rest in silence. I watch Trench and his wife finish up their curry and go out into the courtyard for after-meal smokes. No point trying to bum one off those tight bastards. They suck back and suck back, and blow out so much smoke the air is foggy. I'm stuck in here with sooky la la and his stupid boyfriend. I forget about my sore hand and leave it too close to the hot bain-marie lights. The cut burns so much I might have to punch someone in the face or cry. Trench and his woman stub out their smokes and come back in. Their movement triggers the goodbye again.

'Thank you for visiting the Park. We hope you ha—'

The lights of the café blink out. The bain-marie fades to black. The spotlights outside are slower. I get a last view of the sunset-coloured courtyard and then it's blackness and darkness and yelps of surprise. A crash in the kitchen. Keith cries out. The cries turn to screaming.

'Jesus.'

Andy jolts in the darkness, takes off in the direction of the yells.

'Calm down,' Angela's voice says over Keith. 'Someone help him.'

There's movement toward the gift shop. A soft, hairy body — an animal's body — slips past my knees. 'What was that?'

Three torches pilfered from the gift shop puncture the black and stutter toward the kitchen. The screams have turned to sobbing, but start again when people get near. The kitchen is lit for a second. Keith with his hands over his face, shirt wet, Andy crouched over him.

'Hot oil,' Glen reports through the gloom. 'He upended the deep fryer. Burns are minor. He'll be alright. We better call a meeting.'

Kimberly is pushed into my arms. I can't really see her, just feel her warm bony body, damp undercarriage, her shallow, frightened breaths in my ear.

'What's happening, Granny?' Kimberly whispers.

'It's not the fuses,' says Glen into a walkie-talkie. I can just make him out. The CB radios fizz. 'It's been cut at the mains. We'll have to transfer the food to the aquarium. The generator's going so we can eat from there. Right now, we'll follow the fire plan and meet at the food store. Over.'

The zoo trains run on electricity, and only a couple of Park utes are nearby. The rest of us head over to the food store on foot. Our steps heavy along the paths. Kimberly wants to be carried, a sack of soggy potatoes. 'What's happening?'

'They're going to tell us about talking to animals, darl. That'll be good, won't it?' She clings tighter. I hustle my steps. The darkness makes the other sounds big. The slam of wallabies through the bush, and my swollen-up feet trying not to trip. Banksias flare like sparklers in the torchlight. The ant hills, gravestones of old, old cities.

The power is off at the food store too. We assemble in the prep room and wait. Kimberly's elbow digs into the rib just below my left boob. That might be Casey next to me. Glen on the walkie-talkie again. My eyes adjust. A ute takes off and comes back again, and they unload Keith onto a gurney and wheel him past. I can make out Andy moving along beside him.

Angela's voice breaks through. 'Glen ...?'

Glen turns on a torch and shines it onto a folder. He's slow to get to the bit about the animals. Drones on and on about *contingency this* and *risk matrix that*.

'Are they going to say about talking to animals?' Kim asks me, loud enough that those poor sick bludgers down south could probably hear what she said.

'I think they're getting to that, Kimbo.'

'Excuse me, Glen, I'd like to hear more about the talking ... the zooflu as well.' Blow me down, it's Trench. 'What are the developments?'

Everyone in the room starts muttering. I feel for my phone. It's dead again.

'Something about codes,' I call out. Can't help myself. 'Encoding and ... decoding. Means if you're sick with that flu you can understand what the animals' bodies are saying, and the animals can understand you too. I looked it up.'

Glen's sigh punctures the dark. 'That's exactly what it means. Come on, Ange. Even Kim can get this info. We're not helping by —'

'Nothing's confirmed.'

'Bullshit. This thing's massive. I made a few calls to the southern zoos and they're screwed down there. This disease means that everything we knew about our animals is going to change. It'll last months, if we're lucky.'

'Which is exactly why we need to follow procedure.' Ange's voice is freezing in the hot room. 'We made this plan for bird flu a few years back and we've done some adjustments for now. The short of it is —'

'But if we can talk to the endangered species, maybe we can find out how to help them.' That's Liu. Bit of mutiny happening here in the dark.

'Talking to them is exactly what we don't want to happen ...'

The muttering starts to take shape. One voice, then three, coming together in a chant of 'Talk-ing birds. Talk-ing birds.'

'Maintaining a stable environment for these vulnerable animals is key,' Ange yells. 'It's key. That's why ... that's *why* we've closed the gates.'

The whole staff sings over her, 'Talk-ing birds. Talk-ing birds.'

Poor old Ange still shouting. Casey beside me laughing so hard she can't keep up. In the gap between words, a sound. We drop away, listen. It's the dingoes, howling from the enclosure on the other side of the park. And then a responding howl. Close to us.

FIVE

No lights at the row, no TV. The inside of my fridge is warm already in the fuggy night. All over the estate, the sound of the Park's ute engines charging phones and batteries. I get my Holden going to give my mobile a boost too. There's a petrol bowser up at the food store that will keep the cars moving for a while. Encoding. Decoding. And here we are, healthy as horses. The animals around us squawk their mysteries and we're none the wiser.

Without any lights, the night takes over. Owls and magpie geese hoot overhead. Turkey birds scratch up the bush. Wallabies and wallaroos thump all over. Something in my cupboard chews its way into a packet. Let them have it. Let them clean me out. Anything fresh will be mouldy by morning. Even the critters in my yard have come alive. Baby rock-rat Rocky is suddenly grown up and trying to eat his way out the door of his cage. I crouch down level to the pen and fumble with the latch. Don't even have time for a 'Hey there, fella' before he bursts out at my face, bubble eyes glinting in the moonlight. He leaps away and off across the yard, squishes his fat body through the chicken-wire fence and away. No more Rocky. The others are excited too. Without electricity, the whole world has been returned to its proper darkness. Wallamina doesn't get stuck in the corner. Princess Pie stops making her baby noises and lets out a proper caw, black as the night.

—

I get the candles going in my flat and hunt out the cupboards and all my hiding spots with a camping lantern. Find a bluebird earring by the bathroom cabinet, but nothing to drink. Sit on the cold bathroom floor and wait for the shakes to start. They don't. My head is cool as tiles. People start arriving at the gates, wanting to get into the Park. Those of us left in the row come out blinking in the blaze of the hired utes and cars. Ange dashes around, growling orders. The people on the other side of the fence call through the wire. Can they speak to Blondie the python, or Kermit and Miss Piggy the rainbow lorikeets, or Bernie the crocodile? The police and army are too busy explaining to the rest of the country why they can suddenly talk to their pets. They don't have time to keep the Park safe from every nut-job wants to come in. Angela uses up the juice on her mobile trying to hire extra security for the fence. She starts up one of the Park vans to charge her phone, then makes another call. When she talks to her dad, her accent comes back and her whole voice changes — harder and sweeter at the same time, a boiled lolly. Only a few hours later, white utes with roo lights and bull bars jump off-road and bounce up the gravel past the tourist cars, toward the gate. One takes out a low tree with a sick crunch. The men who get out are built like brick shithouses, wearing loose T-shirts with slogans like 'Hunt the Grunt' and 'Game on'. They station themselves at the gate and the fence.

'Piggers,' Ange tells me.

'Never thought I'd see the day.'

'They've organised. Call themselves Land Patrol now. They were all Dad could get. Also ...' She rubs her face, mashing the tired back in. 'They're infected.'

'They're sick?'

'Apparently it's okay. This disease likes to be within spitting distance. Make sure Kim —'

'I won't let anything happen to our girl, Ange.'

—

Next day, Angela throws Kim out of the car on her way past. We go into my unit and stare at ourselves in the bathroom mirror, check our eyes for sick.

'You look pretty, Granny,' Kimberly tells me, standing on the toilet lid.

Eyes clear and grey, skin a bit pink. Fresh bandage around my throbbing hand. Even my head feels sure — a faulty compass come right. 'I scrub up, don't I?'

We pull our ranger shirts over our nighties and head down to the fence. The tourists are still at the gate, clumped around their cars.

'Who are they?' I shout at one of those pig hunters. He turns his head, a bit slow. Even at a distance I can see he's sick. Red eyes blazing in the pearly light.

'They want to come into the Park,' he yells back.

Nice cars, burnt people guzzling bottled water like there's no tomorrow. It's hot and getting hotter.

'Southerners,' I tell the guy. 'Come up from the cold to talk to the animals.'

The fella leans forward to peer at the people. They straighten up like kids at school waiting to be picked for the sports team. Must be about fifteen cars out there, packed to the gunwales. 'All got pink-eye,' the fella yells.

'I had that one time,' Kim shouts back.

He pulls his mask aside. He's good-looking. Dark, like my Lee. In different times I might have told Ange about him.

'Not like this. Get up close and you'll see.' He points to his own eyes, squinting with red. 'Once you've got it? You have to be tough. Keep your head or you'll be a lock-in who won't leave the house. Either that or some crazy who waits outside a zoo to talk to an elephant. These are people who will have whole conversations with their dogs, you know.'

'I want to talk to a dog,' Kim tells him.

The man straps his mask back on. 'No, you don't. My hunting bitch was a tough, mean, fighting machine dog that didn't take shit from nothing. But what she had to say once I knew what it was she was saying —'

'What'd she say?' Me and Kim at the same time. Snap. But the guy turns away. A tall woman my age starts waving her arms around, trying to get our attention.

'How did you get in there?' she calls.

'I work here.' I point at my shirt. 'I'm a ranger.'

'Can I take a photo?'

I shrug. Why not? Lift Kim up so she can be in it too, and the woman snaps away with her phone. Then we wave them all goodbye and go back to the row, where the TV sits dead and the backyard bandits just want to eat and eat and eat. Me and Kimberly check each other again for symptoms. She pulls down the saggy bit under my eye and peers in.

'It's pink!'

I look for myself. 'That's just how eyeballs look, mate.' We check hers: the same. I smooth the wrinkles out of our shirts while Kim has a cold shower and then I brush the nests out of both our hair. Mine ripples silver and gold. Don't even need any makeup. We've only got Weet-Bix with water and sugar for breakfast, crackers and spread for lunch — even that dog kibble and birdseed is starting to look good — but I'm feeling stronger than ever.

We're late to do the feed. The day is already blasting. A hair-dryer wind down the empty bush tracks to the enclosures. No one minds, except the animals, and all they can do is clamour at the cages when we come through dishing out kibble and dried bugs and seed. The zoo train sits at the café station. I know it'll be dead, along with all the other electrics, but we climb up anyway, try the button. It doesn't even chug. It's tough to get around the Park without the old train.

Plenty of Park utes around but they're locked up, and Glen's always on the other side of the park with the keys. We scoop our buckets and go on foot, like the other rangers do. The Park roads bend and shimmer in the heat. Me and Kimberly hit up every dinky solar water fountain along the way, wetting our hair and our arms and guzzling the water that doesn't get chilled anymore. We fling still-cold fish over the fence at the stinger station, shove mouse mix through the wire at the food store, and push seed, defrosting mice, and kibble through the wires on death row. Then we head up to the dingoes. Take the cooler route through the jungle walk — wooden walkways that flex over the powdery blue creek. We spot turtles scooping through the water, in and out under the border fence. The turtles' way. By the time we burst out the other side at the dingo enclosure, it's so hot only Mister and Buddy rouse themselves from the shade. They drag their bones back under the trees, barely a wag of hello. I call and crane my neck for Sue, but she doesn't come out from wherever she's hiding.

'Remember to tell the other rangers, Kim. They better check on her later.'

Kim nods importantly. We hold sweaty hands back through the Park. Her ranger top hangs from her like a dress. She refuses to take it off.

By dusk, more people have arrived at the front gate, camped along the bamboo-edged road that leads from the highway into the Park. They want to see the animals, and the Patrols are wearing thin. The good-looking guard hits the air around him, ducking away. Tears off down the road — the fine, hummingbird wings of a micro bat flickering over his head. Another guard doesn't come back from his dinner break. Ange rings the cops. They never arrive. She joins me and Kim outside the row, ripping at a nail and watching the perimeter fence. The hot day melts into gloopy night, the air heavy all around us. I put

Kimberly in my bed and find some juice boxes, warm in the fridge. Angela sniffs hers, sips.

'Think we've got some sort of humanitarian responsibility to feed them?' she asks me, staring out at the cars. 'Tania's doing a diploma in development. Said that.'

'We should be scabbing off them, more like.'

Those tourists are burning their headlights like they've got all the power in the world. Dashing around the bush that spans the Park to the highway, chatting to every little furry thing they can. Their hysterical laughter, sobs and gasps bounce off the trees. The gruff shouts of the few remaining Land Patrol when the tourists get too close to the fence. Tired and hungry, they cook up sausages and fold them in bread — the sweet stink of tomato sauce on the smoky air. My stomach groans. Tonight's staff dinner was packet noodles off little camp stoves up at the aquarium. Everyone too fucked to do a proper meal. The fence people retire into their tents and swags and vans; us back to our dark houses and the stink of rotting, mouldy fridges and hot linoleum. Just before sleep I remember that I never got an eye on Sue in the dingo enclosure. Can't remember a time when she hasn't come out to say hello.

My phone rings. It's so dark in my little flat that the brightness flares, and it's a moment before I can make out the name on the screen: my Lee.

'Go outside,' he says.

'You alright?'

'Just go outside.' I open the front door, stick my head out. 'At the fence.'

Outside is all lit up with hot stars and a fat moon sliding toward the horizon. I go down the short path at the front of the row and peer along the exit road to the fence where there's a figure — and I know. When you've birthed someone, you recognise them in any light. He has a way of standing: wonky, but graceful as a dancer. Such a shock when he shot up out of his pudgy baby skin and grew bones like wings, all angles — and that grin. Lee has a way of ducking his head and peering up at you through his hair with his bright, black eyes.

'Baby boy,' I say into the phone. 'What the hell?'

'Saw your photo, you're internet famous. Come to the fence.'

'I've got Kimberly.'

'Even better.'

I go back inside to haul Kim out of my bed and onto my hip. She's boiling hot, smells like dribble. Barefoot down the warm road I go, unable to keep the smile off my face, even though I know it's best not to encourage him. Because if you give him an inch. My baby. My boy. My little man. Stranger with my skin standing on the other side of the fence. Lee is thinner and taller than I remember, dark stubble sketched over his chin. Mirrored sunglasses, and the slow grin below them a heartbreaker. His voice has changed too. The vowels flattened, like dogs in trouble. He's been on the heroin by the sounds of it — maybe got off it in time to kick the habit, but not so quick it didn't knock his voice for six. That voice twists my guts, wrings them dry, but it doesn't make any difference to know.

'That's your daddy, isn't it?' I tell Kim. She buries her head in my shoulder and peers out through a gap in her hair.

Lee turns his grin on her. 'Hello, Possum.' She hums with uncertainty and clings tighter. In her house, Lee's name is said in spite. Even six-year-olds can spot rotten love. She mumbles something.

'What's that, Angel-face?'

'I'm not allowed to call you Dad.'

'What about Uncle Lee?'

Kimberly giggles. 'Uncley!'

Lee nods in my direction. 'Let me in, Mum.'

I look along the fence. The few piggers that are left stand at the gate, all serious now there's fewer of them.

'I already bribed them to talk to you,' Lee says. 'Nothing left.' He spreads his hands to show me all he has: a thin body, a faded blue backpack, ripped jeans, and a love-worn singlet with 'Che' written on it.

'You shouldn't go too near those fellas, Bub. Or anyone.'

'Let me in, then.'

'You'll have to camp out, just for tonight.' My heart smashing itself against the fence. To talk to your baby through wire! 'I'll get my swag from the cupboard and throw it over. It's comfy. In the morning we'll tell Ange. Maybe —'

He looks away, laughs. A bitterness to his smile where there used to be honey. 'There's got to be another way. The piggers said this fence is electrified, but I can't hear it.'

'It's been cut,' I say before I can jam my fist in my stupid mouth. Lee's sunglasses sparkle, catching light from I don't even know where. I try to backtrack. 'You'll never get over that razor wire.' We all know it's too late. Even Kim knows, and she's a kid.

'There's the turtles' way,' she puts in. Lee comes up closer to the fence. Touches it tentatively. It's true. The power's off. 'What's that, Sunflower?'

Kimberly sits up and brushes some hair out of her face. 'The turtles go in and out under the fence. They go under the water in the creek, and when they come up, they're in the Park.'

'No kidding?' Lee smiles at her and she smiles back, and there it is. They smile the same.

'She's just talking about how we feed the turtles. I'll get the swag.' I move to leave but Kimberly writhes out of my arms and takes a step toward the fence.

'What about crocs?' Lee asks, crouching to her height.

Kimberly shakes her head vigorously. She's an authority on crocodiles now. 'They're not allowed in the creek. The rangers tell them to keep out!' She looks up at me to confirm. I know the bit she's talking about. A swimming hole up the road. It's beautiful there. A small waterfall crashes between the banks.

Lee pulls his blue pack on his back. 'Guess I'm a turtle, then. Do I look like a turtle?'

Kimberly nods solemnly, her thumb drifting up to her mouth.

'Lee,' I call. He's gone. The bamboo has replaced him. Trunks thick and speckled orange as the necks of giraffes. 'Shit, what'll I tell Ange?' Lee appears again, his smile catching the moon.

'Hey, Mum, what happened to your hand?'

I hide it. 'Caught it on some wire. Be careful, love —' He's off into the dark.

Back in the bed, Kimberly slumped into an open-armed sleep beside me, I think about him slipping into that water. Remember going there to smoke doobies with Graham, how the rock pools glow at night with some inner light that comes up from the sandy bottom and shows the fish going about their business. Glowing.

I get up, sit at the kitchen table and pick through my ashtray for butts, blazing the cool smoke again and again in the dark. The idea of Lee underwater won't leave me. I see his body fight against the current made by the little waterfall, then under the submerged fence. For a moment he is lost in the shimmering blue. My son is just another boulder, a shadow or a weed. He's trapped down there. Caught on the wire like Sue the dingo, except that Lee can't breathe. I suck smoke. I won't let him stay like that. I see the surface on the other side buckle — his beautiful nose cracks through. He makes it. Lee always makes it. Something about my son: he's a free boy. He's been a free boy like that since he was born. How something so pretty could come out of two ageing rev-heads like me and Graham, with scraps for hearts. I passed Lee to his dad, and Graham said, *Why doesn't he look like me? I heard he'd look like me.* It hurt to laugh. Did he think Lee looked like the farmer next door? It's true, though — Lee doesn't look like anyone. He's got Graham's hair and his black-as-a-burrow eyes. He's narrow like I used to be. But the look he wears about himself, the air that comes with him into a room, the light in his eyes that isn't from anything but his own insides: that's free. What's it like to be free? Ask him. He'll say things like *as a bird*, or *freedom is something you can touch but never hold*. He's always talking like he invented inspirational postcards. I guess when you don't have steady love, and you don't look after your children, and you don't have a house or a job — even keeping a date with a woman is a bit too hard — you can act free. Lee doesn't mind. Lee doesn't mind about anything. He lights up a room. He could light up a coal mine. He even made Angela happy for a second. We helped them to buy the campervan. They were going to have Kimberly and take off across the desert to the coast. Ange grew up overseas with buckets of money but real strict boarding schools, the lot. She saw Lee's bare feet and smelled his particular scent — sun sweat, lemon juice, and smoke — and she reached out for freedom. For that weird beauty that's worth more than money or guts, even in this part of the world. They were supposed to be having a break when they got pregnant, but Lee didn't mind. He said, *have the baby and we'll live at the beach and rent a house from a friend, and I'll get work in a kitchen*. He didn't add that, not long after Kimberly was born, he'd take off without either of them.

Lee gets to the row hours later, half drenched, backpack covered in mud, grinning beneath those stupid mirrored sunglasses he somehow managed to keep on under water.

'Full on,' he murmurs. 'That was one of the most intense experiences I've ever had.'

Kimberly is slumped diagonally across my bed, one arm abandoned, the other clutching Hello Bear. Lee peels off his clothes and stands in the middle of my lounge room in the candlelight, naked as the day, still wearing his sunnies, and inspects his body with a torch for leeches. He's skinny, but toned and brown — tribal-looking tattoos down one arm. There's one leech, right up near his brown ball sack.

'I'll let you get that one.' I hand him the vinegar. The little sucker lets go of Lee's thigh and falls off, and I chuck it outside for Princess Pie to peck in the morning. Last man sat on my couch naked was Andy. It's hard not to laugh, with Lee there in the candlelight like an ad for couches, and Andy, the old round ranger. Lee knows he's beautiful too. My flat and the row seem suddenly shabby.

'Shameless,' I tell him. Chuck him an old towel. He tucks it around his hips. 'What'll you do now you're here?'

'Spend time with my mum. Get back to where I came from. Maternal energy. Quality time.'

Bullshit, but it makes me smile long after I've crawled in beside Kimberly, the little space she's left.

The sun is up and bouncing off the walls by the time I stagger out in the morning. Some mosquitoes got me by the fence last night, bit the shit out of my ankles. My door is open and there's Lee out the front of the row on a plastic chair, shirtless, wearing the jeans I hung up to dry last night, sunnies still on. He's bouncing Kimberly on his lap and chatting up Casey and Liu, who are practically popping out of their ranger shirts. Casey puts her hand over an infinity tattoo on Lee's bare shoulder and throws her head back with laughter. She's an idiot, but I get it — there's something about a fertile man. Liu hangs back. She and Lee give each other a secret smile. She's good-looking, young, grumpy too, and boys like that. She stares deeply into his glasses and her own reflection. Lee just behind it, but he's not quite there. He's on the make, playing the dad, bouncing Kim on his knee, but he keeps glancing over his shoulder into the bush at the side of the road. There's a wallaby there, crouched on its haunches in the shade of some scraggly trees, fat snout twitching. Lee looks at it and looks at it. He can't stop looking at it. The women don't notice, but I do.

'See you've made yourself at home,' I say.

'Here she is.' Lee shoots another glance over his shoulder at the animal before turning his smile on me. 'Total goddess. Mothers are so *valuable*, aren't they?'

'Yes. And that is so sweet.' Casey looks like she wants to become the mother of his children right there on the front path with all of us watching.

Kimberly points up the road. 'Here's *my* mum.' Angela's car pulls into the row. I clutch the door frame. Known her almost a decade now and she still scares the bejesus out of me. Lee's smile for her is brilliant, though. Either he's the best actor in the world or he still thinks she's beautiful. Hair blazing, uniform tight in the right spots, fists clenched, eyes set to kill. Casey and Liu fade to nothing, scurry up the road to work. Kimberly has the good sense to get off Lee's knee and take refuge behind me at the door.

'What the actual fuck?'

'Ange, I feel so blessed —'

'Did you let him in?' She turns on me.

I nod like a dumb idiot, but Lee, God love him, stands up between us.

'I broke in, Ange. I found a weak bit of fence and thought I'd come say hullo. And now I'm here ...' His gaze is taken again by the wallaby. Makes a choking sound in his throat — the animal hooks away.

Angela stares at him funny. She leans in. 'Take off your glasses.'

My turn to step between them, knowing what I've known since I first saw Lee in those stupid specs. Kim is on me like a limpet, dragging me back. 'Lee was just leaving, Ange,' I call. 'He was just —'

'Take them off.'

'These?' Lee tries to smile. 'They're supposed to reflect souls. I met a yoga teacher out east who told me —'

She rips them off his face, drops them on the dirt, rears back.

'Lee?' I ask. He looks over at me with eyes like paint. Pink paint.

'My dad's got pink-eye,' whispers Kimberly.

Ange is so mad she forgets he's diseased. Shoves him hard, and he staggers back. 'Did you know you were sick when you came here?'

'If you could hear them —'

'Tell me, you little shit.'

Lee rubs the back of his neck. Glances with flaming eyes into the bush again. 'You got some great animals in here, Ange.' We all stare at him, mouths hanging. 'I mean, talking to a ghost bat. What a trip, right?'

I wait with Lee inside the row while Angela paces around out front, yelling into her walkie-talkie about another emergency contingency. We've got so many emergency plans now you can't even breathe unless it's part of a spreadsheet. Kim is with us because she's hugged Lee and might be infected too. I try distracting her at the table with the scrapbooks and pencils, but Lee is more interesting than our sanctuary. He's on the couch, staring with bloody eyes at the corner where the front window meets the display cabinet. I keep all my memories there, photos and everything.

'Hear it?' he whispers. I listen. The bush mutters in the hot wind outside. 'Hear it? They've been here. Right here. You can't smell them or anything?'

I shake my head. 'No.'

Lee looks up at me. 'Mice, Mum. They're in there, talking with their fur — and I can tell you what they're saying.' He points to where the wall has buckled in the wet-season rains, left a cavity, a broken tooth of plaster. 'They're hungry as.'

I grab his red-and-tan packet of Brumbies and roll myself a smoke with shaky hands. Kimberly stares at Lee like he's a bird from outer space. 'You're scaring your daughter —'

'Nothing to be scared of. They're just hungry.' He cocks his head and listens again. Rolls himself a cigarette too. 'The smokes block it a bit. Dull the senses. It's intense, you know?'

Outside on the porch, Wallamina decides it's feeding time again. She butts her head at the door. Balances on her tail and tries to thump the glass with her rear legs but misses. Lee sinks back into the couch.

'Holy fuck.'

Kimberly's been told to not go near him. She edges closer. 'What's Wallamina saying, Dad?'

Lee stares at the animal. 'It's like acid. Has Kim had acid?'

'What do *you* think, Lee Bennett?'

'Okay, it's like I can feel everything. I can hear ... everything, the taste. The smell is awful and it goes for, I don't know, days and great, great distances.'

'The smell does?'

'Yeah, and it's bright, even in the dark. And my skin. I can *read* every movement. Every muscle. Can you imagine?' Me and Kimberly shake our heads. Lee whispers, 'And they can too.'

'Who?'

'The animals.'

'They're sick too?'

'They're always saying stuff. We just, you know, didn't get it.'

Kimberly hops around like she needs to wee. 'But what's Wally *saying?*'

'She's saying ...' Lee stares at the wallaby through the glass, the cigarette blazing in his fingers. 'Nah, it's too hard.' Kimberly goes and pokes him in his bare shoulder. I know that poke, and it hurts. 'Okay. Okay, wait. She's like, she doesn't want to be outside. But she doesn't want to be inside neither.'

'That doesn't make sense.'

Lee sits up a bit. 'She's pretty messed up, and it's not just that she's mentally ... you know, mental. There's something wrong with the vibe of this place, something wrong with all the animals in this park. I mean, it's a zoo, right? They're all in cages.'

Kimberly folds her little arms across her chest and glares at Lee, just like her mum would.

Lee squints at Wallamina. 'And she's obsessed. Obsessed with that corner over there.'

He points over to the bit where Wallamina gets stuck.

'That's just the bit where she gets stuck,' I tell him.

'Nah. Nah, she reckons there's something there.'

'What?' Kim whispers.

'Some other wallaby.'

'But there's nothing there.' Kim turns to Wallamina. 'There's nothing there. It's just a corner.'

'There's another wallaby there, she's sure of it. Look, I don't get it either. I don't really know what they're going on about most of the time.'

'What about Princess Pie?' Kimberly points at the crow, who is listening to the ground, one ear cocked for grubs.

Lee shakes his head, his hair flopping like black fingers over his eyes. 'It's just the furry ones for now. But I heard some people are bad cases. Talking to the birds and reptiles, insects even.'

'If I was sick, I'd talk to all the animals!' Kim flings her arms to take in the world, then sneezes. You wouldn't think that much mucus could live in such a little body, but there you have it.

'You wouldn't want to be in here for long,' Lee tells her, while I wipe her face with bits of toilet paper. 'I thought it'd be great, but they're all institutionalised. Messed up in the head. Outside the gates the animals are free. I met these great chicks who said they were going to the coast to hear the southern whales sing. I should've gone with them. They said if you get underwater you can understand the words. Tell you the meaning of the whole world. How blessed would you be then?'

The coast, the coast. Always promises of the coast. Kim is hooked. 'Can we do that, Granny?'

'Don't think your mum would like it, do you?'

Kimberly shrugs and goes to press herself up against the screen door, where Wallamina and now Princess Pie have gathered. Me and Lee roll Brumbies and sit in silence. If everyone wasn't so shitty with us, it'd be nice, like a party.

'Nothing yet,' Kimberly reports every two seconds, then goes back to testing the animals like microphones. 'Hello? Hello? Wallamina, can you hear me?' Wallamina, meanwhile, is beside herself, can't handle the barrier of the screen, hops in circles, strikes out at the crow, wants skin and food and whatever. Lee keeps himself turned away from her antics. For all his hoopla about bonding with them, he seems pretty keen to keep the glass door closed — the whole row like a furnace at this time of day. Spends the rest of his 'blessed' time hiding out on my couch under a blanket of smoke.

Angela comes back into the flat like she's part of her own stampede.

'Too late,' she announces. Her mouth twisted and sore. 'Casey and Liu went straight up to the rangers meeting, and Casey hugged everyone there. Our quarantine is broken. We're all exposed. Are you even listening to me?'

'Sorry,' says Lee, turning from the back door, shaky hand through his hair. 'It's that wallaby. She's ... intense.'

'Jesus Christ.' Ange sets in on Lee: *irresponsible and selfish and dangerous and not fit for nothing. Arsehole. Sociopath. Dickhead. Never going to see Kimberly again.*

'What does it matter anyway?' Lee mumbles. 'She's not ...' He stops. They both glance at Kim, like the girl will go pink-eyed and animal-crazy before us. Kimberly gets nervous under their gaze. Sniffs her snot and pulls her thumb out of her mouth. Pulls Ange down to kneeling so she can wrap her arms around her mum's hard shoulders.

'Are we going to get pink-eye like Dad? I mean, Lee?'

Angela sits back on her heels and puts her hand to Kimberly's forehead, holds her gaze. 'I don't know, kiddo. We'll have to wait and see.'

'If Granny gets it, she'll be able to talk to the animals for real.'

Angela turns her hate face on me.

'Maybe we won't get sick?' I suggest. Lee bobs his head in agreement. Got to keep positive. There's a yellow sticky note above my bed says, 'Wake with a smile, run a mile, do it with style, love all the while.' You can see where Lee gets it from.

No one wants to go near Lee. His burnt eyes and the way he keeps staring off into the bush. Muttering. They open the gate and shout at him to hurry the fuck up. Last I see, he's wandering down the exit road, blue backpack dried stiff with mud. When he passes the big Jurassic Park gates he thanks the guards. They nod at him because, except for the dickhead part, he's not really a sociopath or all those things Ange said. He's a free spirit, and a polite one — I taught him manners, and who has manners these days? Every time I see the back of him, I think it's going to be the last. He's always going off to do stupid shit. Once he hitched across the country without a wallet to see if he could get by on being nice — he could. Next I hear, he's rocked up to an office in the city wearing a borrowed suit, pretending he works there to prove corporate society is a machine. Lord only knows what he'll get himself into now he can talk to the beasts. He turns left up the highway, toward the city — a miniature figure, hazy in the dry-season light. A mirage of heat blurs the bitumen. Ange lets me watch until he's gone, then she's at me like a terrier. Usually, she doesn't get up in my grill when Kim's around. She's so furious she doesn't even clock her little girl there on the couch with her thumb jammed in her mouth, staring at the dead grey TV. I forget my rules too. Roll myself another from Lee's tobacco pouch while Ange gets it out of her system. When she takes a breath, I come clean to her about how he got in, the turtles' way. Her walkie-talkie crackles. She tells Glen to jam an extra bit of fence down in the water so nothing can get in or out — a job my ex would once have done. Glen and Angela mutter to each other over the radio, bicker and consult.

'I can't risk infection,' she tells him.

'You've been around Lee, so if you're infected, you're infected,' Glen shouts back through the static. 'We need you up here.'

—

Angela doesn't want to leave Kim with me, and I can't blame her. I pack the smokes away and fix Kimberly a snack, like that will make Angela's mind up for her instead of the fact that she's got no one else — she's stuck with me. When she's gone, me and Kim try to do some scrapbooking. She turns to the ripped-up cattery page that I taped back in. Throws her plate of Vegemite and dry crackers on the ground. The plate is plastic, but her food goes all over my nice clean floor. While she's busy crying on the couch, Wallamina pushes her busy nose through the crack in the screen door and hops right inside for a free feed.

'Look at that,' I tell Kim. 'Wally is saying: "Wowsers, this is my lucky day. People say ducks are lucky, what about wallabies?!"'

'I don't care,' shouts Kimberly.

I usher Wallamina out again — clumsy hops over the linoleum — and go to sit with Kim on the couch.

'Remember what you'd ask the animals if you could talk to them?' Kimberly unearths her face from between the cushions. She looks overheated. '"Hello, are you my friend?"' I tell her. 'That's what you said.' She nods slow. 'You know what I'd ask them? I'd ask them what they want. Most of all out of everything.'

'What would they say?'

'Which one?'

'Dingo Sue.'

'She wants Buddy and Mister to give her all the bones.'

Kimberly wipes her nose on the back of her hand. I get her more squares of toilet paper and she fills them. 'What do you want, Granny?'

'Me?'

'Yeah.'

'I guess I want it to be Christmas time again. When everyone's here. Your dad and your mum and you.'

'And Grandpa?'

'I don't know. We could invite some of the staff. Andy. And Mona. I'd make something on your mum's barbecue, like lamb chops, and we'd sing "The cattle are lowing, the baby awakes". What do you think about that?'

Her thumb is back in her mouth. She gives it a satisfied suck in answer. Stares out with flushed cheeks and glazed black eyes to the backyard, where Princess Pie is stabbing the ground with her beak. One wing out to keep Wallamina at bay. The insects fizz and flick through the trees. The murder birds start screaming.

SIX

But it's not like that in the morning. In the morning, the heat soaks the curtains. The wrinkled-up sheets we lie between are damp. On the pillow beside me, Kim opens her eyes and they're dawn-pink, two roses sprouting on her little brown face. All the nights of the dingoes' warnings: 'Something's coming! It's here!' and now here it is, in the body of my little darling. I pick her up and try to cuddle her like a baby. Kimberly wriggles from me and won't let me put drops in her flaming eyes. I examine my white moon face in the mirror — eyes still grey as a southern sky, but my nose is blocked, skin prickling with its own heat. Kimberly has pasted herself to the glass door in the kitchen, watching as Wallamina hops slow circles around the yard. I crouch down beside her.

'You know what she's saying, love?'

Kimberly stares at the wallaby. Wallamina circles tighter and tighter.

'Kim? Is she saying, "What's around the corner? What's around the corner?"'

Kim turns her new eyes on me — the whites now pink; black irises a rosy sheen. 'No.'

'What, then. Kimbo?'

My phone rings.

'How is she?' asks Ange.

I swallow. 'She's sick.'

Angela chokes, can't talk.

'She's up and about, though,' I say after a while. 'We'll have some Coco Pops. She seems okay.'

'Bring her here. You may as well. Half the staff have it.'

I tug at a roll of toilet paper. 'Not me.'

'Well, that's just great, isn't it? That's just fucking great.' She hangs up, then calls back to tell me I have to feed animals in all the sections except the aquarium and the bird forest — everyone else is too sick to do the mammals. I feel sick. Could be the start of zooflu. The feeling of everything I wanted rushing at me like night birds. Scratching and ripping — no joy.

Once I get away from Kim and the staff and their red-eyed scowling, I feel a bit better. Breeze on my skin and wispy hair. The stink of leaves on poo on piss on fur. Something dead. Something lively. The Park beautiful this way. My luck runs out when I get to the food store. Casey and Liu are out the back, gaping in slack-jawed wonder at the series of bedraggled cages on death row. Ange would lose her shit to see them sitting cross-legged in the muck on the floor of one of the enclosures, staring at a spotted quoll. The look on Casey's face like the rapture you see on those late night happy-clappy god-botherer shows. Sort of TV my old mum used to get into. Face flung open, sore eyes widened, mouth gaping. Drowning in glory. The quoll darts over to a branch, rubbing its red furry chin along the wood.

Casey trails after, sniffing the branch and muttering. 'It's okay.' Turns to Liu. 'How can I tell him it's okay? Why does he —'

'It's what they all think,' Liu tells her.

'Think what?' I call in.

Liu blinks like she's forgotten how to be a real person. 'That we're predators. That every time we come near them we're trying to eat them. I'm trying to tell them we're safe, but they don't get it. Or I don't get it. Because their bodies. It's hard to ...' She turns away, pink eyes blazing.

'Why don't you tell them we're here to protect them from the wild beasties outside?'

She acts like she can't hear me, goes back to murmuring. All around the yard there are cages filled with animals calling out and shuffling around. The squawk of a parrot with a bad wing. An olive python shifting in her sandy tank. A couple of little wallabies doing circuits around their enclosure. Casey and Liu twitch and frown, heads darting. They call out to those animals:

'Hi, hello, I'm Liu. What's your name?'

'They don't have names. Probably,' I tell them. 'Why don't you ask them what it's like to be covered in fur? Or what it's like to fly? Or why they get tricked by food every single time? That's what I'd ask.' But I can't ask. Or I can but I don't know if there's an answer. 'Ask them —'

'Jean.'

'Yeah?'

'We're busy.'

Don't look busy. Look like two animal-crazy sheilas asking boring questions. Liu puts on her bitch face and goes to cross the yard to the parrot enclosure. Something on the ground pulls her up short. A long reptile tail, four stout legs, and a long, ancient face. Liu starts laughing, the way you laugh at a horror movie — a cackle that covers a scream. The lizard glowers at her through the top of its head. Casey peers out from the quoll cage.

'Can you talk to it?'

The lizard doesn't move except for its heartbeat pumping behind its ears, then it darts a thin pink tongue.

'Did you? Did you get that?' Liu turns to us, pointing at the lizard. Starts her creepy laughter up again. 'He can *taste* me. I'm like deadly salt. I'm poison. He says ... he ...' She gets back to staring.

The sun has tipped over now, poured its fire into the Park. I get away from Casey and Liu, and cross the barren yard toward the food store. Doug is sitting outside the door on the baking ground, cradling a wallaroo joey like a baby. The animal's thin grey legs stick out at weird angles, a bundle of soft, grey, moss-covered sticks — one up near Doug's face, another straight out the side. The joey blinks at Doug with alarm because Doug is blubbering. Big tears that make the orange stubble on his chin twinkle. Skin so white it's see-through and going red in the sun. Jolts when he sees me.

'Thought you were Ange,' he says, wiping his face. 'We're not supposed to be interacting with them. Supposed to just try for business as usual. But he's ... he's calling me Mum.'

I snort. 'Calling *me* Mum, more likely.'

'He thinks you're going to kill him.'

I lean close to that joey. Try to pick up some meaning. The joey looks back at me with liquid eyes. 'He likes me.'

'He thinks you're going to kill him,' Doug says again.

I back off. The joey kicks out. 'Everyone can talk to them except me, is that it?'

Doug doesn't answer. He's back to dripping his fat tears all over the roo.

Inside the food store it's quiet and empty — cool metal prep tables in the snot-coloured dim. My body has sucked all the heat from the day to radiate it back out through the slash in my fucked-up hand. Expect steam when I wash my burning skin in the sink. The water hurts my face and I shiver, now freezing. Drag the cold-room jacket on and collapse onto the gurney we use to examine sick beasts. I'm there like a bat with her wings clutched, my ancient fingers grabbing the air. The shivers pass again into heat, then cold again but not as bad. After the next flush, I feel good enough to sit up and take the jacket off, wet with sweat. A spider sits splay-legged in the corner watching a fat blowfly do wheelies through the air. Someone runs past the food store with a sound that is half laugh, half cry. I snort my nose on a bit of paper towel, and the room stinks like antiseptic, hay, rotting fruit, and mice. The feed in the buckets is waiting to be dished out. Half-rotten fruit that needs to be used today or it's gone.

'It's just you now, Jeanie-Queen,' I tell myself, edging off the gurney. Legs steady enough. 'Business as usual.' Whistle through my teeth like some cartoon rooster, reeling around the food store, saving the day. Keep my sore hand out of the way and go at it one-handed. Kibble in my pockets for bribes and treats. Get going on the mouse feed: the grains, the seeds, the pellets. Whispering — Doug talking to his baby wallaroo. I got real work to do. I grab a couple of soft apples and dice them up wonkily with a big dirty knife on a chopping board stained with fruit from yesterday or the day before. No time for cleaning. The voices grow louder but muffled.

'I'm busy in here,' I shout. Give the bucket a mix with my hand. 'Can't hear you.'

The voices stop, start up again. Yellow mist, a sickly gas, seeps from behind the swing doors that lead to the hall, the mouse rooms, and the gas chamber. The pipes must be busted, the gas left on. It curls like clouds, leaking poison under the door. If it kills those mice we'll be buggered — nothing to feed the snakes or the raptors. I dump the bucket, take a gulp of fresh air, and launch through the doors, beating at the off switch with my grimy hand. It's already off. No gas. Gas. Wisps from the mouse room — must have leaked in there. All the breeding pairs will be dead. The whispers louder. I can almost make out words.

'Hello?'

The gas is thick. They'll all be dead. I haul open the heavy doors to see if I can save even a couple of them. Dozens of mice sit up on their haunches, alive, horrified. Gas rising, not from the pipes, but from their bodies. Not squeaking, screaming. They scream bloody murder, the death of everyone, death in the cages and death in the walls. All the little kids in the whole world die. My poor old Dad reaches out from his early grave. Disease eats my face, crunches my bones until I'm rotting, empty, sucked dry by raptors, bones left to dust. I fall back, fumbling. What's left of my body? Blood and bits, a carcass. But I'm whole. The mice are whole. I'm going fucking crazy. There's no scream- ing, just a whole bunch of fat-arsed mice with their noses in the air.

Run.

I look around. Someone said it, clear as speech. 'I'm in here,' I call out to Doug.

Run.

It's glands from the

body. It's crops

and

killing and shelter —

'No, it's ...' Who's talking? 'It's just Jean.'

The small white bodies in the cages shiver. Gases rise off them, and a squeak comes out, and together they make: run.

On a

hillside. Run

to the wall.

You go, I'll

make my way, one

and everyone.

Everything. The body. Run.

I run. The door behind me heavy with all those little words. The gases push out in clouds and hang around my nose and eyes, jitterbugging my brain. Everything. The body. Run.

Who's talking? Who's here? Casey, Liu, and Doug have disap- peared. I slide down the outer wall of the food store until my bum hits ground. Mice don't talk like that. Mice talk about eating and fucking. It's just my ears, curled like dead leaves. Deathly quiet now.

Only the rumble of distant motors. Whispers from the tree hollows.
I push myself up to standing, to some sort of hope.

Glitter.

'What?'

I can see its

glitter,

give

it to me.

Closer to the hot road there's the blessed noise of an engine — a Park
ute by the sound of it. Grows distant, melts away. In its place is panic.
They've left me. Everyone has left the Park and me in it. With the
mice and the gas and whatever the fuck is the glitter. I get my body
unfrozen and do what the mice told me to do: I bloody well run. The
Park streets empty. One of the Park utes is stalled in the middle of
the road, out of fuel. I keep going. Round a corner, a bulk of scent
nearly knocks me flat. Personal. Someone you don't know waving
their rude bits around, then it's gone. Birds are making nonsensical
sounds above but, all around me, trails of glowing messages have been
laid out overnight. In stench, in calls, in piss, in tracks, in blood, in
shit, in sex, in bodies. A big boy wallaroo has rubbed his scent, slick as
oil, over the grass at the road edge. It's like running alongside a urinal
in a pub. Piss cakes wafting from the bottom of yellow streams. Shake
my stupid head to clear it of the meanings, but they form out of hops,
barks, and whiffs. I see these words as: *King* and *ours*. Bits and pieces,
no damned order or sense. A drunk on the street. Kimberly talking in
her sleep. Until they close like clouds, moving from blobs to ships in
full sail, and I see the sense, loud and clear:

Fuck me, I'm

a King.

Panic rises like vomit from my gut. I shove my hands over my
mouth and nose and run hell for leather.

—

Someone else is running. It's Trench. Never been so happy to see that stupid grey suit. I let go of my face to call out but that makes him go faster, coat-tails flapping. There's a toilet block by the zoo-train pickup point for the aquarium. Trench gets in there, slams the door and locks it.

'Trent,' I call. Pound on the metal. I can hear him whimpering. Can't say I blame him. 'It's me. Jean.'

'No,' he shouts. 'No.'

'Let me in, matey. You can't leave me out here.' There's a pause while the bastard thinks about this, then the door is unlocked. Inside it's pitch. I feel for the switch, remember about the electricity. The only light comes through gaps left by a few missing bricks.

Trench pants heavily in the dark, swallows loudly. 'It spoke to me,' he says. I nod, but he can't see me. 'The wallaby spoke to me.'

'I just talked to mice.'

'He said he wanted to be in the sky but the trees won't let him.'

'The mice told me to run.'

'What does that *mean*?'

'I don't know. I'll hold the door open,' I tell him, 'so there's a bit of light and you can wash your face. You'll feel better.' I can't hear him breathing anymore. 'Trent?' My voice comes back at me in the concrete room. There's moving and humming in the dark. I follow the voice to a corner. 'Someone there with you?' I hear a scuffle. He grabs my arm. I nearly shit myself right there.

'Dog,' he says.

My heart in my throat. 'Dog?' No shapes form in the dim.

'I thought you were a dog. Talking.'

I back up until I reach the wall, feel around for the door and wrench it open — sun like sheet lightning.

Out on the road, nothing talks. The alien drone of the insects. Trench calls out from the toilet block, 'Jean?'

'What?'

'You're still there.'

'I'll go get someone. Your wife. Okay?' No answer. 'Okay?'

'Okay.'

He's not going anywhere. I jog up the short path scattered with leaves and pandanus. The Night House is only 200 metres away. That place has more animals packed inside it than any other section of the Park. It's also where the rangers might be — holed up to find out what a lizard has to say. At least the animals are contained there. At least they're not up in the trees, muttering,

Those

old feet.

'I'm not listening to you.' I squint up at the branches. 'Hello?'

Forepaw, flat

pad — I got

good ones.

Bodies chatting away like I don't even exist. No point reminding them they'd be up shit creek without me to feed them. Whatever little mammals are in those trees are wild.

Turn around and I'll

stick it

in. Your

feet are fucking

ancient.

Turkey bushes flower purple all along the path. I grab a couple to shove in my ears and nose. It'd be quieter if I could stick to the centre of the melting road, but the short cut is down a sandy track between the trees. My ears short and muted. Eyes darting this way and that, like a tourist who doesn't know his face from his bum. The sunlight green through that low canopy. A hissing sound that makes me speed-the-hell-up. Something scratching in the undergrowth. Silence as I stand and plough on. I stop and crouch low, like I can listen better below the wall of stumpy trees. A short, strange cough up ahead. *Keep it together, Jeanie.* Stop those little thinks from travelling up from your gut and getting into your head. Swallow it down. I swallow. My bitten-up hand throbs for me to keep moving. Pick up a wobbly dried leaf of pandanus, and hold it in front of me: the floppiest sword you've ever seen. It slices at my finger, leaving a smile of dark-red blood.

An orange-footed bush fowl bursts from the bushes — has me damned near pissing myself. No messages, just a body. I laugh and it scatters, orange-toed, into the brush. *Eh oh eh eh oh!* Nonsense sounds — no meaning. My pulse settles. Force myself to crunch along the path, tranquil, like when we first moved north. No point rushing around like a freezing southerner. When your blood and the air are the same temperature, you've got to let them go easy on each other. One step after another. The mutterings dulled and the bush turkey quiet.

Just as I skirt around a mossy stump, a voice calls to me like a childhood song:

Queen.

It rips through my itchy earplugs. I know it. Not Kimberly or Lee or the little things in the tree, but someone so familiar that I skip, God help me, and start toward it.

A whiff of

Queen.

Slowly tug the flowers out of my ears and squint through the trees. A fly to my left. The stench of the forest, private as an armpit. Sweat pooling cold between my boobs. My special someone calls again.

Queen

is here.

'Ange?' Angela won't be calling anyone *Queen*. It's someone else in the bush. I see caramel. Meet with a face so familiar it could be mine. Takes a moment for me to understand it's not human.

Every

thing.

'Sue'. I stumble back into a pandanus. We're both breathing hard. 'Can you hear me, Sue?'

Copy that
Queen (Yesterday).

She's right there, escaped from her enclosure, sitting politely in a clearing with one of our rainbow lorikeets in her mouth — metal ID band around the bird's leg. Kermit. Or Miss Piggy. I could never tell which from which. Sue's face is stiff with what I guess is blood. She isn't talking through her mouth or her mind but, like the mice and the things in the trees, through her whole damned body — upright and narrow, very proper in her way. Her voice isn't made of words either. She's speaking in odours, echoes, noises with random meanings popping out of them. A twitching rear paw. Creaking sounds of welcome in her throat that don't say what they should say. No hello or hi, no formal greetings. It's:

My front end
takes the food
quality.
Muzzle
for the Queen
(Yesterday).

'You said "Queen" again.'
She steps forward.

Queen. Open me
up.

'Jesus, Sue.'

What.

'What?'

The noise its face
makes.

I crouch. Really take a look at her. I've spent the last seven or so years staring at Sue, but I never saw her white chest talk two ways. One for the open road, the time of the whole world, the wild dogs out there. The other way for inside the cage, the safety of locked doors and a hand on her back.

A hand on

my

back.

Her body crackles around the parrot.

It's

all (mine)

Queen's.

Everything in me says this is bad: an edgy dingo is a dangerous
one. 'I'm not after your bird. You can –'

Maw

it.

'Why don't we go back to your enclosure to do that?'

She bursts forward, body dancing. You'd think it'd be easier now
that we can talk. *Back to your yard, good dog.* But her twitchy paw, the
rumbles in her throat, her smooth pelt, and her smart-as-a-whip ears
all together say,

Gasping

over the

lock. (I'm

mingy.) It'll call me and

I'd like

to get a drink of

it.

Doesn't make a lick of sense. I speak slow so she can understand
me. 'Why. Don't. We. Go. Back —'

Barking

mad.

I stare at her. Try another tactic. 'It's dangerous out here. You'll get
hurt.'

What.

'You've got to go back to your enclosure.' The smell of metal comes
from her forehead at the mention of the cage. It gets in my nose too.
Same smell as is on my hands when I've been hauling gates open and

shut all day. Locking up Sue and the other creatures all safe and sound.

No whiskers on

the inside. (Out.)

'You have to go back. Come on, we'll go for a walk.' Pat my thigh. 'Come.' *Pat pat walkies* had so much damned power yesterday. Now it seems stupid next to the rippling chorus that's coming off her white furry socks.

The

best thing is to

make

a plan.

'You come with me. That's the plan.'

Not

the barking bandits. The

minstrel.

The singer. The stinky

Queen (Yesterday).

Clear my throat. 'That back paw.' She lifts it a little.

(Yesterday.)

'What happened yesterday?'

The

one made of bones and

biscuits. The (Yesterday) party.

I'm here for the

Queen.

'Well. I don't have any fucking idea.' Her messages grow teeth.

Bloody

colony.

I stand too quick. Trip on a rock. 'Back off. Back off, you —' Bitch? Mongrel? Mutt? What words? She backs off. Puts the floppy rainbow lorikeet on the ground between us, real careful. It lies there like a palette of paint. The dingo blinks her willingness to make the deal easy as possible.

That's

the

way.

That's it. (Tussie-mussie.) That's

it right there.

That's —

'Alright, Sue. Just ... just stay. Sit, you know?'

She sits. A crazy giggle bubbles in my throat. Find some kibble in my pocket. Sue snaps it up, no gratitude or nothing. Just,

The body of my

mother, tang

of blood.

My mother

tongue. The Queen

(Yesterday).

'What's in that head of yours, Sue?' Stupid question, but her ears are on me.

A Band-Aid is

ripped

and every

hair comes with

it.

'A Band-Aid.' Dingo Sue doesn't know what the hell a Band-Aid is. If I've got my mouth, she's got all her flesh and bones. I'm reading her body like some language I barely remember from a high school textbook. *Bonjour madame, connaissez-vous le chemin de la gare?* Let's go to the station. Or, where the hell is the supermarket? I can parrot the words, but the meaning is in scraps. Then there's a waft from Sue's under-bits — small talk from a dingo's bum that's nothing like reading at all. I start shaking and can't stop. Sue calls,

Horse

Queen (Yesterday).

That voice fills my jaw like it's hollow, she's water.

'Hang on.'

Where

does it hang.

'Be quiet. So I can think.'

She's quiet for about five seconds before her body starts letting off hisses of meaning that build and burst.

I want to be a

princess. (Stakeholder

here

and

here.)

Two songs playing at once. Gets me in my guts. I need a drink and a smoke and a sit down before I spew out of all my holes at once. 'I'm serious now. You have to stop.' What? Talking?

Stay.

(Run from

it.) Stay

now.

'Yeah, stay.' I back away. 'Stay there, okay?' The bracken clears to sand beneath my feet and I turn, running. Her reek calls,

Bowel movement (short and golden).

Sit

(Yesterday), stay,

all the way down the track.

Casey is stumbling along the road between the aquarium and the bird hide.

'Casey. The dingoes are out and I don't —' I stop. She's frowning at the ground. Jerks her head skyward. A fly scoots past. Casey surges toward it.

'Insects,' she says. Her voice has a buzz to it. 'Can you talk to them? I can. Those ants.'

Ants follow ants that follow other ants in a streaming black line over the hot tarmac. All along the stark, empty road, small black shapes missile over the ground and through the air.

'There's too many of them,' I tell her. 'You'll go nuts.'

She blinks at me. I go to say it again, but she smiles. 'Oh no. No. No. It's biblical.'

'Biblical?'

A fly circles. She's lost to it. Led by her ear down the road, following a bug.

There's no one in the café. The doors hang open. More flies in the bain-marie — their round black figures buzz, meaningless. I gun it up to Angela's fast as my shaking legs can take me. A wind filled with bits of sand whips up and throws me around. Inside, a message.

King.

I feel it.

Angela is stationed out in her yard, legs planted. I get the fear when I see her, but her anger-eyes aren't for me. She's peering up at the dusk sky. I look up too. Powdery pink, pale as an egg.

'I messed up, Ange,' I tell her. A shadow passes overhead. 'One of the dingoes got out. I messed up —'

She reaches out and grips my arm with her muscly fingers. It hurts. I try to prise her off. She holds on like she'll never let go. Two shapes appear above us. A pair of enormous white-bellied birds that hang overhead, on black wings like reaching hands. Our old show sea eagles: pair of cranky old buggers with smooth heads and eyes like a sea in storm that only a few rangers could ever get near, Ange one of them. They spin above us, then pause.

Angela yanks my arm. 'Get inside.' Starts us running, her face twisted in terror. She lets go of me and flings out her arms. Too slow to stop the sudden rushing of black-and-white bodies falling from the sky like missiles. One of the birds buckles, stretches out a claw like a blade that runs along Angela's face and pulls away within a nick of her eyeball. The eagle is twenty metres in the sky before Ange can cry out. Before the blood beads on her cheek. A scary stripe, but not deep.

'You're alright, Ange. It missed. It missed. It —'

She turns her pink eye on me, blood beading beside it. 'The sea eagle doesn't miss. That was a warning. Oh my God. I am warned.'

'Warned?'

'To feed them. I heard ...' She swallows. 'I felt the claw tell me how it would take my eye and what it would do once it got it. I felt it louder than I hear you.'

'You're talking to birds now? You understand all that?'

She gasps a sob. 'Enough of it.'

'Well, tell them.' I point at the sky. 'Tell them you're their friend.'

'I'm not their friend. I'm their predator. I'm their prey. They're *hunting me back.*'

I drag Ange into the house and sit her on the couch. Kimberly appears in the doorway, thumb in mouth, pink eyes brimming.

'Poor little duck.' I bring her close and wait for the tears to run out. 'Can you talk to birds too?' She shakes her head. 'Good thing.' I wipe her face with the hem of my shirt. Her skin cooler now. Get her busy finding antiseptic cream. Catch my eyes in the hall mirror. Minute steaks sitting on my face. Red glowing, like they're hot. Kim with those same bloody peepers. 'We'll get your mum fixed up, won't we? Doctor Kim and nurse Granny.'

She isn't fooled. She watches her mum out the corner of her eye. Ange is waving her head about wildly at the dimming sky out the window, hair a bushy nest.

'They're hungry. They're used to being fed every day and on time.'

'Ange, what did that eagle call you? Queen or something?'

'No. Only the mammals do that. Dogs. Dingoes. Probably to do with a hierarchy of smell. Redolence.' She squints at the sky through the window. 'The eagles call me Sinew. Bits of ...' She shoots a look at Kim. 'We should never have released them.'

I steer Angela into the bedroom. Raid her medicine cabinet, surprised to find some hard stuff in there. Pop a couple of Valium into my breast pocket and two in her mouth. She settles back in the middle of the mattress, obedient for once. So like Kim when she's tired. Her face puffy and young, mouth softened in a 'too'. I want to sing her a nursery rhyme, but they've all got animals in them. A prayer my mum used to say to me at bedtime comes instead.

'Matthew, Mark, Luke, and John. Bless the bed that I lie on. Four the corners to my bed, four the angels round my head. One to watch and one to pray, and two to bear my soul away.'

Angela eyes me. 'What's that?'

'Little rhyme. Help you sleep.' I repeat it again and again, like Sue the dingo with her Queening. Except sensible. Helpful. Not batshit confusing. Ange watches me with stubborn-as-hell eyes. The room grows hot, then hotter. My Matthews, Lukes, and Johns swim and stumble. Have to swallow a couple of paracetamol and give myself a cold wash in the scrubbed shower. Out the shadowy bathroom window, the tree-mammals mutter evening nonsense.

It is

more visible

if you pull the skin with your

blanket.

Rub my own skin with a fluffy towel. Who's talking to who is talking to who anymore? Back in the bedroom, Angela has finally closed her eyes.

'She's sleeping,' Kim loud-whispers into the pillow beside her.

Ange half sits in a final burst of worry. Grabs my hand. 'You need to look after her.'

I push her back to the bed. 'You'll feel better if you get some shut-eye.'

'You need to look after her. I'll be so busy doing. A new plan for this stage of the disease. This is an opportunity to work with the ... all the animals. We need to coordinate a risk matrix. Contingency. And preparedness. And transparency. And make a plan and get everything ready. All those birds in the aviary. Seven hundred. And thirty-two. Or. Do a count. You need to count them. You need to look after her. Okay? Okay?'

'Alright, Ange.' She's still clutching me, so I gingerly lie down too. 'Okay?' Her grip loosens, and her hand falls away.

SEVEN

We shove toilet paper in our ears and tie tea towels around our faces in the dawn light. Kim's cloth has a kangaroo and an emu on it. Both our noses have cleared. The tea towels whiff of fat and soap. The path to the food store where Angela's campervan is parked is only 200 metres, but it feels like we're crossing a minefield of berserko messages. Presence and time stretch out like a map. I keep shivering, and not with fever. My skin cool, my body hair pricks and then settles. Eyes on the bush, looking out for a sandy behind and a chatty dingo face.

'Are you getting this, Kimbo? Are you feeling that?'

'Huh?'

I shove my tea towel aside. 'Can you feel it?'

She nods. Takes out her toilet paper. 'Like electric poos. My poo's electric.' I can't stop laughing. 'Shoosh, Granny.' I take my tissue out too. Nothing. Then, that whispering. The wallabies and wallaroos bouncing about in the weird green light. The voices off their backs, out of their tails. Calling,

Happy isn't
happy. Happy
isn't the only
happy.

'Don't make much sense, do they?'

Kim turns her red eyes on me, head to the side like she's one of them. 'Yeah, they do.'

'You can't get any meaning out of that.'

'Yeah.' She pulls the towel off her face and juts out a tiny, exposed ear.

The bosom is

a plot

between the feet and the

ground.

'They're saying they're safe when they're bouncing. They like to be up in the air.'

'What's so special about that?'

'They live on a trampoline, Granny!'

I stare at their bodies. The whole world a trampoline.

You're

better

than the dung that

comes out of

pricks.

'Okay, well I got that.'

Kimberly sniggers. 'You got to *look* at them, Granny.'

'I am.'

'You've really got to try.'

I frown at her but can't make it last. Little bugger has all the stubbornness of me, her mum, and her Granddad Graham combined. 'How, then?'

'Well.' Kimberly puffs up to twice her size, and that's not much. 'You have to look at all their whole body all at the same time, not just the bits.'

Get

together,

says a tail.

Sip it —

an eyelash.

Musky fog from a bum calls,

Fancy.

'But the bits say different things.' I edge forward. The roos shriek,

Blood

fire.

Bound off into the bush. Once they're gone you can almost touch the quiet. Like when a noisy visitor has left the house and you just want them back again. Feels like Friday morning — like every time Kimberly leaves.

Glen is in the car park, trying to use his walkie-talkie. A couple of small wallaroos skip around his feet, calling him 'it', giving him a hard time.

It. It.

Now fight with

it.

'What? No.' Glen gets back to the radio. 'Okay, just tell me where you are.'

It. Fuck

the King.

'Poor Glen.'

'But they think Glen's their dad,' says Kim. 'See?'

I blink. Can barely make out their sweet, pointed faces through the fug of messages from their furry ears and hinds. Those joeys with their heavy haunches and thick tails. Paws calling about how they will be King. Mouths still pursed for their mum's milky teat. Eyes on Glen's legs coming out of his khaki shorts. These meanings come together, make a question:

Is it

King.

'Where's Ange?' Glen asks me.

King. Here.

Over

here.

Glen waves them away. The wallaroos hook off, screaming songs of strangers, the whisper of death, and the end of grasslands.

'Jean?'

'Yeah.' I blink. Glen's tapping his walkie-talkie against his thigh like it's Monday and he's late for an all-staff. I don't even know what day it is.

'Where is she?' he asks again.

'A. N. G. E. is sick.'

'Mum can talk to the birds now,' Kim tells Glen. 'Snakes too.'

I grab Kim by the shoulder. 'Reptiles? You sure?'

She's got the constipated look of someone who wasn't supposed to say what she just said. Looks down at her boots with salty regret. Glen isn't coping with this news either. Hands on his knees, head hanging between his shoulders. From the hollow of the big tree, something sighs,

Glitter.

Glen squints at it. 'You girls get what they're saying?'

'Kim can. She's got an ear for it, don't you, Kimbo? What does glitter mean, do you think?'

Kim shrugs but she can't help it: she watches sideways the undertones and microscopic sounds spilling from the tree,

The dazzle

of

it.

She points to her armpit. 'They like the water on our skin.'

Glen wipes his hands on his shorts. 'Our sweat.'

'They like our glitter.'

'Yeah,' says Glen, 'our glitter.'

'They've got a weird way of expressing themselves, that's for sure,' I tell them. Glen and Kim drag their ham-steak eyes away from the tree. I poke the air. 'They think you're their King.'

'Their dad,' Kim says.

'They're calling me "Father-Son",' Glen says, quiet.

'Is that something to do with your tribe?'

'My *tribe*? Are you talking about Djabugay people? Because —'

'Maybe those wallabies are your totem animal or something?'

'Jesus, Jean —'

'Well, it's difficult. You don't make it easy.'

'Monthly cultural awareness sessions for three bloody years aren't enough for you to know when you're out of line? To learn how totems actually work and how important they are to people?'

'The sessions are on my day off.'

There's an anguished scream from the direction of the aquarium. Glen stops glaring at me and groans. 'Trent's wife. Scared of the wallabies. Who the hell let them out?'

I open my mouth to tell him about Sue, shut it again. I'm not too keen on having a loose and chatty dingo about either, but I know Glen. He's handy with a shotgun. A predator's not in its proper place, he'll shoot it until it is.

'I'm due to feed the rays,' I say instead. 'I'll look in on Trench's woman on my way.'

Glen sucks his lip. 'Alright, then. I'll meet you there in a bit. You got your radio?'

I pat my hip. A tough cop.

'Keep it on you. It's going to get gnarly without ...' He nods in the direction of Ange's house. 'We need contact. With other actual humans. Even if they are fucking idiots.' I guess from his look he means me.

Outside the storerooms, Kim reties the tea towels. The store stinks to high heaven — rotting fish, rotting fruit, all decomposing together in the heat. And there's Andy, wrist deep in muck, throwing container after container of feed into garbage bags.

'Don't say a fucking word,' he tells me before I can crack a smile under my wrapping. We work alongside each other — me and Kim with the clean dry food in our buckets, Andy with his stinky mess.

'You got a tipple?' he asks after a while.

'Chucked it down the drain.'

'World gone mad.'

'I think I pissed Glen off. Asking about his past.'

'Glen has a past?'

'His heritage.'

'Fucking hell. Leave him alone.'

'What do you mean?'

'You're always at him. You're always at everyone.'

A voice has crept in. *Oh,* it says. *Oh.*

'How's it going with the animals?' I say after a while. Andy breathes out his nose. 'Look,' I tell him. 'I know it seems like they don't make any more sense now they can talk but Kim says they start to.' I nudge her. 'Tell him, Kim.' She hides her head in my hip. 'Well, she says it works if you take in the whole picture. You've got to try to think the way they —'

'Shut up, Jean.'

Oh.

Oh.

'Come on, mate —'

'Shut up.'

Chance I'm a blue
colour. We
won't eat that
again.

Andy points at the mouse room with a rotten carrot. 'I know exactly what they're fucking saying. A depressed mouse. Who the fuck wants to hear that?'

'Keep the graphics down, thanks. Kim here.'

Plastic
leftovers. How
long.

Andy's face is red as his eyes. 'You think I don't know how they'll eat the cages, the hay, maybe their young before they starve? I know. Don't think I don't know. I just don't want to be the one in here when they do it.'

'Why are you here, then?'

Andy mutters something.

How long until

we

get there.

'What?'

'Keith dumped me, I said. He's off to sign up for the Land Patrols. "Game on". All that.'

'Well, I'm sorry.' I'm not sorry. I feel sore and pleased. Go to touch him but we're just animals too, and I see that he might bite.

Me and Kim pop the feed buckets in the campervan and head toward the aquarium. I bend my tea towel–wrapped face to take in hers. She blinks over the picture of the emu, nods bravely. We drive the baked roads with the windows up, battered by the smells and rumours and stories that rush in, even through our masks. At the aquarium, the generator grinds away over the gurgle of pumps and swishes. The hungry creatures in the tanks list through the dark water. Iridescent fish that shiver behind coral with sleek, silent bodies. Kim pulls her mask off, and we grin at each other through the murk. If Trench's wife was hiding out in here, she's not anymore. In the tanks, khaki creatures cling to watery shadows. Turtles. A freshwater crocodile with sharp, protruding teeth. Fleshy-lipped rays soar overhead in a domed aquarium — planes through tunnels of water. Kim's grip bites into my septic hand.

We turn a dim corner. A small wooden sign says 'Bernie the saltwater crocodile, 3.5 metres'. Kim's favourite enclosure. The glass shows a cross-section of pond and land. Up on the dry bit, a little door connects to the outside, sun sliding in through the gaps. A walk-way around the top of the pond means that the rangers can deal with Bernie without having to actually touch him: dropping chickens into the water and knocking him out with a tranquilliser gun if they need to. Bernie is alone in there now, submerged and hovering in the centre of the pond. The size and look of a fallen tree. A gnarled, woody rep-tile, lit by the skylight high above the water. Perched above a long jaw lined with teeth sits his yellow eye. His gaze trained above him. Still watching the surface, he sinks like he's being lowered on a platform. Small clouds of sand rise at his massive feet where they land. Thank all my lucky stars I don't know what he's thinking.

The door that leads into the enclosure from the outside rattles and Angela ducks in, face striped with tears. I let go Kimberly's hand to rap on the glass. Angela takes a few steps forward. Kimberly touches the glass too. Ange ignores us. We pound harder. Yell. She only has eyes for the pond. Beneath the surface, Bernie is watching.

'Hello, I'm a person,' we hear Ange say. 'A human. I want to talk to you.' She says it slow and clear. We all know very well Bernie has the best hearing of anything in the Park, even underwater. Bernie heard Ange get out of bed this morning — he's been waiting ever since. He stays perfectly still, but his body must have said something, and that something ripped through the water and popped in a bubble of meaning for Angela to hear. She sucks her breath, glances at us for the first time through the glass. Her face says, *did you get that?* I grab for the walkie-talkie at my hip.

'Emergency. This is Jean in the aquarium. Ange is in the croc pit. I repeat, Ange is in the fucking croc pit.' There's a crackle, then nothing.

'Why is Mum in there with Bernie?' Kim's voice wobbles. 'You're not supposed to swim with crocodiles ...' Angela steps a little closer to the water.

'Ange. You better come out of there. Your daughter's right here. See?'

Ange shakes her head like my voice is a blowfly. Waves me away.

Kimberly starts drumming on the glass. I join her. The croc shifts his interest to us.

'Get out of there, Ange. Angela. He'll ...'

Kimberly looks up at me. 'Will he eat her?'

'No. Of course not, love. 'Course not.'

I try the walkie-talkie again. No one responds. The thing is broken. Kim's face is pressed to the glass. I should protect her — she doesn't need to see any of this — but I can't look away either. A horror show happening metres from our skin. Angela crouched by the water. I bash on the barrier again.

'Angela! Jesus fucking Christ.' She's down on her hands and knees, her ear to the pond and she's grinning, *grinning*, then she stops. Frowns. Jerks back, dripping. I see something in her eyes. Not fear. Recognition. She didn't know something — now she knows, and it's not good.

Bernie pushes on the sandy bed of the pond with muscular legs and launches up to break the water. Ange stumbles away from the churning pool.

'No, I don't,' she says, voice quaking. 'I don't.'

The croc seems slow, cumbersome when he launches, but he's faster than her. He surges forward, breaks the surface, and in a heartbeat he's up on the bank. He latches on to Angela's leg with yellow teeth and a guttural roar. Ange is screaming, yelling, arguing with him. 'No. No. I said I don't want to.' The croc gives a sharp tug, dragging Angela half a metre toward the water. I grab Kimberly's face and push her against my stomach. Her yells rattle my guts.

'Where the fuck are you?' I scream into the walkie-talkie. Something taps the surface of the water. A bird dropped down on a hook from above. The blood spreads like a blush. I keep Kim pressed to me and edge closer to the glass, trying to get an eye on who's above, but it's designed so the tourists can't see. Designed so chickens fall from the sky and no one ever actually has to get in the pit with Bernie. The croc is paused by the events in his enclosure. Half in and half out of the pond. He twists a little, dragging Ange to the side. The bloody chicken is behind him in the water. Ange on the small beach, one leg in his mouth. She tries to reason with him, arms waving.

'Please. I don't want to. Let me go. Let me go and I'll leave. No, I didn't say that. Do you really think —?'

'Stay still,' I tell her. This time she listens to me. Keeps her arms down. The only thing moving in the enclosure is that dead chicken. Bounce, bounce over the surface of the pond, bloody as anything. Bernie lets go of Angela's leg and turns his giant self in the water. As he launches for the chicken a gunshot goes off and through him. Again, blood drifts up, smoky. Another shot. The crocodile jolts. Ange cries out. Reaches for him. But whatever was holding Bernie to life lets go, and the croc hovers below the surface, suspended.

'He was talking,' Ange says, still on the ground, leg all bloodied up. 'He said he wanted to play with me. Play with me. Until ...'

EIGHT

'Look, we'll chop this guy up,' says Glen. 'Give the staff and the animals a big last feed. Tomorrow we release all species and close shop. We tried Angela's way. We tried to save them, but now she's lost the plot, and we've got to save ourselves before we go nuts along with her. Agreed?'

We nod — me, Trench, and Doug standing around Glen in the food-store car park. There's blood in our cheeks, as well as our eyes. Up in the branches, bodies jeer, throwing down clouds of scent. I squint, listen. The creatures in the trees — maybe sugar gliders, rats — mutter dissent. Their voices make me edgy, and I'm not the only one. All four of us glancing up, then looking away quickly — heckled by rodents. Angela's face when she was talking to that croc, like someone falling in love with a monster. Beauty and the Beast. Only Casey is enjoying herself now, arms wrapped around a tree, talking to ants. Glen clicks his fingers, brings us back again. He's got skills. Knows how to do things like make a little hole with a knife in the thick croc hide, push a bicycle pump into it, and blow air into the skin to make it bubble. It slits easy, then. He hands me a knife to cut the sinews that hold the membrane to the muscle, so Trench and Doug can pull. The scaly skin comes away from the carcass like rubber.

It

glitters.

'I'll show those animals who's boss,' Trench mutters, threading a rope through the bullet hole in the crocodile's head. I climb into the ute and back it toward the pit. Bernie's big tail swishes at the air like he's still swimming.

Glen's hip buzzes. Liu calling in from the surgery attached to the food store. Ange's wounds are surprisingly minor, she reckons — eight stitches. Liu is more worried about trauma. Got Ange dosed up to her eyeballs on antibiotics and codeine. I ask Kim if she'd like to go over there, sit with her mum and play nurse.

'You could stick Band-Aids on her face,' I say, but the poor kid has shut down. Can't stop sleeping. I worry about the zooflu. Feel her head. It isn't any hotter than mine, so I park the campervan close to where we're skinning Bernie and set her up on the foam bed, where she drifts off to sleep. Once, she cries out and needs me to tell her there's no croc in the cupboard of the kitchenette. I point to where Bernie is outside, half undressed, skin to the waist. Figure it might be best for her to see that big old lizard dead and dismantled. Not sure if that's good grandparenting or if I should be reported. But she nods, seems relieved, and goes back to sleep. It's not like anyone else is setting such a great example. Ange talking to pumped-up lizards. Casey over there, ear to bark, chuckling and hissing at the wood. The beasts higher up in the tree jeering,

Killers.

We scrape the last of the scales off.

Killers but

I'm the

Dad.

'You're not the bloody King,' Trench tells them, wiping his tacky hands on the wood. 'I am.' He covers their glittery chatter with croc blood. It's effective. They fall quiet.

'They said "Dad", not "King"', I tell him over the last rattle of terror from the mammals. Trench grabs the trunk, snagging and ripping his pants pocket, but scaling it with ease.

'Who's Daddy now?'

He catches the rope from a right-angled branch and throws it down the other side. I can hear him telling some creature up there he will bloody well eat them if they don't shut up. They shut up. We pull on the rope from below, hauling at the carcass until it's hanging from the tree like a sacrifice.

Armoured bits of scale stick to my skin. I grab some paper towel and a bucket of water and take it behind the campervan to wash the blood and gore off me. A crunch in the undergrowth. This is the moment when I finally face up and talk to one of those turkey birds. But it's Lee in the scrub, barefoot, grinning like he's just taken a dump. The dirt creeps up his feet and joins with the dark hair curling around his ankles. Dust a layer over him like a skin that sifts and sheds when he moves. His eyes ablaze in that tan.

'What the fuck, Lee?'

'It's a travesty.'

'You better get out of here, darl.'

He fishes a tailor-made cigarette from the pocket of a Park shirt he's pilfered and lights it, hair dangerously close to the pale flame. The smoke crowds his face, melts away. The shirt is filthy. He flicks a bit of ash from it. I snatch the cigarette off him and suck it down. Laughter in my boy's eyes as I finish it and grind the butt against the side of the van.

'You know anything about a dingo getting loose?' I ask him. He nods. Lights another smoke. He's got some magic, never-ending pack in that Park shirt. 'You let them go?'

'Just one. I emancipated her. She calls me "Never There". For some reason he's tickled pink at this.

Kim presses herself to the screen from inside the camper. 'Hi, Dad.' I put my finger to my lips. 'Hi, Dad,' she whispers, just as loudly. Lee kisses her through the mesh. Her eyes sparkle. 'What's he-man plate?'

'Emancipate, my Magic Mushroom, means freedom. Don't you want to be free?'

Kimberly nods, solemn behind the flywire. Lee nods too.

'Everyone does. Everything does. Way I see it is the domestics — your dogs and your cats — are like Barbie dolls. Rip the heads off them and replace them with the heads from other toys, like dinosaurs or cows. You still do that?'

Kim nods, proud. Her bedroom at home is littered with plastic freaks.

'Hairless plastic lady body, green monster head. The domestics are messed up on thousands and thousands of years of us. They're domestic in a wild body or wild in a domestic one or some train wreck of it all.' He sucks the smoke back and breathes it out in words. 'With these poor little guys in here, the captive wild, it's more like an institution. Like a hospital, a prison. They've gone nuts. Their brains are nuts. They don't know whether they're in or out, wild or free, predator or prey. They've got it in their heads we're out to kill them and keep dropping food on the way. We're just messy predators, too clumsy to catch them. That's how all these animals see us. We're not "friend or foe"; we are the enemy, every single time. Sure, there's respect there because we hold the food. What they're hoping is if they hang round and do what they're supposed to, we'll drop something.'

'That's no excuse for letting them go, Lee. And no excuse for being here either. You've got to leave.'

'Tell us about the whales again, Dad.'

Lee grins at this. 'That's the best bit. There's other animals, isn't there? Mammals that aren't domestic, and they're not in jail, they're wild and free. They're singing. Refrains. Repetitions. Notes you can't hardly hear. Deafening choruses. Songs so sad and so happy those words don't even begin. Can you hear it?'

'I can hear it,' Kimberly shouts.

'Darl,' I hiss, 'shut your gob.'

We all hush. Listen to the shuffling, scratching, and murmurs in the bush —

That's my

ear

pit —

until Lee can't hold his tongue any longer. 'Zooflu is a gift,' he whispers. 'It is. It's a gift. Those right whales down south. Come into the bays. Come to chat and can you even imagine what they'd have to say? Blow your little mind, right? Going to head down there soon as I can find a car.' He casts a pink eye over the camper, and I've got such an itch to slap him.

Kimberly strains against the mesh. 'I want to see the whales.'

Lee nods at her. 'Find out the mysteries of the deep.'

I move to stand between them. 'We're going to cook a croc, and you're leaving, Lee. Before I'm out on my arse with you.'

Lee lingers. 'Got some money, Mum?'

I go find my wallet in the van. There's almost a hundred and forty in there I haven't had the chance to spend with the Park all closed up. I give him the hundred.

'You should come with me. Bring Kim. It's better out there. The phone towers are still up. There's power outside. Except for all the army and pig hunters, it's better.'

'Get out of here, hun.'

He wipes his half-smoked cigarette along the ground, puts it in his khaki pocket, and goes in for a hug. Stinks like rotting.

Bernie smokes all day over the fire — the air is heavy with him. The croc corpse looks like a model made out of pink play dough. By night, he's cooked. We smother the coal under him with buckets of water from the reservoir, then start a new fire pit to sit around. Andy emerges from the track to one of the houses — wet and clean of the putrid food he's been in all day. Casey is cross-legged on the ground at the very edge of the light, whispering to the insects flicking about her head. Ange is still in the surgery, with Doug ferrying plates of croc meat to her. He doesn't stand a chance but he's not doing it for nothing. On one of his trips back to the fire he turns out an impressive collection of half-drunk bottles of whiskey. Nobody has any tobacco left. With all of us there, the other mammals stay clear — eyes shining from outside of the firelight, snouts of the released wallabies and wallaroos whispering warnings and lines of flight. Messages from their muzzles like the chop, chop of helicopter blades.

I've got you,

says one to another.

Where. Where. Same

way as

always.

'Don't mind me,' I duck through them.

Watch

it.

'It's okay. I'm just —'

It will

eat your babies.

'Good lord.' Make it to the food store and into the surgery, where Ange is laid up on the gurney, eyes inflamed in the dim. Foot all done up in bandages, nothing broken. I try to get her up and she grumbles, bleary.

'Best thing to do when you fall off a bicycle? Get back on.'

'Leave it.'

'Come on, Ange, we've got a party out there. The animals aren't even ... well, you don't have to mind them. And Kim needs to see that you're alright.'

This gets her. She leans heavily on my arm, lets me lead her, badly limping, out into the night sounds. The stinky, foot-in-your-face sounds. One eye on the dark sky for the sea eagle's claw. A bush stone-curlew screams its murder from the scrub. Angela just smiles politely, nods at the bird. Joins everyone around the fire and pulls Kim in for a hug. The girl falls asleep as soon as she hits Angela's shoulder. After a while, I pop Kim back in the bed of the camper with Hello Bear. Trench carves more bits from the crocodile carcass and piles it on plates. The meat is smoky, soft when I suck on it. Looks like pork, tastes like sea fish, chicken, and brackish rocks. Doug keeps filling my cup.

'The angrier the croc, the better the meat,' I tell everyone.

'Yeah.' Doug raises a disposable cup from the vet clinic and winces at the taste. I stumble over to sit by Andy.

'This is alright, hey? Sitting here drinking in front of the boss? Where's your cup?'

Andy doesn't have a cup. He stares all serious into the fire. 'I tried Kim's way of talking,' he mutters. 'Looked at their whole bodies.'

'She's got a head on her shoulders, alright. Gets that from her grandmum.'

Andy's voice breaks. 'I heard ... heard the pregnant mice say that they'll ... what do you call it? ... *self-terminate* because things aren't right. They can do that. Did you know they could do that?'

'You need a drink, mate.'

'You think this is a laugh. You think Angela trusts you. Don't bet on it.' We watch Liu help Ange into a park van headed for the house. I call out that I'll look after Kim, but that just makes Ange struggle with her seatbelt, trying to escape until Liu talks her back. 'She knows you'll fuck it up soon as you get the chance,' Andy tells me as the ute drives away.

I drain my cup. 'You're just pissed off because your fella left. What happened? You tell him we've been doing the dirty every other month? Missionary style on the double bed. Queer guy with a straight eye?'

'Fuck off, Jean.'

I leave him to his mouse problems. Stumble off down the gravel road until I'm out of the light circle and on a sloping bit of the drive. The rocks creak under me, quietened by my streaming piss. Splashes up my ankles. I shuffle my feet out further. Mind glazing over in the friendly fog where nothing comes or goes or speaks to me. This is the way to get through the animal apocalypse — stay drunk and smoke durries. I was doing it right all along, never knew it. When I stand again, my knee and hip joints have seized into position. They pop, sting while I pull up my underpants. I wander down the road a little, give my stiff old body a bit of a shake-out.

Stran … ger.

'I don't know exactly what you're saying,' I call, 'but as long as you don't tell me to fuck off like those other bastards, we can be friends. Alright? Hello?' The brush is soft, quiet as a bed. My festering hand a dull throb with my head. I lie down and close my eyes. Wake up later with the weight of having done something wrong pressing at my chest. The booze worn off. I can hear whispers, hisses, terror. Something pisses gently on me from above — the urine shouts,

Mine,

mine, mine!

'Hey.' I scramble up, wipe my face. 'Hey.' The being above screams,

Chew through

me.

'Why would I want to eat you?' No answer to that. I get myself back to the fire pit. An empty circle of chairs. Coals still smoking. Even the stars have disappeared, covered by a layer of ashy cloud. Drag marks along the ground from where something's grabbed a chunk of the leftover croc and pulled it into the bush.

The camper shakes as I climb the little steps. The mattress bare except for one small blue sock, no girl. Kimberly is gone. Hello Bear missing too. The night beats at the glass.

'Kim. Kimberly!'

The car park vacant. I rush to the food store. Call for her through the stinking rooms. The mouse bodies scream that they're dying. Out in death row, the mammals startle in their cages. The wallabies thump the ground with their hind legs, hiss and snort, telling each other,

I woke up. Where I

was

beaten and —

But Kimberly isn't there. She's not anywhere.

Where.

Where.

I start the camper and gun it back to the row. The trees come up too fast. Swerve and skid over the gravel to my flat. A rectangle in the dust where my Holden used to be. My TV gone too. Feel in the dark for the top shelf of the refrigerator — the revolver cool in the padded bag, and the bunch of cash. A note on my kitchen table glows in the dark. 'Communing with whales. Peace and love.' Lee's mirrored sunglasses watch me from the bench.

God help any critters that appear in front of the camper when I screech through the Park to Angela's. She's asleep — bottle of those pills beside the bed. Kimberly's rainbow room is empty, bed unmade. There's a creak on the boards, and Angela is in the hall in saggy undies and a singlet. Boobs akimbo.

'Where is she?' Her voice slides around on itself.

'She's not here?'

'Where's Kim?'

'She's with me. Don't you worry about it. She's sleeping in the van.' Angela makes to go outside, but I put my hands on her shoulders.

She tries to push me off, misses. 'She's not even yours.'

'No, she's yours. Of course she's yours. I'm just Granny and I'm looking after her.' Say it so firm I almost believe it.

'She's not even your grandkid. She's not even Lee's kid. She's not even anyone's. She's just mine and hers.'

'Lee is ... he's still her dad.'

'Nope. Nope nope nope.' Her eyes bat shut. She sways. I get her to the bedroom — starting to smell mouldy in there. Back down in the van, I shut the door. Dawn bleeds through the night. Kimberly's black eye above me in the sky, pink disease creeping over the horizon. I stare up at the house. Kim's house and Angela's house. *Not even anyone's.* Climb the stairs again.

'Whose is she, then?' I ask. The house is quiet. I realise I'm shouting, still pissed. Angela can't hear me, though. She's passed out on her back on the bed. Barely breathing, but breathing. 'Whose is she?' I shake her. 'Ange?'

The papers in Angela's desk are neatly organised. I find Kimberly's little passport with 'Cannot write' in the signature. Her birth certificate: father 'unknown'. The gin and bourbon bottles watch me from the kitchen bench like pensioners on payday.

I finish off the rest of Angela's fancy wine, steering the camper with my knee as I skull. Wait until I get back to my little dark lounge room for her gin. Tastes tropical, even without tonic or lemon. The sky turns lemon over the row. Lee's note on the table. Princess Pie and Wallamina like moths pressed against the sliding door. Wallamina hurls meaning at the glass.

If it's
got clean whiskers it will
know what's
down.

I open the door. She falls in.

I see it,

says Wallamina's ear.

Has

it

got clean whiskers.

'Sure have. You want a drink, Wally?'

I pour a shot on the lino. She sniffs at it, rears away.

Down is what's
down.

'There. We're mates now.'

I saw a shadow of
me
up but the law
says down.
'Wallamina.'
It
pongs.

'*Wallamina*.' I grab her by her narrow, hairy shoulders. 'I'll leave the door open all the time and you can come in and out of the house whenever.'

It tangs like poison
anus.
'What?'
Fuck its
face.

She leans back on her tail and bats out with her muscly hind legs. She's slow but so strong. Her claws rip through time. I see what Angela saw in the eagle's talon: everything that's past, everything that's happening, and all the things to come at the same time. I see my mistake. You've got to show them who's boss. I stand, tower over her. Go to pick her up by the tail, but she bounds away out of the house before I can catch her. Makes her way back over to the corner of the fence. Patch of worn-out earth.

Where's my milky
mum.
She's here. She's
here.
I
smell her tomorrow.
'Wallamina. Wally. There's no one there —'
Tomorrow is where the milk
is. My milky
mum.

Inside, Princess Pie makes short hops across the table. If she's saying something, it doesn't mean much to me. I get closer. Her hisses and squawks like a tuned-out radio. Stretches her wing and her leg at the same time. Clever girl. Clever, quiet beastie. In the bush, other things whisper, jeer. The sun heaves itself over the tree line and turns the kitchen gold. The note on the table, 'Communing with whales. Peace and love.' I'm sobering. Turn to the bourbon. A shot for peace and a shot for love. One for the whales too. Stuff that note in my mouth and swallow it. Gag but the note's gone. The tiger on my boob crouches. An old trick was to flex my pecs and make the tiger jump. Used to make Graham and Lee laugh. Now I realise the tiger wasn't jumping but breathing. One wrinkled breath after another. It's all we can do.

'It's all we can do,' I tell Wally and Princess Pie. 'You can't just steal a kid and take off looking for whales. You got to breathe.'

Where

has my life

gone.

It's hard to breathe. The light is sickening. Under the table it's cool. The lino wet with gin. Burning and chilling at the same time. I stick out my tongue and lick a bit. That's really funny. That makes me laugh. I want someone to see how funny that is.

Motherly.

Big fucking dingo in my face. Yellow teeth set in deep black gums. Tongue lolling. Ears forever cocked. I sit up and bash my head on the underneath of the table. Doesn't hurt so much as knocks me flat. A thumping sound. The animal gone. Sit up again, look around, and she's crouched by the fridge. I shit through my ears. Dingo dog. Fucking Sue.

Flesh and

blood. (Yesterday.)

'Get out, Sue. Go on.'

Not

yet.

And then right up to my face.

Tomorrow.

'Get out, I told you.' Her body half twitches away. Whispers,

Tomorrow

is not from the

tin. (Don't

fight.) It's

on the nose.

The bingle on my head and the start of a killer hangover. Lie under the table staring up at the flaking chipboard. An abandoned web. Sue chanting,

Fresh

flesh, Tomorrow

(get

into it).

Her body sings a picture of Kimberly. The bruises on the girl's scrawny legs. To Sue, Kim stinks like the freckles not yet appeared on her skin, like the wee that will need to happen in an hour, like the washed sheets she slept on, and the sting of adventurous fear when she took Lee's hand.

No locks for

Mother (the

metal tooth).

Run

for Tomorrow.

'Look,' I tell Sue like she's a normal person. Andy in my kitchen trying to sober me up with coffee instead of a living, stinking wolf who can remake my grandchild with the smells in her behind. 'If "Tomorrow" is dingo for Kimberly, you can forget it.'

Morrow —

'Out.'

Takes a big bag of courage for me to crawl from under that table and grab Sue with my bad hand. I nearly pass out from trying.

Meat

diet.

Sue gives my infected hand a sideways sniff.

(Gnawing.) The respectable

smell.

I get her by her ruff and drag her with skittering nails over the lino to the front yard.

'Stay,' I shout. She starts dancing, whining high and urgent.

My mother was a

little angry full

of

off-road sand.

'Great. So glad we can fucking talk now.' I shut the door on her. A combination of everything Sue — her yawps, her reek, whatever it is — gets in through the gap under the door, hits me with meaning. I hang off the handle, the words. *Tomorrow. Tomorrow.* Open it up again.

Tomorrow takes

a

lot of

paws.

'Can't you see I've fucked it up? My own boy took her.' Start blubbering fat tears.

There, Mother. There

(Yesterday).

She points her nose like she's Skippy the bush bloody kangaroo. The ruff on her back raised, excited, not in anger or hunger. I wipe the snot and tears onto my forearm, peer down the road where she's pointing. Kimberly again, not on the road, but in Sue's every twitch and stink.

Tomorrow

and Never There (shit

on it). A

tinge of

small.

An idea bumbles into my stupid brain. I get over to the camper, grab Kimberly's tiny blue sock from the bed, hold it out to Sue. The dingo comes around, sniffs.

Mouth love. Good

morning,

Tomorrow. A rabbit's dream (goes

south).

Hello,

plastic (eat

your eyes out).

All together, this makes up Kimberly, but not a Kimberly I've ever known. In Sue's drool and eyelids and paws, Kim is an animal — a stinky thing but also patient, important. It's the stretch of Kim's neck, the small catch in her throat before she talks. Kim as something about to happen. Sue keeps talking but not as crazy. Her nose tells stories about Hello Bear. That soft plastic body covered in dribble.

Slavering sweat

and a little bit of that

eye

snot.

Songs about Kim, songs about the teddy bear, and also the stench of a note: south. Sue shoves her nose in the sock and back at the air. Goes down the road a bit, sniffing. Running alongside Sue's body like a river that won't bunk its course: south.

I shake my head. 'I'm soaked here. Sozzled. I can't drive ...'

The dingo lets out a whine and, in it, I'm the den to come back to and a poison pellet all at once. I see Kimberly again on Sue's tongue. Sue has my girl on her nose and here's me alone without even so much as a whiff. Useless, pissed. Lee's note lodged in my belly. The keys to the camper digging into my hip. Blood made of bourbon. Communing with whales.

NINE

Half the traffic lights are out. The camper's got low revs, takes off like a baby elephant. I plug in my phone, pull a slug of Angela's bourbon, wind down the windows and gun it anyway. Beside me sits a dingo dog. Some wolf, some kelpie camp mutt. Her sandy behind on the shotgun seat. Panting, she draws in great gulps of the hot air. A flash of tooth.

Rabbit.
Oh shit. (Dead bits
of me.) That one's
for the ground. That's for my
gums.
How about
there. And there.
And —

'Why are you helping me, Sue? I mean, why aren't you with your brothers?'

She peels her nose from the window. Amber eyes swirling.

Its whole face is
a desert with water. It's
whole (Yesterday)
mouth
the sky.

I turn back to the road, blinking. In her fur and her spit, the tick in her eye, there is a feeling for that time all those years back. I went out to the desert with the rangers. Heard a grunt under a bit of tin, and lifted it up. Instead of the big snake I was expecting: fat puppy bodies. Three there, but it was Sue, the small and tan, that I reached for. Picked her up. They say not to do that. I picked her up and put her in my bra, next to the tiger. Back at the Park, the two brother puppies opened their eyes overnight and saw each other. Maybe they tried to look at Sue, but she kept her lids down until the sun. When her eyes split, she squinted, and there I was, sniffing in that good sweet hot milk baby smell. My face. A desert with water in it. Big compliment probably, coming from Sue. Now, this grown-up dingo, beautiful as the day she was found.

I know it

stranger. Hello.

'Yeah, hi, Sue.'

My pack. It

wants something.

I'll get

it Mum

(Yesterday).

I stare at her until she looks away. Nervous licks. 'Okay. What's with this "Mum" business? I *was* "Queen".'

What.

'Why did you call me Queen?'

It's a

warm sky

fire. The hot

meat mother.

Oh.

I taste the

pack. I smell it

(Yesterday).

She darts forward. I swerve half off the road in fright. But it's her pink wet tongue that meets me, not those switchblade teeth. Spit wandering over salt and rot and obedience, and also something that isn't coming back. See myself through Sue's eyes, stretched out over the gritty plains — beaten down, gone as yesterday. Kimberly is the road ahead and behind. Can't see Lee anywhere. I steer the van back on the proper side of the road. Wipe a sweaty palm on my leg.

'If I'm the Queen —'

Mother.

'Whatever. Will you do what I say?'

It wants

something. (Run.) I'll

get

it.

'Don't bite me, how about that?'

What is its

gospel want want

want.

'I want to find my kids. Just to find my bloody kids, okay?'

This way and

this. (Dig

deep.)

Sue's nipples call want, want, want. Sue's snout, the ripple of the pores along her muzzle, those black lips: *this way*. A whisper of other dingoes so soft down her spine. Try to look and smell and taste the air around Sue all at the same time, like Kimberly said. The smell of engines and rain on concrete and fried food makes up a city. Lemonade, cheap soap, and roll-your-owns make up Lee. The smell from Sue's hairy armpits, the microscopic sounds in her throat, the quiet and constant song for blood across her gums all make: *south*.

—

South. We've got to go into the desert, until the sand runs out and turns to water. The highway through it shivers in one long line under the blue shock of the sky. Everything swaying on an inland wind that blows the disease across the country. Wire strung out between neat, sun-bitten fence posts, empty paddocks with chewed grass, power lines overhead. The birds rise up out of the paddocks, fling themselves at the clouds, saying I don't know what and don't want to. There's people in those paddocks too. Army looking up at contrails across the sky. Big black packages that float down on big black parachutes. Once, a helicopter. Land Patrol arrive in utes splattered with what I hope is reddish mud. Spotlights catch the sun. They try to get to the packages first, but the army are fighting fit. The piggers only manage to nab one container to heft back to their truck. The army surround them, there's words, they walk away. I slug back that bourbon and watch the copter until it disappears. Press the pedal.

'I'm coming, Kimbo.'

We'll be

there

Tomorrow.

People reckon that animals are just machines, reacting to every-thing. 'Kimbo,' I say again.

Sue's fur responds.

Tomorrow. (Smelly

womb.)

'What are you thinking about, Sue?'

What.

'In your head.'

She starts panting, panic waves around the car. A picture of her leaping out the window, landing on her feet and running until I lose sight. That horizon, empty of Sue. Another scene overlaps, noisier and brighter than the first: Sue with her muzzle on my thigh.

'Don't get so stressed, matey. "What are you thinking?" is just

something people ask each other when they're close, you know?
Always used to piss Graham off. "What are you thinking?" I'd say.
And he'd say —'

Its want is

in

the past.

'Graham? No, we're through.'

Sex in the warm

place. (Fuck it

every night.)

'None of that.'

Decay

underneath.

That stops me asking her what she thinks. Even so, she's sensitive
as grass. Takes one sniff in my direction, and her fur rustles, whispers,

Good

cat.

Tucks a paw like a pussycat and feigns sleep.

The land is wider outside the Park, the air different. Hotter, drier. If
the Park seemed empty, this is fucking desolate. Maybe it was always
like this. Maybe I've been inside too long. Seems like there are more
burnt trees than before. More abandoned cars, rusted to lace. More
rubbish kicking up in twists of wind. The world has been tipped
sideways and all the creatures — people, everything — have fallen
off.

'Where the fuck is everyone?'

I can trace the

kill.

'No, Sue, it's alright. Just sit or whatever.'

She sits like a regular dog. But those dingo eyes. That nose.
Catches a scent of something, bolt upright at the window.

The longest mother

in a

cage.

My foot eases on the pedal until we're paused at a big dusty intersection, Sue's body sparking with recognition. The turn-off to the old person's home where Mum'll be on her gurney by the window. Talking cats and dogs wandering by. Maybe they'll attack the old folks. They can be violent, those ferals. Or they used to be before they talked. My poor old mum doesn't know that — she'll be scared out of what's left of her wits. My heart peels off in two directions: south to where Lee and Kimberly are; west and not so many kilometres to my mum.

My band,

my party. (My

itchy

place.)

Sue's not talking about Mister or Buddy back there at the Park — her brothers. She's talking about me and the people in my blood. Her blood too, she reckons. I get the strongest feeling of nursing Sue, her furry muzzle to my boob. Feel that warm shot of the milk release. Swipe a hand at my nipple to be sure there's no dingo attached to it. She's still there on the passenger seat, taking me in with ochre eyes.

The party is

starting. (Watch the tooth.)

The

best thing is to have

a plan.

I slug at the whiskey bottle. The bourbon fizzes in my brain.

'A plan. Right. Here's a plan for you: we check in on Mum. Arrange to send her up to the Park, where Ange or someone can take care of her, then we get back to looking for Kim.' Sue stares, waiting for more. 'That's all I've got.' Still as death. Like she's pulled another skin and is hunkered beneath it.

'Well?'

What.

'Do you think I should keep going after Kim or go check on Mum?' Some parts of her body — her paws, her black nostrils, and the fur around her neck — open up at the idea of keeping on south, a thick stench of meaning. One of those desert flowers that blooms once a year.

The

muzzle line.

But her ears and the silky down between her claws point to the nursing home road, like she can already hear Mum calling for tea, a bit of cake.

(Hold it

steady.) The best plan is

a plan.

'"The best plan is a plan."' I get the van in gear. Beats the pants off my inspirational sticky notes.

The nursing home is ratty-looking. Rubbish bins overflow outside the windows. Crows caw and pull at their contents — having a great old crow time. When I open the door, Sue nimbles over the seat and leaps over my shoulder like it's nothing at all. I duck — still not sure about her teeth, even if they can talk now — and she's gone.

'Sue!' I call. '*Fuck*. Sue.'

What.

Scares the breakfast out of me coming around the back of the van.

'What are you doing?'

Territory.

'What territory? Get back inside.' She does so, muttering,

All safe

now

(report nothing).

I check out the trashed parking lot. The rubbish. The crows. Rusting access-parking signs.

'What am I looking at, Sue?'

Nothing.

Everything.

This changes quick smart to,

Forever,

when I go to close the door on her. 'It's not forever. It's for half a second. Five minutes max.'

I leave her sucking at the gap in the window of the camper like she's dying in there.

(Fucking

life.) This is

forever.

The maze of halls inside the nursing home is designed to fuddle the dementia patients so they don't escape. Aircon on full, and a mural of a Paris café so those old birds can imagine they've flown better places than here. The spot where Mum's gurney always sits. Vacant now. *Forever*. My breath hurts.

'Hello? Ranger calling ...'

No answer. They'll be dead in their beds. A noise up the way: someone's survived. I burst into the dining hall. The whole place has been rearranged to face the doors that open onto the front garden — a view of the rubbish. There's ten or so old girls pointed at the windows, watching those crows tug at old spaghetti and plastic bags like they're toy intestines. Almost don't recognise Mum, sitting up in a wheelchair in someone else's giant purple muumuu, whiskery hair on end and a pleased-as-punch expression. Karen, the main carer, is there in her blue nylon shirt and black slacks. One of the cooks too, apron on. Staring at those crows. They've got the sherry out and everyone's having a tipple, even the staff. I grab a couple of the little bottles, shove them in my pockets.

'Here I am,' I tell them.

Karen starts. Stares at me like Mum does — like she's never seen me before. Blinks bloodshot eyes and remembers. 'Hello, Jean. Isn't it great?'

One of the crows near the window makes a noise. A birdy sigh. I would have thought I was the only one heard it, but the old girls get out their gummy grins. Karen moves closer to peer at the bird. One of the bald residents starts to laugh and laugh. Even Karen cracks a grin. Glances at me.

'Can't you see her feathers?'

'I see them.' I peer closer, oily black. A couple missing.

Mum is staring at me with her bloody eyes now. Shaky hands to each side of the chair, the little muscles in her arms set to pop out of her skin as she wheels herself closer to me.

'You're not listening right,' she says in a voice like someone pretending to be a crow. 'Give her a sniff.' I haven't had a proper conversation with my mum for about three years. 'You're too busy,' she goes on. Pink eyes shining — maybe not with recognition but someone's at home in there. 'That's why you can't talk to the birds. We got nothing else to do. Better than TV.'

I clear my throat. 'Got to find my grandkid, Mum. Your great-grandkid. You remember Kim.'

I don't think she does, but her quivering hand takes mine, gentle. 'Go find your girl. Then come back and talk with us old birds, okay?' I blink back stupid tears. 'We'll be here. Unless we're dead.' She cackles with her gums on show. I forgot she doesn't have teeth. Hope against everything that Kim gets to see me when I'm old as that.

There's still a giant bloody dingo in the camper, paws all over the seats. An oily sweet smell coming from up the back tells me she's pissed on something. The bed, it turns out. She's made a good go at eating the mattress too. The van looks like the inside of my head feels: like a wild dog has been having a party in there. Chunks of foam thrown about.

Sauce bottles toppled and landed at angles in the cupboards. A bag of chips split, ground through the shelves like sand. Sue in the middle of it all, clumsy. Pinging from the sugar and salt.

The bug,
the bug.
'Sue.'
Listen to the bug
under the
world. (It bites
back.)
'What bug?'
Sue paws the floor.
Under
the world.

I lift the linoleum. There's no fucking bug. Where Sue has pissed, the liquid dries sticky and gritty on the sheet. I go at it with some detergent and the dishcloth, but it's grim, hot and dry.

There are other cars on the road, but not many. I see Lee and Kimberly in my Holden over and over again — the black bumper a lure ahead. Speed up, only to overtake a freaky-looking guy, then a woman with a cat, then three kids wearing what look like pelts. The sun shifts up in the sky and settles over the road like an oven grill. Abandoned cars are marooned on the verge. I stop and check them for petrol. There's a bit of clear hose where Ange stores the spare tyre and jack, but when I thread it, most of the tanks blow empty. A little red Mazda bubbles. Suck until the gas touches the tip of my tongue and then let gravity do its thing. One jerry can fills with petrol and most of another. Every bloody time I open the door, Sue jumps over my shoulder, patrols the campervan, and leaps back in, reporting back.

A dead nothing (alive like
Yesterday) no

good to anything. The bugs,
the bugs. The water in the
sky.
'Can you still smell Kim?'
South.
'Any more detail on that?' Closes her eyes.

A few kilometres later, I slow to stop again. A small transport truck with wooden slats for sides is stalled smack-bang in the middle of the highway. I can't get around it, but I gather my hose up in case this baby runs on petrol. Pause at the sight of two people standing on the other side, going at each other hammer and tong. Their faces wrapped up like they're fumigating, pointing angrily at the truck.

'We are,' says the woman.

'We are not,' says the man.

Hello.

Hello.

Someone in the murky depths of the tray.

Hello.

It's with

us.

Visited a children's home once with Mum, carrying bibles to do the Jesus work. The kids on the balcony called *Hello* like that. Shy but desperate to be seen by me, who at least had a mum to grab me by the hand and pull me past.

Hello.

'You broken down?' I ask the couple. 'Who's in there?' They ignore me. Keep bickering.

'We're doing it,' the woman tells the guy. He folds his arms, and the woman rips into him. 'I'll go fucking crazy. I won't drive any further. I'll leave, just watch me.'

His pink eyes narrow. 'That's money in there.'

'Money didn't talk before.'

Hello.

It's

with us.

'Stuff this.' The woman stomps away up the road.

The guy sizes me up. 'Porkers. Good ones too.'

Hello.

Hello.

He lets out a shaky sigh. 'Can hear that *hello*-ing all the way up in the bloody cabin. Still got a five-hour drive ahead. That's good money there.'

'Well, I need to get past. Trying to find my son. My grandkid, you know.'

'You let them out, then.'

He throws the keys at me and stomps up the road in the direction of the woman. Lost their manners along with their minds. I fish the keys off the ground. The movement is noted by the pigs in the truck. Their snouts through the slats.

Go on, go

on.

We've got a scary face. No.

Oh. It went

away. Where.

Where.

Under the front seat of the campervan I find an ethnic-looking scarf with little mirrors on it, smelling very faint of sandalwood. Wrap myself up in that and Lee's sunnies. For all their damned reflection, they don't do much to block out the messages of,

Piglet,

coming from Sue's whole body.

'You know about pigs, Sue? You're a bit Kelpie. Can't you help me herd them or something?'

Piglet.

Outside it

pops. Inside
it slithers.
She starts dribbling, and her saliva says,
Pop.
'Fucking hell.' I shut the door on her.

Hello. Hello. It's
something
salty.
They go quiet at the rattle of the keys at the gate. I wrench the big
metal door open and pull down the gangway.
It was here
before.
There's around thirty of them, crammed ear to tail in the hay- and
shit-strewn bed of the truck. The smell seeps into my scarf — sweet,
like they're already dead and cooking. One squints at me, a thick
crust of infection in both her eyes. Her tail calls to the pig beside her,
an ear for the outside and her snout for my left armpit. I squint, try to
see the whole pig.
Got a
light.
'What?' A ripple through the darkness, like laughter.
It brings the
sun.
Another one pushes forward.
Is there
more.
I clear my throat. 'I don't know. You better get out of this truck.'
Those that are facing me peer up. The others are too crammed in,
and couldn't crane anyway — pigs don't have necks they can turn or
move. I remember that about pigs. The few times I went on hunts with
Graham and his mates: pig dog skipping on scent, dancing over it,

then barking, sharp as birdsong. A high yelp that bounces around the riverbeds, then the lock on to the pig's thick ear. Graham would wrap his hands around the pig's bony hind legs and grunt to lift him up. The dog's body tucked in close behind the boar's ear so she can't get bitten. Knife right through the neck, the pig still breathing. Graham would plunge it past the layer of black hair and pink skin so it was held in place by the flesh, jiggle until it started gurgling with thick dark blood. The pig would feel it then. Take a final breath and die quiet. Can't look at a pig without thinking of its meat, its afterlife on my plate.

The closest one edges forward into my memory. I blink back guilt, hoping she can only read bodies, not minds. She's got those thick haunches and a brutal head, eyes that squint into my soul. A blast of meaning from her cheeks.

Is it

good.

At first, I think she means me. Swallow, nervous. My eyes on her stomach, tasting her salted. Then her ears twitch, and I can see from the muttering black hairs that she means, *is it good outside?* Seems to me she'll die whether she stays in the truck or not, so I tell her, 'Sure. It's good.' Die in a pen or die in the bush. 'It's all good.'

What is

it.

I look out at the wasteland of orange dirt, tussocks, and clumpy trees along an eroded stream. 'Grass. And creeks.' These hogs have probably never seen a creek. Just hoses and concrete. 'Mud.'

In the

wallow.

Some start to edge down the gangway on narrow hooves. Suck in gusts of air. One behind the other.

Your bum

is our face. More,

more.

I've seen battery hogs before — of course I have. But not out and about. Not staggering around and trying to walk, calling to whatever they think is 'more'. Glazed eyes that strain like they've never seen sunlight. Skin stretched over bodies fed to the point of bursting — something between swine and meat. Saw some animal liberationists on the street in the city one time, saying factory farms were the same as Nazi camps. I called them bloody racists too. The pigs clatter past me down the ramp, fucked-up eyes on the road ahead, calling,

Hello

is it more.

Those animal nutters were wrong, but not in the way I thought. It's not the same as the Nazis: that was us doing to us. What's this? One pig stops by me, a burst of stench from its hind, echoing my thoughts.

What is

this.

I crouch down. Stand again, quick smart, trying to hold my breath but the meaning surges around me. The heavy squash of cheek by arsehole by infected snout. A foot rotted and impossible to get to in the squeeze. The piglets squealing. Lee screaming in the back seat where I can't reach him and Graham won't stop the car. Just keeps driving faster.

What is

it.

'It's ... keep going. It's grass.' I say it to every pig that passes. 'Mud.' Wave my hand down the ramp. 'Just keep going.'

Is it

that way.

'Sure, that way.'

I breathe through my nose again with the last of them. Out over the bitumen on uncertain hooves. A hurt sow sits on her haunches, then lies down on the verge, panting unevenly under the slathering sun. Another weaves blindly over the asphalt toward her, flies spinning around her head. They push their noses into each other.

Send me
a postcard,

the sick one says. Postcard, indeed. What the fuck. I watch more closely. The meaning bright off that tight skin. All the little bits saying,

Leave me,

and,

I'll hear about it,

and,

Don't you see
it. Move on. There's
more.

The ones that can walk stretch their legs, for,

More,

more, more.

I stand at the top of the truck ramp watching them break into a group trot toward the next paddock. Skin rippling. Hooves carolling. Know that heart-in-your-mouth run. Know exactly what 'more' is. I've seen it in Lee and I've had it too, at times. These pigs are half dead, they're stumbling around, blind, mad, and fucking *hopeful*.

TEN

A motel that's also a dead petrol station and a minimart sits like a block of lard on the highway, the only buildings of a scabby little town just north of the desert. Three guys stand out the front holding guns. Their once-white T-shirts tagged with 'Game on' in black marker. By the looks of them, they've eaten every pig they ever killed. Inside the shop, a woman behind a counter clears the gunk from her lashes with a wet wipe.

'Haven't seen a campervan since last week.' She's got a face mask dangling around her neck and scratched-up sunglasses perched on her head. 'Hardly any cars through here today at all.'

'I'm not on holiday.' I show her the few photos on my phone. One of Lee, me, and brand-new baby Kimberly up at the hospital in the city. Graham had left by then, and Lee was about to. I look half drowned with pride. Lee is sheepish, staring off at something past the camera.

'You seen this boy?' Find the photo of an older Kimberly at my house with Wallamina. 'How about her?'

'The wallaby?'

'The girl.'

The woman shakes her head and the mask bobs around on its elastic at her chin. 'They've got to be headed for the city, though.

131

Everyone's going there. I don't know why. People getting killed at that service station — just for petrol!' I start ratting through the shelves. 'Don't go looking for a hand drill,' she calls. 'I don't sell them, never will.'

'What do I want with a hand drill?' I mutter. The store looks looted. Packets on the lower shelves ripped into, their contents eaten. The taller shelves cleared. The newspapers are only a day old, though. Front page all about the race for a zooflu cure. Seems they gave a whole bunch of mice a flu like ours, but when it came to blitzing it with strong antibiotics, the little buggers kept telling those scientists where it hurt.

'Personally, I don't think they're after a cure at all,' the woman says. She's snooped up beside me to poke at the paper. 'They like everyone in a state of emergency. Easier to manage. That's why we're all taking to desperate measures. Have you seen that video?' I shake my head. She gestures to the piggers outside. 'Don't bother. I keep those guys here instead.' At the back end of the store, a message twists like smoke through the half-empty shelves,

Oh.

Oh oh it's

all the

babies.

Pictures scurry up my spine. A furry arsehole, a scratched-out burrow, my whole life a nest. The owner grimly ignores it. 'You should get a guy,' she tells me. 'You can't trust anyone. Especially the army. They pretend they're all about people's welfare, but they help pets and livestock and all sorts of mongrels. That's where our taxes are going — some stupid animal that's suddenly got a story. Have you talked to them? I mean communicated? Try talking to them about anything important and you'll soon find out what their brains are made of: grass and dog food.'

On the other side of the window glass, one of the Land Patrol fellas shifts, cocks his gun to where Sue peeks from the van. Before I can get out there to give him what for he throws his head back and laughs, hugging himself. Sue, snout to the window crack:

Can

I have its poo.

I start grabbing anything that's left in the shop. Nappies, a packet of party poppers, a measuring jug without a handle. My hand closes on a thin packet of preserved fruit that has been missed. The rush of flavour. There's a fridge along one side of the wall but it's dark, shelves warm and labelled DAIRY and MEAT with cartons of long-life milk and packaged tofu instead of proper food. Antiseptic and a bandage. The only fresh food is corn and oranges, piles and piles of them. No cheesy chips. No white sauce. No spam. All the wet pet food gone but there's still dry, beef-flavoured dog biscuits. Grab two packets of them for Sue. The creature hidden in the shelves calls,

Oh.

Oh.

Two women stand close to each other in an aisle labelled CANS. They're big and young, with strong pink arms in singlets, even though the wind that blows across the desert outside is cold. One holds a tin. The other grabs for it, and they fall into each other until the one with the tin bites the other on the soft exposed flesh of her upper arm. Pushes away, gripping the prize. Back at the register now, the owner of the store says loudly, 'I don't think I should sell that to you.'

Oh.

'Fine, I'll just take it then.' The tin clatters on other things in a basket.

'I'll call my guys,' the owner says.

Tell every one

mother

is coming.

The woman laughs. 'Those dudes couldn't catch a mouse.'

Oh.

The door chimes her departure and the owner appears around the corner of the aisle.

'What was in the can?' I ask while I lay my hand on an open box of air freshener.

'Fish. It was our last. It's all gone.'

The woman on the ground scans the empty shelf, then examines the bite. Not deep but it has drawn bright blood.

Oh,

oh. Yes.

'I'll get some Band-Aids.' The owner disappears again.

'She knows I could sue her for this,' the woman tells me.

'Is there still suing?'

'Yeah. True.'

The bite looks sore. 'Was it worth it?'

'If you had a husband moaning at you like mine it was.'

Oh.

Oh.

We edge away from the shelf where the creature has found something. Its messages twitch out at a speed that makes my teeth hurt.

'My son was vego,' I tell her by what was the tinned meats shelf. 'I had to learn all sorts of things. Spinach, that's alright, we grow that here.' Look around. There's no spinach. 'Chickpeas and lentils for the protein.'

'You sound like the government. With that nutrition ad. Husband says it's all a conspiracy anyway. The pollies and the greenies are in it together, he reckons.'

'Yeah?'

'Yeah, they've got you programmed. You think it's a flu, right? Bullshit. It's in the water.' I spy an oval can of spam flush against the back of the shelf. The woman keeps going. 'Animals can't even talk, you know that? The water's making us hallucinate. We think they're saying things but it's just us, imagining it. Makes sense when you think about it. It's not like anyone has died from this flu, except the suicides.' She glances toward the hidden creature, but the animal has taken its gases to another part of the store. I dart out a hand. Hide the spam behind the dog biscuits.

'You're not supposed to be taking pets around with you.' The woman nods at the biscuits. 'Government says you're not supposed to travel with them.'

'Thought it was all a conspiracy?'

The woman dabs at the bite. 'I don't fucking know. I just want to find some meat for the husband so he'll shut up.'

The owner comes back with a new packet of medicated wipes, antiseptic, and Band-Aids. I offload some of the broken crap I'm carrying and grab corn and oranges instead. Find a jar of coffee, some out-of-date bread that looks weirdly fresh, Vegemite, biscuits, baked beans, lollies, and long-life juice.

'I'll take some smokes too.' Only Sunset Reds behind the counter. The owner names a price five times what they're worth. A sign reads CASH ONLY. I don't have enough. Start rejecting things — the lollies, the biscuits.

'Just the smokes, then. And the dog food. The spam, the antiseptic. And some phone credit.'

The woman nods absently, one eye on the customer and her out-of-it-looking husband, who has now come in through the door. Part of his skull shaved and a bloodied square of plaster stuck to it with medical tape.

'I'll stay with you,' I whisper. 'You know, until they go.'

The owner snorts. 'They'd all starve and die now if I closed up shop. Here' — she pushes a pair of black plastic sunglasses, a face mask, and ear plugs at me — 'I have to hand these out now. Waste of time.'

I take the stuff. 'Leave you to it, then. See you,' I tell the other customer as I go past.

'That the bitch that bit you?' I hear the husband slur. Once upon a time I would have taken him on. But Kimberly is out there some-where with my son. Sue locked in the van with no water. Ange going lulu with the lizards back at the Park. My old mum talking crow. All that keeps me moving.

My whiskey hangover kicks in between the minimart and the campervan, starting with my eyeballs. Almost miss the big fuck-off horse snorting and slathering in the middle of the car park. Two kids astride.

'What are you lot up to?' I call. The horse takes me in. 'Hey.'

The sweet hand

is here.

'Is it?'

It's

here.

I creep forward with my phone stuck out, trying to get a few snaps. The beast's otherwise glossy coat is nicked with scars. The minimart owner follows me out and stares up at the kids like they're the riders of the apocalypse.

'I told you not to come back here.'

Here.

Here.

The horse's song is measured as a metronome through its soft, hairy nose.

And

it was grass.

'We thought you were closing,' one kid calls over the horse.

'Yeah, we thought you wanted to clear out,' says the other.

'Don't need to. Got security. Hey. *Hey.*' The Land Patrol guys over near the camper ignore her — they've taken up with another animal: sandy bum and greedy snout. One of the men pushes a treat for Sue through the window gap. The horse keeps muttering.

The lawn
wins
tonight. So does
the
heartbeat.

The air itself becomes a rubbery muscle, stretched. My own body pulled to snapping. The shop owner's face contorts. Then, we're released, snap.

'If I see you around here again,' the owner shouts, backs away, but her heart isn't in it. She clutches the doorframe, turns her attention back to the Land Patrol.

'You going to protect me here or what?'

One of them points at Sue. 'You should talk to the dingo.'

'Not bloody likely.' The woman's back in that air-conditioned box before the animals can say anything more. My eyes are caught on the messages sluicing off the horse's body. Every limb calls in a different direction, but all four agree on a clear run, some space to see forever. Those kids have got her on a short rein.

Listen
to the pinching
fingers.

'She's frightened,' I call out.

The angry
world comes
closer.

'Nah, horses are like that,' says the kid riding near the horse's neck. His voice wobbles. That he could still go through puberty in all this. 'They got good memories but. Never forgets a face. We call her Elephant now. She used to be called Slayer.'

The angry,
says the horse,
world.

I edge close again. 'Why don't you tell her it's okay? It's okay.'

A truck screams past like hell on wheels, and for a moment the whole world *is* angry. The kids are mouthing off, their words taken in the rush.

'What?'

'I said, where have you been, woman?'

'Yeah, and how'd you get out here? You're not from here. My dad says no one has petrol. Except army and the piggers, of course.' The boy shoots a longing glance at the pig hunters, their ute, their guns, their meaty arms. 'He says to bring petrol back if I find it, and he'll give me more food.'

'Your dad sounds like a real catch.'

'Yeah.'

'I'm looking for my son, his little girl.' The horse watches me with her moon eyes. The fine whiskers on her chin whisper,

It is a perfume

place

here.

The boy reins her in, sharp on the mouth. Her skin shivers with meaning.

What a smelly

little foal.

The hard bridge of her face. She rears back at my touch.

Subject!

Then her skin flickers, settles. My body fills with rain and I shiver too. She sniffs me.

It has

sugar hooves.

Kimberly. My girl stretches a hand — apple in her palm. Sweet. Takes me a moment to find words. 'You saw her?'

Its face is

hungry.

'You either got to yell at her or talk to her real gentle,' the boy at the back advises. 'She'll spend her whole time going on about feelings and shit otherwise. Don't come near her with a boot neither. Dad gave her a beating with one, like, one thousand years ago. She never lets go of anything. Ever.' He pulls a pre-rolled cigarette from a red-and-tan packet and lights it, reclining on the horse's rump. Smoking to the sun. The other kid is half asleep, draped over Elephant's strong neck. I smile, try to make my face nice. Reflected in her glassy brown eye is a psycho clown.

'Help me, Elephant? Seen my girl?'

This
place is
homely.

I look around at the grease-stained concrete. The empty road edged with clumps of dirt. 'It sure is.'

The horse brings her silken nose closer.

A paddock
for a soft
hand.

I open my palm and she inhales it.

What hoary
sugar. That little
foal in
the sand.

'She probably means the desert.' The smoking boy sits up again.

Big salt. It's
a dead whale
search.

'Dead whales is what they call petrol. You've got to know how to speak animalese.'

The boy draped over the horse's neck opens his eyes. 'I know who she's talking about. This morning at that other petrol station —'

His brother punches him in his leg. 'That wasn't this morning.'

'Fuck off it wasn't.'

'It was two days ago, idiot. And it was right here.'

'It was whenever that hippie guy gave me all these smokes.' He fishes out the Brumbies packet from his shorts pocket and crushes it. Lee's brand. 'Oh yeah. Days back.'

'Was there a girl with him?' I say it too loud. The whites of the horse's eyes shine, a man's raised arm. The boy gives her a little stroke and her pupils return to liquid brown.

Sweetie.

'Little kid, yeah. Gave Elephant some old apples — best day of her life. The girl totally sooked out when she had to leave, but. Some old person gave her an ice-cream.'

Was it strawberry? Did it make her feel better? Is she okay? Is she okay?

Salt,

says the horse.

It

stabs.

The boy flicks his cigarette — a tiny firework in the hot air — then digs his heels into the horse's ribs. Body to match her thoughts. Hooves on the bitumen.

Go.

I need a rinse under the tap and a lie-down, but the piggers are still gathered around my camper, deep in conversation with Sue. One wipes an eye.

'Yeah, mate. Haven't seen them in ... shit. Where's Rabies now?'

'With the rest,' says another. 'In the pound.'

Sue throws pictures of meat from her snout. Memories of every cage. The stench of fear creeps over the concrete, crawls up shorts and jeans legs until one of the piggers clutches his head, shakes it, pokes a beefy finger through the window gap so Sue can lick it.

Is it a

friend. (Follow.)

'We could be back for breakfast,' the pigger tells the others. Turns to me. 'Nice dog ...' I shoot the fella my best smile, but that just sets off a ripple of nausea that builds in strength toward my guts. *Sugar hooves. Is that its friend.*

'Um, lady. You alright? She's having a heart attack.' I'm too queasy to give the little bugger the slap he deserves. 'Motel's good.' He nods to the building attached to the shop. When I turn back, he's at his ute with the other men, storing his gun in the tray.

'Where do you think you're going?' The minimart owner has returned, yelling over the car park.

'Find our dogs.'

'I don't want dogs here.' Scuffs slowly after the screaming tracks they leave on the concrete. 'I told them I don't want dogs here.' She looks around for someone who cares. Stands on her tiptoes as I open the campervan.

'Here we go,' I warn Sue, but the wild notes of *territory* leaping from the dingo's flesh have the woman slumping back to her shop. Sue, meanwhile, gets stuck into her patrol.

The burrow is
clear. (Watch out.)

Tail muttering,
I need more
details.

I fold my arms, watch her circle the van. 'Those piggers could have shot you.'

Guard
dog.

'Yeah, right.'

Wild
cat.

'If that's what makes you feel —'

Sit and
stay.

She's seen me gazing at the motel vacancy sign. Her body stinks of pictures. Shadows made by moonlight. Paw-footed through the sand.

I'll call the

others. (Help me.)

Let

them —

'No.' I grab her by the scruff. 'No howling. I'm your pack, remember? And tomorrow we can go hunting or do whatever. Not tonight. Please, Sue. I need to sleep it off a few hours before I drive us both into a tree. No good to anyone dead, right?'

What.

'You have to stay.'

Where.

'Here.'

The best

plan —

I slam the door.

The woman at the counter is a hulking, older version of the one at the servo. Sisters, or mother and daughter. Her body swaddled in clothing, bits of material, a tea towel around her face.

'Any animals?'

'Just me. And I don't piss on beds.'

'What?'

'Nothing.'

'Where's your mask?' she slurs.

I grin at her. 'Been on the sauce, love?'

'No.' She straightens herself. 'It's just medicine.' She reaches into her nylon pants pocket and produces a bottle of purple cough syrup, unscrewing the gummy white lid and slipping the bottle under her tea towel to take a nip. 'You're supposed to wear a mask. Not supposed to talk with the animals.' She takes a dainty sip. 'New government flyers

142

say that. And on the internet. Keep to your kind. You stay in your territory, they stay in theirs. Let dogs be dogs and cats be cats and birds be birds. You want some?' She points the purple at me. I shrug, take a sip — tastes like childhood. Ask her where I can get a feed and a proper drink. She points to a notice, 'Closed indefinitely', written on hotel stationery and stuck to the restaurant door next to another 'NO ANIMALS' sign. A chip machine hums in the stark hall. Not a bug in sight. I push coins in and take the packets out to the van. Dip the chips into the spam while Sue goes for some dog biscuits on the van floor. When I lock her back in for the night, she comes to the window and pants at me — her breath leaves a heart on the glass.

Too

much moon. (Howl for

them.)

'Quiet, okay?'

But

it's too much

moon.

Can't see a moon for the cloud cover. Her messages of *too much* follow me across the car park and into the hotel room, where I can close the door on Sue, put my phone on charge, and keep one ear cocked for mice or whatevers talking in the walls. Unlike the minimart, this place is true to its signage — clean of creatures. The shower water scorches my face and scalp. Soap bubbles turn brown and circle the drain. Sitting on the floral double bed in my towel, I take nips of the nursing-home sherry. The liquid courage is too slow when it comes to dabbing antiseptic on my infected hand. Skin bloated around the cut. Test it with a finger and cry out. Someone on the other side of the window responds.

'Hello?'

Not even the swish tide of another car on the highway. Another squawk. Out the window, the old woman is sneaking her way across the car park toward the van. By the time I haul my filthy clothes back on and get out there, she's charging back.

'That ... that ...' A dense spray of spit from her mouth. 'That's your dog?'

'She's okay.'

'No, he's bloody not. He's —'

'Is she hurt?'

The woman grabs my arm. 'You can stay with me, love. Don't you worry about it.'

'What's happened to Sue?'

'He's ...' The woman looks searchingly at me. 'He's an animal.'

'Yeah?'

'Says he wants to eat me from the inside out. That crummy dog is going to *kill* you.' She shouts this. I'm already at the van. Sue's dark growls:

All the
same
meat to me.

The clouds have parted, leaving the lit-up ghost of a dingo, a pale and vengeful ancestor on the passenger seat beside me. I bet they can still hear Sue ranting from the other side of the car park.

That meat is
haunted.
(All the
entrails —)

I pull up again. 'Hey. Hey Sue? You wouldn't ... you're alright with me, aren't you, girl?' Her hair shifts. Body ripples with messages that join like drops of water in the sea.

Milk shine. (Leave it for
the pack.) Its
door
is barking.

I touch her gingerly. 'You wouldn't bite me again, would you, Sue?'

Its anus

is

my north.

'Jesus. I'm just asking you this one thing.'

Mother

can bite its

pink.

A picture of me sinking my teeth into Sue's scruff and shaking. The dingo limp in my mouth. Enjoying it, almost. 'I'll hold off the biting, thanks.'

It

can.

'Thanks.'

Shake some dog biscuits into my hand and let Sue snuffle them out of my palm.

Now

Yesterday.

Eat the bitter

bones.

I put the last one in my mouth and suck it, then spit it out. Sue is right at it.

'You like that cardboard chicken shit?'

I want the

fresh warm

heart.

'Yeah, and I want a beachside unit and a man called Jack Daniels. Where are they?' Scan the unhappy highway. Want my little darling by my side, five hairless fingers on the scrapbook, drawing a new cat.

We eat some more of those chips and Sue settles on the passenger seat, her tummy groaning from the weird food. I close my eyes but all I can see is the road, Lee's and Kimberly's faces bouncing along it and Sue running just behind, snapping at their ears with her wolf teeth.

—

A Greyhound bus lights the camper with sweeping gestures, sighing to a stop near the minimart. The few shaky-legged passengers make their way down the stairs and pat their shirt pockets and handbags for cigarettes. One has a lighter and shares the flame around. The driver comes off last and takes off his bus-driver top, worn grey singlet underneath. He busies himself with the underneath of the bus, hauling container after container of petrol to refuel. Once he's finished, he wipes his hands on the shirt and lights a cigarette too. My ranger shirt is grey as one of the cleaning rags I used to wipe over the tourist bathrooms and the gift-shop floors. I rub my teeth with the hem, run fingers through my damp hair ends. Shut the door quietly and make my way over. Whispers from under the overflowing skip outside the supermarket. The rodents are doing their night shift in there.

Only you be careful
with the
light,
light. Back up and follow
up.
Follow the
tracks.

I make a wide circle around their meaning. Aim for the bus where the passengers are clumped together outside the door. A woman and a man a bit younger than me. Family of four kids and a haggard dad. Two young women with pickled-looking faces. They're all in the same black plastic sunglasses as the ones I got from the service station. Bright foam plugs trumpet from their noses and ears. Shift their masks to their foreheads and necks. They've got smokes. Hunched over their phones watching some video. Bodies secret and dull. Only the obvious gestures get through — a folded arm, a crooked finger, a toothy smile.

'Seen a blue Holden sedan? Classic job?' I ask them. 'Young man and a girl?' Remember my manners. 'Please?'

The driver takes his cigarette from his mouth. 'Lots of young men on the move. You got a better description?'

'Dark. Black eyes. Good. Girl's got a head of hair, name's Kim. She's good. Good —' So many tired hours with Sue I can't get the words to flip off my tongue. The man eyes me.

'You alright?' Smoke billows around his words. He leans into the circle of other passengers and they follow suit, muttering. Turns back. 'You into talking to the animals? You got a dog in there?'

I check back to see Sue's fool face peering through the driver's window. Try to will her down with my mind, but we're not at telepathy yet.

'A pet. It's normal.'

'There's a new normal now.' The driver sucks on the smoke again, nods at my head. 'And around here, not wearing a mask means you've gone animal. I'd put on my protective gear if I was you. Put that mutt in a cage. Cops are pretty serious.' The driver throws down his cigarette, grinds it out with his foot, and then stoops to pinch it tenderly between his fingertips, bound for a little box he keeps in his shorts pocket. Fussy and filthy. Reminds me of Lee. 'It's people like you spread this thing around.'

My fists buckle. 'What?'

He doesn't repeat himself. I stomp back over the concrete toward the camper. Sue springs out like always, but this time she heads for the bus. Her name catches in my throat as she starts doing her show, all prance and friendly, but with added bonus communication.

I

like

to play.

She throws messages at them like a wind-up doll. The people trip over themselves to back away, then draw forward at her body talk. Sue sweeps tail and nail — showing them the emu dying on a road kilometres away and into the yesterdays, the weeks, the years.

The old poke

(in the

puppy
place).

My sneakers don't make a sound when I cross back over to the bus. Someone yells at Sue, 'Can you tell me about my brother? Is my brother out there?' just as I click open the undercarriage. Grimy white containers I can lug two at a time. Sue doing her routine.

'Good girl,' I mutter — like she's a lap dog, and I'm carrying treats for the both of us.

'A Holden sedan, you said? Blue?' the driver calls. I'm legs-on-the-dash in the front seat, resting my arms a moment with Tammy Wynette, trying not to smoke through my rations. Sue worn through from the theatrics. The driver shouts about how he's got a two-way, can ask the trucks if they've seen Kim and Lee. Doesn't notice his bus is a bit lighter as he climbs aboard. I turn Tammy off to hear the crackle of the driver's two-way casting out over the cold flat land, sometimes hitting a moving truck, or a family on a farm, a cop car. Up above, the stars scatter across the sky. The animals in the bin return. I climb out to see the gas from their bodies. Gas like from the mice at the Park, but these guys are lean, brown, wild. Their messages affectionate.

Look at it
approximately. The
world
is up and down.
That's your property.
Watch
when I use it.

Seeing them talk makes me feel like a nice alien has landed on my heart.

Only me and you and all
of us with music on

the

tracks, the

tracks, the tracks.

Makes me think about Sue and her ideas about me as her pack. Some old shiny thing from yesterday. Ancient monarch in tatty robes. A rock comes pelting through the dark and hits the side of the skip. The animals shriek and scatter. The young woman aims another that clangs its target, and the messages slip into crevices. A muscle in my knee starts to spasm and doesn't stop. The driver picks his way back over the car park, lugging a couple of small jerry cans of fuel, packet of smokes in his mouth. He doesn't know I've got a liquid goldmine tucked in the side of the camper. The driver sets the cans down and presses the smokes into my hands with his gloved one. 'They help dull the old senses.'

I jam one in my face, light it and suck back. When I've got a lungful, we both give coughing laughs. 'Been a while,' I tell him, my tongue loose again.

The driver lifts his sunnies to his head. Eyes like a fresh coat of pink paint.

Is that

its

friend.

'Yeah.'

'You talk to that dog, then?'

'She won't shut up.'

'Bloody hell. Who'd have thought a few talking mutts would throw the whole country out? Got to lock down, I guess. Don't want this thing spreading to places where they've got tigers and tarantulas and God knows what. You talked to a snake yet?' I shake my head. Think about Blondie up there in her cage. The things she'd say. 'Me neither. You see them dead all over the roads — people swerve to kill them. The cops and those army boys, they've all got the zooflu, even if they pretend they don't, and they go a lot easier on you if you smoke.'

We smoke for a bit. I don't want to ask in case they're squashed flat on a road like snakes, but I have to know.

'And how about Lee? My son and my granddaughter?'

'One of the guys did see someone of that description pull up here a day ago.'

'The horse was right, then.'

'What's that?' I shake my head. 'Heading south,' he goes on. 'Whole convoy of a hundred or so, with animals. They're on track for the ocean and it's a long two-day drive from here. He said this young guy was sitting on the roof of a vintage car with a little kid and a guitar. No, a ukulele, singing a tune. That sound like your boy?'

The bed stinks only a bit of dingo wee. I sleep. Sue comes to lick my face in the night.

Territory.

When I slide the side door open for her patrol, she melts into the night. Doesn't reappear. The worry keeps me up, but at some point I conk out. Start awake again on dawn, thinking I can hear her howling for friends. Instead she comes to put her dry nose in my armpit.

It wants

something

'What?'

Mother's

want. I'll get

it. (Don't.)

I struggle to my elbows. Heart to heart with a hairy dingo. 'Want to find my kin.'

Here.

I'm here.

I flop down again. 'Not you. The real ones.' Her body goes so quiet. It's just a tan ghost that slinks off to sit up shotgun. The campervan clicks and shifts in the sudden still.

'You alright up there, Sue? Need some water?' She's disappeared into her own body. The Greyhound bus gone, the minimart shut and empty. Magpies in the rubbish outside, their bodies silent as Sue's.

ELEVEN

The road is shortened by the shimmer ahead. I lean back in the driver's seat, chaining smokes. Ride the hundred. Me and Graham used to ride the hundred all over the country. See how far we could go on a tank. He always had us rigged out with spares, but there was that buzz of getting stuck out in the desert in a tizzed-up car, keeping warm by loving on the back seat. Lee reckons one of those nights was his creation story, but I think I probably got knocked up after a day of boozing at a desert hotel. Half close my eyes at the memory. Graham's barrel chest and pointy little rump. The surprising curve of his dong. I tip one hundred. Face at the window. The van slams. A body. Sue slides forward and hits the dash, legs and paws yelling,

Firestorms. Of ripping

rain.

I bat my hands around the van, looking for heat. It's coming from Sue's head — fear licking up her eyeballs.

I

have a hot

side.

'You got a fright. It's just a roo.'

Mother will

burn.

'Can't you help me shift it off the road, Sue?' We both look at her dainty paws. They say,

Fire (leave

Mother). Fire (Mum

burns).

Sue's fire ranting tugs my nerves through my ears while I lock her in and turn to face the roo, sideways on the road and talking out its pain bits.

Down,

it says.

Keep down. I

know

this.

The marsupial's soft brown eye like glass, blood a tear from its mouth, breathing with effort.

I know this,

but

it has been

a while.

'Shit. I'm sorry. I didn't see you.' Like the roo is some person. The kangaroo lifts its head — its broken leg twitches — then down again with a sigh, looks away.

This is dangerous,

Small. Stay

under the

covers.

Who's it talking to? 'Look. You just came up out of —'

We

know this

place so well, don't

we. Small.

The roo's stomach lurches. A whisper from under its skin. I dare a hand close, push against the hot fur and close around something

hard. A set of legs, then a tail and a head. A joey — alive. The
kangaroo's big eye rolls and she makes a noise, *tok tok*, through her
bleeding mouth.

Kick it in

the snout

hole,

Small.

I pull the joey into my arms. The mother bucks much as she can
— she's so broken. Then her body empties, her eyes slide. She looks
off past us and up the road where she was headed. Eyes stuck on the
part where the bitumen turns to throbbing mirage. The joey is hardly
anything at all — barely hair, barely roo. Wrapped in pink skin, fine
grey fur.

'Sorry,' I tell it.

Hungry.

Its ears and fur and stench.

Need

her.

I think about trying to drag the big roo into the van so the joey
can feed off her until we find a vet. I think about trying to keep Sue
off them. I think about Kimberly and Lee, how every minute is one
more from them. In the end, I do what I have to do. Put one hand
around the joey's head and the other around its body.

Hungry.

Hungr—

Wring sharply until I feel the crack. It goes quiet, limp. I lay the
little roo, very slow, next to the big one.

One stretch of road turns into another and everything's red. See that
roo across it in blood and bone. The echoes of *hungry, hungry* in
my head. Clutch the steering wheel so as to stop my shaking hands.
Hungry. Sue's nose scanning my hands for the roo stink.

Eat
it,
she tells me.
Crunch through (my bony
love) —
'Shut up, Sue.'
Break
it.
Suck the
eye.
'Fucking —'

A big white sign on the side of the road flares out — Old Sanctuary Mission — bleached by the sun. A town of dirt roads and squat trees. I gun the car fast through those dusty streets looking for people. Anything to take away the fur and meanings. The silence when they're dead. A Holden is parked outside another smashed-up service station. I pull the van right up to it, my heart climbing out my mouth. But it's a green car and there's a dead woman in it, about the same age as me.

'Poor thing.' A glance at Sue to see what she makes of it. Scared she'll want to eat the woman or something. 'You think it's zooflu? Are people dying of it now?'

It goes
to the picture
place. (I
do too.)
'Dingo heaven or something?'
It breathes the same
air.
'I'm sorry, matey, but this one is —'

The dead woman opens her eyes and we scare the living shit out of each other. I wind my window down with jittery hands — gesture for her to do the same. She shakes her head around like some rabid dog.

'Trying to find my son,' I shout. 'My little granddaughter. And somewhere to get a proper feed. You alright in there, love?' She's still shaking her head. 'What do you reckon, Sue?'

Sue comes over to look out the window and the woman goes apeshit. Starts banging on the horn and screaming and yelling. Sue is right there with her, shrieking,

(Hide.) It's

going to die

anyway.

Woman screaming. Dingo snarling. Even with all this noise, no one comes out. No one saves that lady. I bully Sue over to the spare seat and get us out of there.

The place is a ghost town. Streets like someone swept them clean with sand. I'm about to drive out the other end, join back up with the highway, when we reach the Old Sanctuary Mission Hotel. A shed-like pub with a big hall attached to it. My Holden sedan, just sitting there in the carpark. There's Graham's paint job. There's the rust, creeping down the shell. There's Hello Bear sideways on the dash. I have to get out and touch the car to know it's real. A peace symbol drawn with an adult finger in the dusty windshield. Car unlocked. I snatch up Hello Bear and march toward the pub.

Inside, it's night.

'Help you, love?' A shadowy figure behind a bar. My eyes adjust. Scabby place — I've partied in a billion like it — plastic chairs and tables, concrete floor, crusty couches, and a pool table. No Kimberly. No Lee. Girls' and boys' toilets empty, shit-smelling. Spider in the corner — body quiet. When I get back the man behind the bar is waiting. No mask, but enormous wads of toilet paper in his nostrils and ears. His eyes are flaky and red. Packs of tailor-mades on the counter. He carefully ashes one balanced between the fingers of pink washing-up gloves.

'Young man and a little girl come in here? Their car outside?'

'They were here. Not now.'

I reach for his cigarettes. He doesn't stop me. 'Where the hell are they, then?'

He thinks about this. 'Their car broke down so I did a trade. Gave them my wife's little run-around-town job for the Holden. The wife's car is just a three-door Micra. I don't know what he was doing swapping his HR. It's a classic, just needs the fan belt —'

'It's mine. Where are they?'

'Gone south.' He pours me a Coca-Cola and sets it on the bar. 'Why don't you pull up a stool, have some breakfast?' My mouth suddenly so dry I could lick the sweat from the glass. I sit Hello Bear up on the bar and down the Coke. He watches me, nods. 'I know a bloke with a whole heap of chooks. Reckons it's only the roos and rats try to talk to him. He's got no problem with chooks. Keeps me supplied with eggs.' He pats his big gut and smiles. Mouth purple rimmed, bottle of that cough syrup in his hand. He pours himself a nip into a sherry glass. Waggles the bottle at me. 'You won't catch them right now, love. They left here yesterday.'

'How was she? Is she okay?'

'Little girl? Happy as Larry.' I push my Coke glass forward and he tops it up with purple syrup. 'She needed a wash, but we're all a bit ...' The man shoots a look at the door, face suddenly as purple as his drink. 'I'd get that blooming mutt out of here if I was you.' Sue stands in the doorway, panting.

Puddle.

The man careens backward. 'You eff right off with that animal stuff. Stop that bitch talking.'

'It's hot,' I tell the guy. 'Puddle just means water.'

'I'm sorry, love.' He shakes his head. 'It all gets a bit twitch and sniff around here after a few beers. If Land Patrol come back here for a knock-off, I'll be done for. I can't have it.'

Takes all my effort to pull money out of my pocket for the Coke and slap it on the bar. The man looks at it unhappily.

'Never said I wanted any of this. I had a wife but she's gone. We've got to stick together. We've got to be ... what's that dog saying now?'

Puddle.

I go around the back of the bar, push the publican aside, and get Sue a drink in a peanut bowl. The man can't take his eyes off her. Chugs back on that syrup with one eyeball cocked. I go back to my already-warm Coke and purple. We watch Sue drink.

Rock.

Metal. (Mine.

Mum's.)

She pauses to clock us. Licks drips off her lips.

Dead

sky meat.

The publican pulls a wad of toilet paper from his ear. 'What's she saying?'

'Just going on about the water. It tastes funny, I think. She calls me "Queen". Show him how you call me "Queen", Sue.'

(Yesterday)

Mother.

She goes back to the water.

'It's from the tank.' He stuffs the tissue back in. 'I guess I thought they'd have more to say.' I drain the glass. The publican pours me another, straight syrup this time, and gets down to give Sue a nip in her empty water bowl too. 'Maybe this'll help her talk properly.'

That cough syrup must be alright because sharing a drink with Sue and this man in a titty-fuck town in the middle of the desert suddenly seems really funny. My laugh tears taste like chips. The publican has bags and bags of them behind the counter in all the flavours: chicken, barbecue, salt and vinegar, plain. We eat them, and then we eat some of those eggs he talked about, and all the time we drink that purple drink, and bourbon and cola too.

—

I tell Sue, 'You know how there's games, right? You know about games?'

Throw it. Please

stop

(Yesterday).

Where is

Tomorrow.

The mention of Kimberly makes my heart bleed through my chest. I take another swig. 'This is a drinking game. Every time someone says um or ah, they have to drink. Got it?'

Where is the smelly

little one.

Mummy wants

kittens in its

places —

'I want you to play this game. The rule is don't say um or ah.'

She doesn't. The publican's name is Jamie Calarco, and he was born just up the road, four years before me, almost to the day. He's got a face like a round stomach. Blue shorts crumpled at the thigh, singlet too long in the armholes, patch of chest that looks sensitive next to the burnt skin beside it. We're umming and ahhing and drinking. We decide to give old Sue a nip of the syrup every time she wags her tail. She gets drunk alright. Takes out her dingo on a couch cushion. Rips it to shreds.

Rude.

(Don't.)

Rude to

keep

me from the trees.

'What's she saying?' Jamie still has that toilet paper stuck in his ears.

'I think she needs to do a piss.'

'Too late.'

The widdle catches the light that finds its way in the painted-up windows. We start laughing.

What.

Sue sweeps her tail uncertainly. Bits of cushion hanging like decorations from her fur.

What.

She's talking through a tunnel. The cough syrup works, a bit. I give her another nip. Jamie thinks weeing on the pub floor is a good idea, and he pops his fat little thing out to take a piss in the corner near the pool cues. I'm laughing so hard I might wet myself. This makes Sue wag and wag, and I pour more and more in her bowl and in my mouth. Jamie pees on his leg he's laughing so hard.

He says, 'You do it. You do it!'

I'm a lady. I take it outside.

Next to the pub, the big white hall crouches on wonky stumps. Its wooden slats stained up the sides like the mark of a sunset tide. 'Old Mission Sanctuary' written again on a sign over the broken door.

Come

on.

A small plastic sack of rat poison slumped by the door. I bet it's one of those damned places they put kidnapped kids back in the day. I've seen the photos. Big old tin-roofed house for a hundred beds. My grandmum — a whole bushel of nutty Jesus — used to have paid work on one, running the laundry. She'd talk about those station days like they were the best thing on this earth: married to the herder, all those blackfellas working for her big white arse.

Come on. We're

dying

here.

The Mission name is still there but the people have gone — the place turned into some sort of animal sanctuary that makes the Park look like a well-oiled machine. What were once washrooms are now Perspex-fronted enclosures — DIY jobs, glued and screwed. Big locks shut tight. A hammer and a crow bar scattered on the floor. Cracks and splinters from where someone has tried to bash their way back in. It's all lit by a fearsome golden light from filthy clear panels in the roof, and there's a noise, like a weak alarm going off.

Come

on.

Come on to Kim and Granny's Animal Place. No animal turned away. Half expect Kim to run out of there, baby wombat under her arm. Thought of finding her makes me take a gulp of dusty air and go in deeper. Floor covered with shit and straw. The dusky stench of poo. The cheeping of birds that (thank the Lord and the Devil combined) doesn't mean anything to me. My eyes clear in the endless twilight, only to be filled up again with the sight of cage after cage of animals, locked in, starved to death or nearly there. No little girls. Just birds, lizards, and mammals. The hairy bodies a mist of whispers.

Hotter

than blood.

Kookaburras in pairs, one dead, the other nearly. A koala slumped in the fork of a branch.

Haven't caught

any

rain.

'Hey,' I say. 'Hey.' The latch won't come undone.

Rain.

Puddle.

'Right. Water.' Past a firmly locked cage where three pygmy possums clutch each other in death. A goanna watches me behind dented plastic. I pick up the hammer to bash at a rusty lock confining two rosellas. It gives. I leave it open, but they're too weak to budge — their brilliant red and green tail feathers discarded on the floor. A pelican in a pit by a dried-up pond limp-waddles to the door and stops there. Another cage of songbirds.

'Water,' I tell them. 'I'm getting water.'

In a little kitchen the water dribbles from a tap into a dog dish. I sit the bowl outside the sealed entrance of the koala enclosure, and the animal stares at me with its button eyes like I'm some sort of torturer.

Find

me.

'I'm trying to get it open.'

Has it seen

my

feet.

'Your feet ... your paws are right there. On the end of your legs. Can't you see them?'

I'm

all done here.

'I know, matey. I know. There's got to be a key, right?'

I'm

cooked.

Jamie is in serious communion with Sue on the floor of the bar, toilet paper from his ears scattered around him.

'I always thought all cats were girls and all dogs were boys when I was a little tacker. I heard that dogs know when their owner's going to die. That true? You know when I'm going to die?'

I point to the sanctuary beyond the tin walls. 'What the fuck is that?'

Find

me.

Jamie squints up. 'The wife. She does the animals. I do the pub.'

'They're half dead.'

'Punters love to go look at them, then come in for a feed. They love it.'

'They're starving out there.'

'Her job.'

'Where is she?'

He shrugs. Sue, for her part, is off her head. She's lost the scent, weaving back and forward, stepping in her own wee, growling at something in the corner. All kelpie-cross. All dingo.

**Bits and
pieces.**

'Give me the keys.'

'Drink this.'

I do. Then start opening drawers and tins and plastic containers. Jamie leans in the door of the room behind the bar — an unmade bed of faded blue sheets and a floral quilt; a TV and the saddest collection of singlets and shorts carpeting the floor.

'She took them.'

'Who?'

'The keys. The wife. I went to poison the animals. All set to do it but when I tried to break the Perspex, I could see their bodies, saying … Here.' He points the purple at me again. 'If you drink enough, you can't hear them calling.'

When the dusk comes — and it comes around like a freight train out here — Sue lifts her head and howls. Me and Jamie can hardly understand her meaning, we're so full of purple drink, but we stop and listen because her insides fill every corner, every bit of air.

**I was passing
by. And …
still here. Where …
are you.**

Outside the walls of the shed, somewhere in the darkening desert, there's an answer. Then another.

Sue responds with howls and fuzzy body talk.

Oh. My
pack ... bigger than
Yesterday —

I have another nip of purple. Her meaning lost to me. Remember the Valium I nicked from Ange. One for Jamie, one for me.

The clock on the DVD player reads 6.47 am. I'm on a couch, covered in a blanket tatty with cigarette burns. All my clothes are on my body, and I pat myself on the back for that. If Sue's got a weakness for wild dog packs, I've got one for sausage-like guys look like they're about to burst their skin. A small pile of purple vomit on the floor next to the couch. Past that is Jamie, laid out on some more manky blankets spread over the concrete, sunglasses, the rubber washing-up glove, and a great big handkerchief stretched against his face. A homemade bushranger. A mental patient. For a moment I think he's dead too, then I see his big frame shudder in a snore. My bladder pushes to bursting. Try to draw my foot out from beneath Sue and think I feel a rumble in her chest.

The whiff of
Small.

'Get off, Sue.' That rumble again.

Little little
(my head).

Jamie's hand shoots out when I try to tiptoe past, wraps around my ankle.

'Petrol stations have closed down now, you know. So as to stop people travelling. They're working on a cure. You could wait for your son to come back.'

'I got to pee, mate.'

He tightens his hold a little but the feeling is more that of a brace than a clamp. Keeping me upright. 'You could stay here,' he says. 'With me.'

I prise him off and go to squat on the stones outside. The

campervan covered with dust. The road too. Stand up too quick and my head floats out to space for a bit. The steady feeling of that hand on my ankle. The idea of staying put. Feller at my side and a talking dingo at my feet. A talking bloody dingo. Inside, it's cool and dark and there's a bar. Bits of tissues scattered around the floor stick to my bare feet. The floor sticky with purple drink. The beer pumps hiss empty but the liquor bottles are full. My hand shakes at the nip. I drop the shot glass. Shatters like ice on the concrete floor.

No. Where is my
south.

'It's okay, Sue.'

Watch it.

(My old
head.) Watch
it now.

'Shhh.' I drink straight out of the bottle. It's rum. The sugar hits my throat before the alcohol does. Jamie crawls across the floor, singlet sagging like skin, until he reaches the bar stool then pulls himself up to join me. Finds two fresh shot glasses and pours both with a sure hand.

'What should we drink to?' he asks. He's got those red eyes, purple lips, a sentimental smile.

'What about —'

Tomorrow.

Sue has snuck up on her spindly legs. I take the shot. She watches it. Another deep rumble.

'You *are* fucking growling at me.'

Jamie laughs into his drink. 'Doesn't want you to have a friend. They're jealous creatures. I guess you keep her around for company.' His eyes dart toward the back door, sanctuary beyond. Sue, meanwhile, bores her ambers into my very being.

Tomorrow, Yesterday.

Tomorrow.

'I keep her around —'

Jamie refills my glass. Clinks. I take it, but it doesn't sit right.
The long road. The
cold
kitten in the
sand.

'Sue's helping me to find my kittens.'

'You mean your kids.' Jamie hitches his shorts. 'I'll go make us some tucker. You'll feel better with some eggs in your guts.'

I think of Jamie back there, making eggs for three, while I'm driving down the highway with a life-sized dingo, looking out for his wife's little run-around car. My kittens inside it. Once the pub is out of sight, I pull up by a dry dam, open the campervan door and have a spew.
I'll eat
that.

Wipe my mouth. 'What?'
I'll
eat for Yesterday.

Sue jumps over me to the ground. I watch her eat it, then I spew again. 'Full, are we? Don't want that second one?'

Sue turns her back to it.

'That's a disgusting habit you've got there, girl.'
A good, clean
cat.
(Never
hungry. Never wasting.)

'Clean cat no spew. Clean cat no eat animals.' I'm starting to talk like her. Or like we talk to the foreigner tourists back at the Park. Loud, like they can't hear. Her tail shifts, whispers,
Yesterday.

'Prefer Mother, thanks. Or Queen. What about Queen?'

Her whiskers tell a story where I'm not fit for the dust on some

Queen's shoe. Her 'Yesterday' tail wags the feeling of the turn of the wind in the south after a stinker of a hot summer. It's still hot, but you can sense the autumn muttering icicles underneath. Graham loved that death of summer. I'm a convert to the kind of country where there's only two seasons. Sue was born up here — it's in her blood and has been for thousands of years. But the way her stench and shiver talks about me, you'd think she was southern born and bred. Both ways and no ways at once, all the time.

The poison

face

of Yesterday.

'Didn't taste too good coming up either.'

Poison face with

no

babies. (Never

there.)

My heart drops into my womb. The long highway ahead and they're on it. Close Sue in the camper and stumble up the road a bit, away from her stupid talking tail. The broken roads and orange dust of a country so big I'll never see the end of it, never find such a small girl. Crows line up on the electrical wire that scoops the air above me. I hardly notice them until one rises up in the dim sky and flops down again. They caw, watch me.

This is

different.

I squint. Looking for whatever mammal just spoke to me. The only critters I can see are the crows above, gripping the power line.

Not

like us.

Shake my swollen head. Breath in my throat. 'No.'

They caw again, glare down their beaks as I hoof it back to the van.

No *food* **is**

to be *prayed.*

I trip over myself getting back to the camper. Grab Sue by the ruff. 'What did you say?'

She licks her lips, nervous.

It won't start from
here. (A
crack.)
It
starts by making the
best plan.

Outside on the powerline, the crows edge closer, messages in their marbled feathers, half-open beaks, arthritic claws.

It.
Game it.

I grab Sue again, bring her close. 'Can you hear them, mate? Can you hear those crows?'

Sue indicates the line of ants marching across the floor of the van.

Their fingers are
engaged.

'No, up there. Up there!' I force her muzzle up. She blinks at them.

Sky
meat.

The crows look down.

We can't eat
it yet.

They rise, flop down.

Lust on that
instead.

I start blubbering. Sue pushes her cold nose in my face and whispers.

It
hurts. (Fight its face.)
It hurts. Stop
it.

Sue flings her meanings around the van, filling it with muzzle, the soft patch of her underbelly, claw, but the messages from outside still come through. I can see what those crows are saying. I can understand the birds now.

'I can understand the birds now.'

Just sky

meat. (It always

falls.)

'But I think they're talking about ... about waiting for us to die out here. Then eating us.' I grip her coat. 'Sue.'

Yesterday.

I'll take care of

it.

Then she goes back to staring at the ants and takes care of exactly fucking nothing.

The face mask is still on the dash, but the earplugs have escaped. There's a packet of tissues on the floor, gritty with feet. Sue takes up glaring at the crows through the window. Her body tenses with the bullshit violence she won't do.

The sky gets

better

in the ground. (Hold

me.)

I spit on the tissues and jam them in my ears and nose. The plastic sunglasses. Angela's chewed-up scarf. The world dims. Sue's meanings muffle. I start the van. A shudder, the death knell. The fuel gauge bounces on empty.

'No. No no no no no no no.'

Irritated

dishes. (There's

love on the

wind.)

'There's no fucking juice, Sue.'

The best

plan is

to

eat. (Run.)

'Eat the crows? How do you plan on doing that? You got wings now?'

Sue stares.

What.

'I'll go batshit here with all of you,' I yell into the scarf, tight around my face. Click the door open a fingernail. Black figures on the line above. If the crows say anything, it's muffled by the tissues and plastic and cloth. Duck around the side of the van to pour three of the five remaining jerry cans into the master tank. If I don't look up at the crows, if they stay over there, it's okay. I'm okay. They edge closer. So close that I can see the messages form on their oil-slick wings through my sunglasses.

Your

turn.

Your turn.

It's sweet and eyeball.

Maybe some of those petrol fumes get to me because when I look up at the birds they seem to say, clear as if it was written in the sky,

Let it be.

Let it be.

Like they're the fucking crow Beatles.

TWELVE

Cold moves over the world like an empty bed. The further south we go, the closer the sky to the van. The closer the birds to my head. I keep my sunnies on, my mouth wrapped, one earplug and wads of manky tissues stiff with spit in my ear and nose holes. Colour flares out. We drive and drive, but we don't find Kim and Lee. The dingo on the seat beside me has electric fur that speaks one hundred ways, and all these ways make up:

Here.

Sue's nose has us skirting the towns. She nudges me.

Here. (On the back seat.)

Says we should go down this unsealed lane that leads to nothing but a seven-point turn, scrubby bushes up the van's arsehole. Does Sue know where my kittens are? Is she keeping them from me? Maybe that Jamie fella was right: she's jealous.

'Do you really know where they are, Sue?'

Deep down.

South? Or buried? Her body flung at the road. South.

'I need a bit more help than just "south", mate.' I screech off the highway, heading east toward a town instead. Sue's body hollering,

South.

South.

'I need help, I said. I'm sick. Sick as.'

It's a big town too. A hospital and police station on either side of a park, people camping out in the middle, looking worn out as me. Noisy miners in a ragged pine tree gossip our arrival,

In the deep know.

Down there.

It's there.

I ease the van into a space on the main street and let it tick around us. Sue muttering,

Runt

muncher,

and other obscenities. The people on the other side of the windscreen are clumsy with tired, but Jesus, the way some of them move. Shuffling along with shaved patches, bandages around their heads, dried blood flecked on their foreheads. Others desperately scrolling through the photos and videos on their phones, *have you seen this kid, this cat, this husband*.

It can

plant in the

south.

'Uh huh.' Get out my phone to find a good photo of Kim and Lee that I can hand around.

Why

listen.

'I *am* listening.'

Up above, noisy miners observe,

It *stayed* the

night.

Now it's up with the *sun*.

How *long* will it

last. Not *long*, not
long.

I point at the birds with my phone. 'What do they mean, "not long"?'

You're a long *way* from it.

Wait *until* it
dies.

Those birds are staring right at me. 'Are they talking about us? Sue ...' A rumble in her throat.

This
isn't how it makes things
grow.

'If I can get into that hospital and get fixed up, we'll have a better chance —'

It is
the worst
dog. Cats have
more. It
will never meet
love.

'Sue, come on now —'

It will never
catch a fish. It doesn't see
anything.

'Will you shut up half a second?'

Why
doesn't it dig its last
hole.

'Fuck's sake, Sue!' Raise my good hand. It hangs in the space before the slap. Sue gives the future where I did actually hit her a sniff, then makes her body go from eleven to minus two. The van so still I can hear the wind testing the cracks and gaps. 'A bit of peace for once.'

—

I pick my way through the debris strewn all over the camper. My body like rocks being dragged along in my sack of skin. Back of my head being torn to shreds by amber eyes as I make it up the footpath to the pale-brick hospital with its people, people, people and fewer animals the closer I get. Tuck myself all cosy in a line that runs down the hospital steps and across a lawn. Human bodies that smell like normal things: sweat and smokes and oil. Bodies that don't say much of anything apart from dull hand gestures and what's coming out of their mouths. Even so, a shudder runs through us when the miners high up in the big old tree start going off.

It's *in* there.

There.

There.

Take it. *Take* it

out.

I do what the others are doing: rip up some of that nice green grass and add it to the other things stuffed in my ear holes. Everyone is facing away from the tree. Those damned birds. The air feels cleaner than what has been blowing through the vents from the road. People in the line look like they've had more showers and better food than me too, but they're still sick. A small girl in a dress like a meringue drops to the ground and whispers at the damp soil.

'Play with me. *Play* with me.' Her dad hauls her up again. A woman at the front starts laying into an attendant sitting at a white plastic table. I take out the foliage to hear what she's going on about, but she's way past words. Finally, someone at the end of the line yells, 'Why don't you eff off and let us have a turn?' She doesn't. Two police waddle over the grass, stiff with riot gear, and escort her away.

At the front of the line is a white table with a big white nurse. I sink into the white chair, and my back cricks and cracks from the days of driving. Ease my swollen feet from my sneakers. The nurse's voice through the paper mask is like one of Angela's online meditations.

'Where is this dog of yours?' he asks, so gentle.

I point down the street in the direction of the van. The cranky bitch has got herself up to the roof of the camper and is sitting there like a beige gargoyle over the side entrance. 'She talks all the time, except when she doesn't,' I tell the nurse. 'And now,' I lean forward, mouth, 'birds.' The nurse watches my lips intently. I sit back. 'I want to see a doctor.'

The nurse adjusts his safety glasses, then seizes a pen in his hairy hand and fills out a card. 'There you go.'

I take it. 'So I can go up to the hospital now?'

'You're registered, all official. Here's a couple of armbands. Not compulsory, just a handy reminder that you've been diagnosed correctly. Okay? Next, thanks.'

'Wait up. I'm *sick*. I need medical support.'

'The doctors are busy with the psychotic,' the nurse says quietly. 'Those who are displaying psychotic tendencies, in danger of trepanning, talking to insects et cetera.' We glance down the line to where the little girl is pawing at the ground. 'Are you talking to insects?' The nurse is up in my face now, filling the world.

'I've got just as much right as anyone —'

'No. You're not. I can tell you're not. I've seen about a thousand of you since yesterday. You haven't even progressed to fish.'

'But I know what the birds are saying. My son has taken off to talk to bloody whales.'

The nurse puts his meaty hands on the table and pushes himself to a stand. His big bald head blocks the sun. 'Would you like the police to help you instead?'

I stand my ground. 'I will not,' I tell him. 'I will *not* be —'

'Here's what you're going to do.' His voice cools, hardens. 'You're going to take your common-case-with-medium-symptoms body and you're going to step it away from my table. You're going to suck up all your righteousness and hold it even if you drown. You're going to open those red eyes and have a look around and see that you're not the only person here today. And then, lady, then you're going to take this card and this armband saying you've registered yourself with zooflu, and you're going to leave.'

I look back down the line at the people glaring at me to hurry the fuck up. Put my infected hand on the table. 'Could you at least take a look at this?'

'Canine could fix that.'

'Sue?'

'All the noise you've made whinging here —' I guess I make a noise. 'Yes, whinging and whinging out your mouth, instead of shutting up enough to let your ego explode. Have it rebuilt by a bird, an ant, a *dingo*.' He sighs. Seems to take me in anew. 'You probably still eat them too.'

'What the hell else am I supposed to eat?'

He laughs. It sounds like someone opening a bottle of fresh fizzy water. Then he stops, his breath taken. There's a little black gnat floating around his head, a speck, gently butting his goggles. I want to swat it away for him but he lowers those goggles, cross-eyed, to see it. Mutters, 'Kiss.'

I point at the kid in the line. 'You're not going to fix her. You're just going to bond with her over bugs.'

'I'm going ...' He blinks at the insect. Annoyed that I've interrupted his little bug-in. 'I'm *going* to get her away from her idiot parents long enough to tell her that she can live two ways — the animal way and the people way.'

Two ways. The turtles' way. I stumble back across to the park. At least the creature talking two ways from the roof of my campervan knows what's up without a stupid registration card and a wristband. Her mutters and messages have drawn a small crowd, glooping around the van, pointing. 'Look. Is that a dingo? Karen, have you ever talked to a dingo?'

Sue through their eyes. That shining coat. Ancient look. I stand back and have a laugh. Sue spots me. Calls out,

Mother.

King.

Time to

go.

'Royalty again, am I? Why don't you show these people your stuff? Earn your keep around here?'

That's a

rotten bits

plan.

'Come on, show girl. They haven't seen a real dingo before.' I put on my guide voice. 'A purebred dingo. Five bucks a question.'

Sue crouches. People thick around the van, pulling down their masks and wraps, red eyes gaping. Some with drilled-in heads. Lucky for everyone Sue's used to being stared at.

'What's it saying? What's the dingo saying?'

Sue's body, rows of nipples, claws, panting out,

Don't eat its

face.

Good cat.

'It's saying it's a good cat!'

Yes

(this is the

sharp

end).

'Can it have vege sausages? We've got some.'

What.

(Don't bite

it.)

'Can dingoes see cancer?'

What.

(Don't.)

'Five bucks a question,' I tell them again. They mill like tourists. 'Have you got a question? Then get in line.'

They shove. I pick a nice-looking teenager at the front. She clears her throat. 'What's it think of people?'

'Ask her.'

The teen smiles at me, then up at Sue. 'Are you wild or tame?'

What.

'I want to know what you are?'

It wants my

lick.

I hope it sniffed

(and licked

it).

The teenager sniggers. Uncertain. Another person pushes through. Rickety smile. She's unhinged, this one.

'Do you eat babies? Do you know the dingo that ate the babies?'

Sue glances around.

(Only

eat them

when they're

gone.)

More people come. 'Why do you kill my chickens?'

Sue throws me a look over the crowd. Panic waves pour off the roof of the camper.

Good

cat. (Tear it

off.)

I see blood and I see how she'll make it.

Sitting.

Staying.

(Surprise.)

The fear in her hairy armpits. Feel of their hands on my fur, leather around my face, tight on my neck.

THE ANIMALS IN THAT COUNTRY

'Show's over,' I choke.

'They're not even native, you know that? You're not even from here.'

Push through the crowd and reach my fingers up to touch one of Sue's white paws. She darts around, her mouth stopping just short of my hand. The people startle, back off.

'That dog's a psycho.'

'He's dangerous.'

'It should be locked up.'

Sue takes to the bed at the back of the camper. The road out of town the loudest thing around now. I drive one-handed, turn my phone on to call Lee. Straight to the 'Namaste' message service. Listen the whole recording through just to hear his voice. Made before it went smacky flat. A hush to it that I never noticed before. Graham's phone rings twice and then cuts dead, no message bank or anything. Heart in my fingers when I type Lee and Kimberly into the search engine, looking for reports of their deaths. They aren't there. They aren't anywhere. The last of the petrol in the tank. Bright, freezing air on my cheeks. Faster I go, the less gnawing in my chest. The quicker the insects splat against the screen. We go on like that for an hour before Sue pipes up to tell me there's rain coming. All I can see is cold blue sky.

'We're going south, Sue. Is this the right way?'

Sue grunts, no.

This

way, this.

Wild dog GPS. Accurate, though. I recognise the landscape — the wonky fences, the pockmarked paddocks.

'This is where Graham lives.'

Its

want,

Sue's rear-end says,

is now.

'Me and Graham are through.' Sue taps up the front to sniff me.

Today is

Yesterday. (Now.)

I turn back to the road.

'Are they really there?'

Sue flings her messages out the window:

(So weak.)

Hardly a

bark.

Her nose empty but my mind full — Graham and all that we were: a family. Hard to imagine but easy to remember the feel of their skin. Human skin. No fur except for in the spots there's supposed to be. Grip the steering wheel. On the edge of his town there's a sign on a post, reads, 'Here lies a former settlement, flooded in order to expand the dam'. I pull up to stare over the lake, once a little valley where people lived. The cross of the old church salutes the air above the waterline. A tern perched upon it like he's the last preacher in the south, calling,

Son *daddy*.

Son *daddy*.

Put your *head* in

it.

I slip and slide down the bank of the flooded town, get my hands in the freezing water to wash myself. Stinks like mud, pondweed, metal. A sickly mist lifts off the lake. Take off my ranger shirt and singlet and give my underarms a go. My nipples pinched and sour. Ribs grinning under my skin. Gut white and bloated. Sue trots along the ring of tide. Paws in, she circles and backs away. Dingoes aren't ones for water. I can see her body muttering, tail musical, but it's not for me.

Stand on the

rocks and
look at the
city. It's full
of dogs.
(I'm the
Queen.)

'If I call you Queen,' I shout, 'will you forgive me?' Sue crouches.
Spring-loaded.

The hunt is
here.

A pair of travelling warriors glaring at each other over muddy
water: me with my tits out, Sue ready to track and bring back the kill.
Kill might talk to us these days, of course, but we're ready.

The streets become so familiar I might be asleep in my own history.
Riding in Graham's cherry-red Holden EK along roads I saw with a
body that held Lee. I could have sucked the salt out of the sea with
those cravings. The farmhouse we lived in when I was pregnant.
Graham's cranky old dad, his quiet mum, and their herd of dairy
cows, all mooing in a row. Near killed all of us trying to get along.
Petrol stations with their pumps hanging. Lucky for me with those
jerry cans, but they won't last long. Geraniums exploding from a
garden. The shocking blue of a painted letterbox. Birds hacking the
sky with their talking wings. My own eyes, pink slits on a filthy face.

We get to the road that borders Graham's farm on the other side
of town. The rain that Sue talked about comes over in sheets, drives
the insects and birds from the skies. It isn't even deep winter but the
air is sharp, cold. The southern sky low and disloyal. The fencing
twitches. The dirt, the grass, and the feed.

What's
that.

'They're cows.'

Is that its

friend.

'I guess we could be friends, yeah. I probably knew their ances-
tors.' I stick my elbow out the window, take one good look at the
bovine bodies, and draw myself back in quick smart. The cows appeal
through the wire,

All of

me.

The whole place smells like milk, fermenting grass, grief and heat.
A wild look of survival in those cow eyes.

Could it tell

my babies I'm

still

here.

Hipbones awkward as stilts against their own weight. They push
against the locked gate, making a distant clanging sound from another world. A past where I was Jean, and Graham was standing here,
and Lee the length of my forearm — no Angela, no Kimberly, no Sue.
Calves everywhere. The sound the mothers would make at the fence
line when the little ones were driven away.

It knows

them. Where are

they.

The paddock gates are open, but cows still hang around inside,
some sick. The ones still standing are being milked at least, udders
full and pink, their black backs glittery with rain. The strongest of the
cow's messages come from their guts. Low, confidential.

It came and

made babies from

babies. Where

are

they.

The first cow in line sways slightly on her feet, leaning against a weak post, rocking it loose. She makes a noise — a deep lowing that to my ears sounds like 'No', but the stink and flick of her ropey tail form a very clear,

Come on,

cunt.

Lifts her leg almost gracefully and smashes a hoof into the post of the holding stall — a crack that makes the other cows stumble and panic.

Fuck my

clumpy teats where

are they.

The whites of dozens of eyes. They start toward me in a rolling, sharp-hooved mass of black and white. Have me going for the revolver and bullets in the glove box. Heavy little thing. Cold in my hand, bullets in their cradles. Just when I'm trying to cock it, the cows veer toward the sheds and stand there in line, edging forward to be milked.

She, then

she, then she, then she,

then she.

These cows want to tell me stories I don't want to hear. Got my own lost babies to find, thank you very much. Turn my back on their big, frustrated bodies and get myself down the empty driveway of the farmhouse. There's no little white car with my Kimberly inside. Just a squat, lopsided weatherboard with a front door flush to the elements, and no eaves or porch to shield it. The few steps stained with decades of mud. Graham's mum was no proud housewife, but she loved a garden. The rose stalks ready for winter. I march past them and up those steps to face Graham and his new missus. Sue watches me from the shelter of a tree that was small last time I was here. Her nose to the roof of the house, body misting like dry ice, messages fighting the air.

Puppet Bearer. Hot

Milk.

That business
with the sky.
(Howl and
root.) In the —
'Sue —'
What.

Her stare has a slice to it. A sudden lunge I can feel in my nose. A teeth-through-cartilage answer.

'Nothing. I just. Let's get this over with.'

No one comes to the door. I rattle the knob, push against it, locked. Graham never locked. The rainwater slops from the guttering into my eyes. I edge past and rap on the buckled pane of what was our bedroom window.

'Graham,' I shout. 'Ham?'

Wipe my eyes and jog around the side, Sue trotting in front like she owns the place. Her chatter so thick I have to brush through it.

Mate in the
old whale and
mate in the sleep —

'Let me handle this, Sue.'

We circle a banged-up green Holden with grass growing from its roof. The back door of the house didn't ever have a lock. It budges, but won't open all the way.

'Graham!'

Mate. (Breed with
bugs.)
Mating.

A grunt on the other side. Something dragged across the linoleum and the door flung open. I catch a flash of Graham's bulk. He sees the dingo and trips over the short step from the sunroom, stumbles back into the hall and down to the far end of the house.

Sue bristles.

Where is its

mate.

I push past her — mate indeed! — and around the old sideboard that has been moved out from the wall. The rain beats its cold fingers through the open door and onto my back. The lights are off. The blackness of the house. The hallway a throat behind an open mouth.

'What's going on, Ham?' Graham recedes until I can hardly make him out in the shadows that gather up the end there. I can't see any sign of his woman. 'You alone in here? She around?' He comes a bit closer and stops by the kitchen door, swaying there in the darkness.

'Took off first sign of trouble,' he says.

'That'd be about right.' I turn to Sue. 'See? No mate here.'

Puppet Bearer

and

Hot Milk (taste

it).

Mating in the

sky —

'What are you doing here, Jean?'

'Lee's missing.'

Graham's face doesn't twitch.

'Did you hear me? I said I'm looking for our boy —'

'I heard.'

'Well, then.'

He steps out of the dim. Eyes inflamed, the eyelids turned out, exposed. Lee's mouth, Lee's skin, Lee's hair if it was silver and thinning. Graham is bigger, hairy on the arms and poking out the vee of his flannel shirt, though his long hot-rod beard is gone. I realise I've never in my life seen his chin — his face looks newborn.

'Haven't seen him in a year,' he says. 'Took Amy Olivia's debit card and drained the account. Wasn't much. Posted a roll of lotto tickets and a sorry note to pay her back.' Smiles flick over our faces at this.

Lee and his notes. 'They weren't valid, 'course.'

'Well, now he's taken Kimberly —'

'Kimberly?' I see that name hit him. Sideways, like a wrecking ball. Sue mutters,

Toy

Breeder.

Graham puts a hand up to blinker his eyes. Block her out. 'Where's the girl now?'

'With Lee, I told you. I've got to find her before her mum finds me.'

'Angela.'

'Angela.'

Pairing

in the sky. (Bug

magic.)

Graham looks at Sue like he might kill her. 'Where'd you get that dog?'

'Dingo. From the Park.'

He snorts. 'Thought I recognised it. Going around with a dingo would have to be one of the stupider things you've done.'

'Come on, Sue.' She stays exactly where she is: stock-still in the doorway, legs planted like they grew there, nose to the air around Graham.

Toy

Breeder.

'Breeder, my arse. Come on —'

Big

Daddy (do it).

I peer at Sue. 'She remembers you too, Ham. Got a nose on her smarter than the brain in your head.' We used to feed each other insults that way, but he's struck by Sue and her,

Puppet

Class.

Her nostrils going like the clappers.

'How would she remember you after all this time?'

Graham shrugs, but I can see his face is lying. That particular way of raising his eyebrows and squinting his eyes. Surprised and ferocious. In the Park, an animal will pull the same move — wagging and growling at the same time — and you better get the hell out of that cage, because it's defensive as fuck, fighting for its life. Graham had that face when I asked him why he was leaving me. Sue says,

Fat man (easy
to swallow)
breeding up in
there.

I stop for a bloody second. Listen to her.

Rear up
in the sky for the
Hot
Milk.
(Sit.
Stay.)

Pull a chair from the filthy table and point Graham into it — right where I used to sit up at nights, smoking through the pregnancy insomnia.

'You got any cigarettes?' I ask him.

'Quit.'

I sit down opposite, put the old gun on the table, and take a breath, inhale the decades. Feel Graham and my old self and all the days and nights I walked up and down the hall, talking to the baby in my gut. I gave birth to Lee at the hospital just up from here, and we waited out a month or so in the cold front room before we hit the road. Never minced words together — thought that was a good thing. He turns his rogue eyes on me and there he is. Wilful old roadie and hothead in one.

Put that
dick
in a cloud.

'How can you even think a word in your head with that around?' he asks.

'She's got a body on her can speak, that's for sure.'

Graham flicks his eyes down my body. Makes me laugh, the little shit.

'Be nice to catch up, just the two of us,' he says. Teeth whiter than they used to be.

'What've you got to say you can't say in front of an animal, Graham Bennett?'

He shrugs. 'I owe you an explanation.'

'Bloody well do, too.'

It takes a bit, but I coax Sue out the back door with the promise of food.

Is it in the
ground or the
sky. (Dead thing
there
and there.)

'Just out here, I told you.'

It's not
on my
tip.

By the time I've shoved the sideboard up against the back door — Sue on the other side calling,

This is
forever —

Graham has the lights on in the kitchen. Table wiped. My revolver wrapped in a tea towel. I lean up in the doorway, watching his big frame bump up against the bench, then at the fridge getting out some rough-cut bacon, then to the stovetop. He's all barrel, sharp bum. The blissful quiet of his body after Sue. Sees me sizing him up, all leery.

Lays a bit of bacon in the sizzling pan.

'If that pig could talk,' I say.

'None of that. It's just us in here, right? Just you and me.'

The pan throws sparks of fat. I can hardly hear the rats whispering in the walls, Sue calling,

Toy

Breeder. Toy

Breeder,

from outside. Graham gets out two plates and a bottle of sauce. The bacon so salty my tongue hurts.

Graham chews thoughtfully, avoids my eye. 'We should never have taken up those jobs at the Park. Should have kept to the road. Maybe we'd —'

'No regrets, mate.'

'I got regrets. Regret every fucking creature I ever met.'

'Who's talking about them now? See you're still milking those cows too.'

We listen to each other chewing.

I swallow. 'Well?'

'Well what?'

'Why'd you leave?' He goes quiet. Once a gambler ... He won't say shit until I lay my cards down. A few days with Sue, and I've almost forgotten how this game goes.

'I did the dirty on you once,' I say finally. Enjoy watching him choke on a bit of gristle. Then he laughs — a rare thing.

'Who was the bugger?'

'Happy. Dopey? You know, with the convertible.'

'Lucky? That fucking failure.'

'Guess that's why they call him Lucky.'

'You know he had warts,' he says. I throw a rind of bacon at his face. 'He did. Now I know why I got them.' He's got his belly laugh going now. If I'd known it would cheer the cranky old bastard, I might have told him a few years earlier. 'Anyway, he wrote that car off.

Not so lucky.'

'He died?'

'No, but,' he points to his head, 'may as well have.'

I think of Lee with Kimberly. Rattling around some death tin like loose teeth.

'So?'

'So what.' He squints, picks up a crumb, cleaves it in half with a ragged fingernail and puts it down again in two. Repeats this, then there's four bits. Then eight.

'You got something to say to me or what, Graham Bennett?'

'You know what it is. You bloody well know.'

Like my hand is cramping from holding on too long, I let go. Graham right in front of me with his words. Used to think we were so different, but here we are the same — mouths that talk instead of fur and smell. The cold bedroom isn't as far as I remember down the cold hall. Graham's body warm: we remember. Rock together on old love and loss. I put him inside me where he fits. We go at it with gritted teeth but neither of us can make it to the end. Graham's chest full. A dint between the ribs that perfectly fits my cheek. His big hands around me. I clutch on like I'm free-falling and he's the only thing solid. I cry a bit, but it's very dark. His cheeks are wet too. Fall into sleep like that.

The wrong
   breeding
   pair.

Sue a silhouette in the doorway. Made blonde by the light thrown up from the kitchen down the long hall.

'How'd you get in, girl?'

Window
   helper.

'Get out of here.'

'She's alright, Ham.'

He pushes away from me. The cold air in the space between us.

'So this is how you want to play it,' he says.

'What's wrong with you now?'

'Come to rub my face in it,' he mutters. Sue's tail shifts.

The seeds

grow.

'That filthy mutt told you all about it, and now you're here for your just deserts. Well, it just happened, Jean. These things happen. And then it kept happening and we couldn't stop it. And I always thought it was my fault you and me could only have one kid. Shooting blanks. But I wasn't. Turns out it was you. Something wrong with your plumbing, not mine. She turned out alright, didn't she? Kimberly? All her fingers and toes?'

'Graham.' I whisper it. It's his chance to stop. To leave it alone.

'That little pervert used to watch us from its bloody cage next to our house. No secret anyway. Everyone knew. Even Lee knew. How did you not know, Jean? Are you fucking retarded?'

I hear murmurs. Rats in the walls, calling,

Follow the

tracks, follow them.

Keep on

singing because

the

train is moving.

Memory noise. Rat noise. Dingo noise,

The teeth on

Yesterday.

I throw myself right at Graham's stupid face. That sensitive nose — I go for that. Starts spurting blood soon as I touch it. I can feel the wet on my fist. Then I'm on top of him again and I don't let up. It's not just his face I'm smashing either. It's Angela's. I rip that fucking mane out of her head. Bash my own idiot skull. Those two, going at it in front of me. Graham's breath like rotting meat — that familiar smell. The immense heat coming off him. He's not fighting back. Just lying there. Makes me punch harder. Go in for a big swing, and stop. His face in the half-light is Kimberly's — her fury and frustration when she can't get something to work. The remote control. Her colouring-in. The right grub for a feed. It sucks all the angry out of me. My arm falls. Sue watching, all hairy and pointy-eared, from the door.

It can mate the big
man now. Go
on.

Graham wipes his nose, chuckles through his chest. 'You're that dog's bitch,' he tells me.

I get off him. 'I'm not.'

'She says, *stay*, and you stay, like a dog. She's leading you around like you're a bit of shit stuck to her bum hairs.'

Sue starts swearing and growling deep in her throat and doesn't let up. Graham growls back — bloody animal that he is. The flurry of big limbs and small. Sue finds a soft bit and holds on.

(Elastic.)

Graham wallops at her and she's off down the hall, him in pursuit. Drag on my clothes and get down there after them. Rooms empty. Back door open. Over in the yard, by the herringbone shed, Graham has my gun up and pointed, not at Sue but at some poor bloody cow. Graham shakes where he stands. He's still naked, rough line of stubble running down his neck, overflowing into thick hair over his belly and dick. The cows shuffle at the fence. Mumble their stories to each other, then turn to us, calling,

I
know that
face.
It holds
children. Where
are they.

Does it know
about the yellow
grass.

Their bodies make pictures that get inside my bones until I'm half cow with skin shivers and nose chatters, pregnant again and again. Least I know what that is. Graham grabs his big gut, doubles over, and a rush of vomit blows out and splatters over the ground. He fumbles at his face, retches again. When he's finished, he squints through the weak light to another voice.

Big
man.

Sue. Picking her way back across the gravel. Careful paws, watching us like a stalking cat. No smart asides. All focus. Her fur mutters,

The burning
takes it
down.

Graham stares at her.

The old fucker
has
no toes.
No
prick.
No tooth. No
insides.

'Shut up.'

No milk. No
meat. No Yesterday.
No —

'Shut the fuck up.' He lifts his revolver, shaking so hard he can hardly pull the trigger — but he does. It cracks the air in two. Sue skits away, alive. Starts back toward us. Graham steadies his hand and takes aim. This time, I move. Punch out and get him in the nose again. The explosion of blood makes him lose enough sight that I can wrench the gun out of his hands. He wipes his face.

'I showed you how to shoot.'

'You showed me how to leave too.'

'Don't be a fucking idiot for once in your life, Jean. I'm doing this for you. Get rid of these blighters and we could start again. Lee'll show up eventually and then —'

'Then what? Happy families? You, me, Lee, and your daughter by Angela? We've been doing fine without you, thank you very much.'

The cows observe me as I back away.

Does it

know.

'I do know,' I tell them. Their skin tightens.

It

knows our

kids.

'Everything you touch turns to shit,' Graham calls over them, rolling sideways to push himself to his knees. Even upright he looks cut out, his big body almost see-through in the wispy light. Sue takes a few nimble steps forward. Leans into my leg, soft with a rib cage under the layer of fur, murmuring,

Old

Puss.

Her skin shivers with mirth.

Hello

Kitten.

'Yeah?' Feel the hysterical laughter bubble up in me too.

I'll show

it.

'What?' Serious now.

I'll

show it

Tomorrow.

My fingers in her fur. She's solid. Real. 'Okay.'
We start back across the yard.
Good
Cat.

THIRTEEN

Cold down here in the south. The morning brings thin, freezing rain, and it doesn't get warm for a long time. My body stinks of Graham: my skin came off on his. From Sue there's no *Mummy, Mummy, I'll do anything for Queen* now. Uses the hard bits of her body — her spine, black nails, rotating paws — to issue gruff commands.

It has to go
up and then it
bends very
slowly
with the window open.
'This way?'
Wait.

I pull over and turn the engine off. The rain keeps up its patient tapping.

Wait. I can see
now —
hopping.
Hopping. Hopping.
Continue.

I steer us along the high, exposed part of the highway. Take a looping exit that spins off in the direction of the city. Up, down. The sun looks inside out, spilling its pale guts all over the sky. The farms on every side are empty. Rubbish and shit blown into the paddocks, coming to rest by sheep carcasses. The few live ones keep their distance from the dead. They ignore us, mutter into their flock. Even from the car I can see their woolly tails twitch with meaning,

One step forward

with you.

The pale kites in the sky note us, though, and everything else crawling over the defrosting ground.

Living is too

big. **Living is too**

big. **Small** *piss,* **there.**

There.

No trees out here, just rain that bites at the windows. We haven't seen rain in five months up north. The only other cars are army. They speed past us, lumps of green inside, camo from head to toe.

The road curls inland toward the city. Sue wants us to turn off at a little arsehole of a coastal town that crouches around a bay like a kid who won't share lollies. Heaving with cars, some moving, some abandoned where they conked out. A new Range Rover in the middle of the road, its fuel door open, cap hanging. Spikes of glass glued onto the doorsteps and windowsills of houses. This is where all the people are — cleared out of the country, where there's too many beasts, and all piled up on top of each other in the towns. Electricity, mobile phones, lights on inside the stores. If anyone's trying to escape the animals, though, they're out of luck. Town birds — your seagulls, magpies, and pigeons — in the trees and on the lawns.

Where *are* **you.**

Here, *here.*

Oh *thank* **you.**

Oh *yes.*

I can poke spitty tissues into my ear holes all I want, but the birds talk through them. Dogs too, weaving freely through the crowds.

Sue's nose freaking out a stream of consciousness.

Female. Male. Male.

Male.

Corruption of the

intestines. (Don't

look at me.)

Let me smell

you inside.

'How about you concentrate on my kin. Kim? Lee?' I cautiously put out my hand. Watch her watching me touch that epic spike her fur has made. She wags carefully. Mutters so soft I'm not sure I hear it,

(It burns slower

in the

cage.)

I go to roll up the window, block out the crowds, but Sue's nose sees over and through them,

Tomorrow.

'What? Where?'

Wouldn't bat an eyelid to find Lee in jail and Kim with him. But Sue's paws remember a cage outside, like the one she's been in all her life until now. Home, of sorts.

'There?' I point out a crappy apartment block that probably looked good for two seconds after it was built. 'There?'

The Smoke goes

through

(the cage).

There's a cat carrier in the yard of a house and a gate beside a shop. 'That cage? That one?'

Cooped

up. In

it.

The town has the vibe of a Christian festival or a hippie love-in. Some animal ritual. Sort of place my Lee would sniff out from a thousand kilometres away. A ratty sailing club clings to the edge of the bay, which curls around to a little headland.

A van arrives bearing a big fat cross, and stops at the foreshore reserve. People flock around it. Bloody Christians, loving this animal apocalypse. Man with a cloth over his face makes his way over to the campervan clutching a big pot. Sue gives him friendly ears.

Is that

its

friend.

I roll my eyes at her. Shit judge of character, girl.

'Hey, yeah, hi,' the man tells her.

Hello

(brave face).

'Hi.'

That's a good

time.

'Yeah, it's good stuff. Get her a bowl, will you?'

'Am I allowed to have some too?' He doesn't catch my tone. All dog, this guy. But he's got hot tucker. Steam catches a burst of sunlight, then escapes into the gloom. The soupy stew is thickened with flour, a few carrots, some globs of purple meat, and it's hot. Wipe out a cup with a manky tea towel and hold it out the door. The man fills it awkwardly, murmuring to a nose and set of whiskers that stick out from his pocket.

'Hate is like love but the opposite.'

'Pardon?'

His pocket replies,

My bones are

warm.

He spoons some into a plastic takeaway container for Sue.

'Love is like … I don't know.'

Warm.

'Must be a burden to you,' he says.

I stare at the man over the soup steam. 'You talking to me, or the animals?'

The man squints. Bright-green eyes rimmed with red. 'I could take her for you. Give her a good home. You want to come with me, nice girl?' Sue — the bloody traitor — stands and gives him her love tail.

'You can stay right there,' I tell her. She sits on it, but her arsehole lets out a smell that whispers how she'd leave me for dust if it meant more of that soup.

'I'm looking for this young man and a little one.' Go to show him the photos on my phone, but it's dead. 'Well, they're in a white Micra. The man might have been singing —'

One of the people outside runs her mouth along the windshield of the flat front of the van, leaving a trail. The dust we've collected on all the roads browns her teeth like she's been chowing down on chocolate cake. She wanders off. Ange is always telling Kimberly not to stare at different people, but I'm staring.

'What's wrong with her?'

The man makes a rat-a-tat motion on his noggin. 'Bless them. Our do-it-yourselfers can get excited, turn nasty.'

'Do-it-yourself what?'

'Do-it-yourself trepanning. Hand drill to the skull, relieve the pressure caused by the flu. Stops all the critters talking to you. You must've seen the video. I can do it for you, if you want.' He nods at Sue. 'You can pay me in dog.'

My mouth hangs open. At the edge of the park, a few people drag a bloody-skulled lady to standing. Another car pulls in. Fear-faced family peer out with matching red eyes. Gullible written on their bodies like they're talking animals, making messages with their skin. The soup man moves over to a woman hauling a pink-eyed teenager and a rabbit in a cage. The woman's face is how I feel — the anger, the fear, and the frustration — but she shoots me a half grin while she stops for the soup, rolls her eyes. *Teenagers!* Roll my eyes back. *Dingoes!* She hands over the cage to the man. The teenager loses her shit and starts crying, talking rapidly to the rabbit. Sue keeps her eye on the man.

It's a long way

(home).

'It sure is, girl, and if you're as good as finding it as you are my kids, you'll never get there. Where are they, huh? Where?'

It wants

something.

'Are you fucking kidding —'

Sue can't take her eyes off the man with the pot. He stores the rabbit in the Christmobile and heads with his soup to a house across the road. A cat licking itself in a front yard next to a big tree.

What eggy

air.

Guy puts down his pot and stretches out his hand, real friendly. The animal isn't having a bar of it. Scoots to higher ground. This guy with his hands out, motioning. The cat lets him know that he's a disease not worth getting, and he huffs away with his soup pot.

What would it

know about

cubes,

the cat mutters, settles back on the grass. Lifts its triangle head to the wind.

Yes,

yes,

eggy.

What eggy

air for

kittens.

'Kittens.' Turn to Sue. 'That cat's got something. You smell it?'

Sue does. She tells the cat,

I'll

eat your skull. (Claws in

my
throat.)

'Bloody one-track mind.' Slam the door and call over the low brick fence. 'Puss, puss.' One of the cat's ears turns toward me, the rest to the wind. 'What can you smell there, puss?' Meanings wick off its whiskers, clink and scatter, the bones under its skin.

My panic is on the
weakest side
of a
kitten.

'*Kitten*?' I watch her whiskers, tentacles in the air. They whisper *kitten* again and I'm over that fence, clearing the empty garden beds, no matter who's in the house. The front door swings open in the wind but no one appears. Bright kitchen on the other side. The cat watches me.

Funny
cat.
Legs all the way from the
head
to the ground.

'My grandkid, is that what you can smell? She passed through here. I mean, probably. She'd like a cat.'

I ate
it.

My laugh comes out a choke. 'She's a growing girl. Don't think you ate her.'

It ate
it.

'What?'

It ate
it.

'We don't eat our grandkids, thank you, no matter what you think.' The door to the house swings wide again. The cat notes this.

All the

kittens.

'You got kittens in there? Mine or yours?'

Ours.

I get the fear when I step toward that house. Grab the cat for company or protection, half expecting it to bite or scratch. Ornate metal tag around its neck: 'Bryony'. She settles against me the way they do — her soft body water, my arms a cup. Difference being that all that fur and cushiony skin chatters and sparks now.

We've

got to feed

them.

'Let's just see who's home first. Knock knock? Kim?' I push through. The kitchen big and cold, and scrubbed by someone used to making one thousand sandwiches for football games. Carry that cat through the empty, spotless, threadbare rooms. A set of metal bunk beds with chipped red paint. A bathroom the size of my kitchen in the row, enamel eating itself in the sink. 'Hello? It's me: Jean Bennett.' Like I'm some celebrity. The cat's stomach lurches.

We've

got

to get them out of

here.

'Who? Where? My kids or yours?'

Ours.

'Well, where are they?' I set the cat down in the lounge room. Cords still plugged into the sockets but no TV. The cat twines through my legs, messages of,

Ours.

Ours.

We're in it

together.

'Show me, then. Hello? Show me where the kittens are.' The cat leads me through like an estate agent, bum hole promising this and that. I wrench open sticky cupboards, look under beds. The place empty of anyone but us. The cat is crooning to kittens I can't see. Disappears while I'm grunting to get up after looking under some chipboard drawers. Find the animal back out in the yard, nose to the air.

So
eggy.

'There's no kittens here. Not mine. Not yours.' The cat takes me in with mirror-ball eyes.

Forget the
welcome
mat.
It
doesn't belong
here.

I point back at the house. 'Two seconds ago we were sharing kittens.'

I've
never met it
before.

'Thanks a lot.' I wait. The cat ignores me, and after a while an icy wind starts up. I scrape my leg scrambling back over the brick fence.

In the warm van I grab Sue. Bring her big rib cage close to my heart. Her body isn't made for holding, but she knows me. She knows who I am.

I'll
get with it
Yesterday.

'How about calling me Mother?' I ask into her stuffy coat.

Its pack is
my
pack pack.

'Tell me about being a pack.' She gives off such a whiff of the old days that I can feel my mum's scratchy wool coat around me. Hear her flat shoes on the gravel while she walks us through the cold to a place that sells garlicky kebabs. There's also another coat, a warm teat, Mister and Buddy alongside. Give them a shove, burrow in, the milk tastes sweet. The hairs on Sue's nipples and ears shiver, chuckling as she stretches sure foot pads. Go to give her a bit of a tussle on the head with my good hand, now that she's back to old Sue. She licks my cheek. The spit says,

Sore

bits.

'That cat was rude, Sue.'

Lick

its old cat wound in the

puddle.

'We *could* go for a drink.'

I gather my bones and practically crawl over to the driver's seat. The pub on the corner of the sailing club is busy already. Just seeing it leaches the adrenaline out of me, leaving my mouth parched for something with a kick to it. Takes my everything not to drive the van through the brick wall and order a shot with a beer chaser from my window. We chug down a tiny side street edged with broken security fences protecting houses that have already been ransacked and stripped. Just past a locked gate, there's a tiny white car. My breath hits my rib cage. No one inside, but it's theirs. It's theirs. I know it's theirs. Bloody big peace sign drawn in the window dust.

FOURTEEN

I grab Hello Bear and fling open the camper door. Sue slips out — last bit of sunlight from the day — and streaks off up the street. Past a house where a woman stands in the bare front yard with a glass of wine and a cat dish like someone who lost her date at a party. Following Sue, my falling breath is punctured, body moving through mud even though I'm tearing along. A snout through a gap in a fence calls out,

Let me
go. I didn't
do
anything.
'Sorry. Sorry.'
But I'm
not
guilty.

Got to keep my eye on my own freewheeling canine. Big crowd gathered in the recreation park by the bay. I can hardly see the water, let alone a slinky dingo or two dark heads of hair. People in masks and sunglasses lurch toward and then shrink back from each other. Some of them with bloody holes in their skulls, others with the same-old pink-eye. Way up above, seagulls loop-de-loop — the colour of clouds. Whispers in wings too far to make out the words. A man with thick bare legs and scuffs on his feet stops in front of me. Hand out flat. A praying mantis sways on his palm.

'You talk to them yet?' the man asks. I squint at the insect. Face like a leaf that fell in love with itself. Body secret. Shake my head. The man shoves it closer. The fragile bones of its green knees. I reach out to touch it. The man pulls the insect away so fast he nearly crushes it. 'Are you fucking stupid?'

Edge away from him to stand by a young woman with a new baby. This lady has got the pink-eye bad, but so does everyone. She stares ahead like there are no people cramming the space between her and the water.

'This a government thing? They making an announcement?' I thumb backward in the direction of the little white car. 'Do you think I can do a call-out? I'm looking for my kids.'

'It's whales,' she tells me. 'Southern right whales. They come here every year. But ...' Her baby wriggles suddenly, then calms. I shake Hello Bear at the kid, but she's too little, she can barely see. Stand on my tiptoes to take in the shitty little beach. It's shallow to a point, then the water turns dark where the sandy shelf plunges to some deep place. Someone in front of us ducks to pull up their pants legs, leaving a gap in the crowd that reveals the broad bay. Shapes in the water, pleated concrete slabs. One of them rises, rolls, and, before it slams, lets out a song that ripples through the park like winter waves.

On my back.

Or,

Return it.

Or,

Home is here.

'Did you get that?' I ask, straining forward.

The woman nods, gaping too. 'Come back. They said: Come home.'

'Yeah. Come home.'

Come home it

has been away
too long.

The young woman begins to laugh, but it's high-pitched and creepy, makes her baby cry.

The people around us take it up — laughing and sobbing — and, god help me, I get tears too. The woman's face is streaming. We look at each other, like, what the hell? But we're babbling. Remembering things we don't remember.

'I had this ... tail.'

'There was bad weather at the top of the water — you remember the storms?' She grabs my hand, fingers wet.

'But it was quiet.'

'That's right, autumn at the bottom. Plankton falling.'

Come home.

'Plankton.'

Come home.

It's late.

Down on the beach, people are getting in with their clothes and shoes on. The bay bleeds up jeans, and billows shirts and skirts. People take a few giggling steps out, and then the sea bed drops them into darker water, chests and chins. Laughter like they've opened the door at home to find all their friends and family yelling, *surprise!* With them, a dark-haired figure. He starts toward the water from the narrow rubbish-cluttered beach. It's Lee.

'Lee. Lee!'

He's wading in with his thongs on, arms flung out. *Surprise.* One thong frees and floats up beside him — a pilot boat guiding a ship. I throw Hello Bear to the grass and push through people, down the sharp rock stairs to the beach and into the bay. Scan for Kim and try to keep a clock on my son at the same time. Up to his thighs. His T-shirt catches on the water and anchors. People float and swim around him, ears and faces down, while eight or ten enormous grey mammals breach the bay.

Let's go

home.

A swimmer comes back in and rolls like the whales on a short wave. His grin frozen, eyes open, half covered by hair, dead. I surge away from his body, yelling for Lee just as he steps out and drops off the hidden sea shelf, clothes bubbling above him like a wet flag. I'm in against a current that's thick with people, wading and floating, alive and dead.

Welcome home.

The bed is

ready.

The waves churn. Salt water in my hand wound. Beneath the water there is a bed. I can have a sleep on it, and I would, but for the foxy yap of an alarm.

Yesterday.

Sue bounds up behind me and into the water. My bad hand closes over the ruff of the dingo's sodden orange fur. That fur whispers,

(Bad

Dog.) Stay

with its pack.

Expect her water-hating dingo self to drown too, but she strains around me, her kelpie kicking in, tail floating behind. She grabs the drift of my shirt. Pulls me away from the whale song. I try to box at her, but a small growl comes from her snout like a crocodile, saying,

Its place

is in the middle.

(Sky meat,

poison water.)

In the

middle with

its pack.

'I'm going *home*, fuckhead —' Wrench my shirt so hard it tears away — Sue has some and I have some. That blubbery call. All those people grinning, nodding, dying. A whole family wades past. The man helps his little boy.

'I want to go home, Dad.'

The man laughs hysterically. 'That's what we're doing, Bub.'

Start to follow them. Take the boy's other hand, like Kimberly's but pudgy. The man smiles at me, tears in his eyes. The whales welcome us — mother's voice on the other side of the womb.

Can't wait until it

gets here.

Up to my waist before Sue cuts in again, snapping and circling.

Stay

Good Dog.

I turn, a *fuck off* on my lips. The little boy's hand slips out of mine as he steps into the deep. I look frantically over the silvery wastes for my son. Only a small bubble of his T-shirt still floats there. My breath stops at that bubble. Then, seaweedy black hair. Gone again. The distance between the two of us. Sue is wet through, her snout hairs and black lips calling,

Sit.

Stay.

The water oily and thick. I'm calling for Lee, but my voice is a man's voice. Lost all its tone, coming up from the guts of me. Foam in the water where his hair was. It rushes through my hands. A wave rolls in and knocks me away, then another until I'm back to shore. The whales are turning, their heaving mass pushing the soak.

We've

waited a long

time.

I wade back in, breath caught. I'm holding it for Lee. A slick where he was. Sue paddles around me, snapping.

Its pack is

here.

A bubble. Another. The T-shirt appears again. I let my breath out and swim forward on the backwash to catch the cloth, the fabric straining with the weight of him on the other end. Again a wave rolls me back to shore, but I know where he is now.

Lee is a bit of material so thin on the water. Could be a patch of cloud making a shadow. The T-shirt sinks. Half my life passes while I fight my way back to it. My breath in and out. The whales call,

Stick close

tonight.

I focus on Sue's yapping. 'Get him. *Him*, not me.' She keeps circling, tugging my hair, shirt, skin. I get my hand in her sodden side and push away through the water to where the T-shirt was. My feet still touch the edge of the sandy ledge, a metre or so below. Crouch through the murk. Under the water, the whales are in full homemaker swing.

Here is where it

came from and

here

is where it sleeps. Here

it remains. Yes.

Yes.

My fingers close on a shoulder, hair. Don't have to see Lee to know the shape I moulded with my own body.

Yes.

The water sucks and resists. He's stuck to something, too heavy for me. For a second I think the whales have got him somehow. Then the sand slurps. I haul, fall back. Lee's body breaches. I swing with the current to see his face, wait for him to take in a mouthful of air. It's so real to me that he does that. This baby sleeping. This boy passed out because he hit his head. This teenager drunk and stupid with it. This man dead. I drag my son through the water, up onto the shore. Down on my knees, face to the cold sand. I breathe, I breathe, but he doesn't. Pump at his chest. Watch for water, air, spew. He's very still. He doesn't say or do anything.

'Lee.' My brain is in so many pieces on the sand. The cold beach squeezed in my fists. A lonely, crunching sound. 'Where's Kimberly? Lee. Lee. Lee-Lee ...' His name loses all its meaning. Overhead, pelicans glide like warplanes, calling,

Up.

Slip in on the *up.*

'Lee.'

Come

home.

And I'm up, scrambling for my girl. Salt water everywhere. I hear the call from below the surface.

Welcome

back.

The waves swell. The bodies shift.

What took it so

long.

Crawl to the water's edge, put my ear to the wet. Voices so clear. Home. I stagger to my feet and wade back in until I'm halfway out to the whales, take a breath, go down.

We're

all here together

waiting.

'Where is she?' I try to say. Gulp a mouth of bay instead. The water murky with sand, weed, and salt. My foot presses down on the sandy bottom and I break through to air. Sue is barking from the beach — too far away, I can't tell what she's saying. The whales are closer. My head so heavy it touches the murk.

Why doesn't it

rest for a

while.

'Is she ...' I swallow water. 'Is she there with you?' Another breath. Sue barks. 'Shut up, Sue.' I go down. The water laps my ears, and I hear faint shouting.

'Granny!'

I stare down into the water — the whales have got her. The whales got my boy and now they've got my girl.

'Granny.'

I'm eye level to the sea. Look across its washed-out forever, broken only by the bodies of all those poor souls. Sue is running up and down the beach and past her, up on the grassy verge, my little girl waves at me from the grassy cliff. The world buckles. I gasp, take in water. Cough it up. See her clear. Waving and waving. I push back. Run much as you can run through water made up of people. Behind me the whales call,

Make

yourself

more comfortable —

Home is dead on the shore. Home is waving at me from up on the verge. Home is where Sue calls and calls from the beach, no good to anybody.

'Granny. Granny!'

Lee's hair is all over his face. His mouth open and awful.

'I'll come back for you, baby. Do you hear me, Lee? I won't leave you alone.'

'Granny.'

Don't know how I walk away from him but I do. Stretch my legs for what's still living. Kimberly now in a cop car, face pressed to the window. Behind me, Sue calls,

I will be with

the sodden

coals. (Sit.

Stay.)

'Fat lot of use guarding him now. You could have pulled him out. You could —'

'Granny!'

Kimberly's face opens like arms when she sees me staggering up the rocky stairs to the bank, scooping Hello Bear from where it's been trampled into the grass. A policeman gets to me before I can get to Kim.

'I'm the grandma,' I bawl, clawing at his dry, narrow chest. 'I'm Granny.'

'You're' — he looks at his phone — 'Jean Bennett.'

'Yes. Yes.' I rush forward, but he gets me by the wrist.

'We've been asked to take her home.' His face like a piece of bark. 'The mum asked us.'

'Angela?' I glance at Kimberly, staring out from the car like the whole world has gone. 'I'm her grandma.'

'The mum says you're not.'

'I'm —'

'We'll get her home.'

'Don't you have better things to do?' We take in the dead and the dying and the mad all around us.

'Yes. But the little one's mum knows people so I'm doing this instead.'

'Well, I'm her guardian. I'm the one that looks after —'

'Not anymore. You and ...' He glances at the phone. 'Lee Bennett. Mum wants her away from the both of you and back home.'

I point to the beach. 'That's Lee down there. That's her dad.'

The cop takes in Lee's body strewn like seaweed on the shore. Arms laid out where I left them. Sue standing beside him so alive. He hasn't moved.

'Apparently, he isn't,' that copper says. A sound comes out of me — a moon sound. A dingo howling. The cop pockets his mobile, moves to go.

'But I found her. I need to tell Angela that I found her.'

The cop grunts but pats past his gun and police shit for his phone again.

—

I dial Angela. The phone rings once before I hang up and try Andy instead. The call reaches over the kilometres.

'Yeah?'

'It's Jean.'

'Jesus fuck, Jean.'

'I've got her. I've got Kimberly.' I can't talk about Lee.

'Where?' I hear Andy scrambling for a pen or something.

'Bay Town. About two thousand kilometres south of the Centre —'

'Look, stay there, Jean.'

'I can bring her back. I've got the van and —'

'No, take her to the cops. They've been searching all over.'

'Yes, but I found her.'

'I don't know how. You must have second sight or something.'

'Sue did it.'

'Sue?'

'Dingo Sue. She found Kim. But then —'

'Fuck's sake. You sit around talking to each other?'

'Where's Angela?'

'Ange is ...' I imagine him staring off through the hot air. Feel like I might freeze to death down here. 'Ange has got it bad,' says Andy. 'Talking to insects now. Out of her mind about Kim.'

'She in hospital or what?'

'You know her. She's made herself an animal-proof bunker and runs the Park with a walkie-talkie.'

A laugh that is half cry bubbles out of me. Inside the car Kimberly reaches, calls out, 'Mummy.'

I duck to see her shape through the window. 'It's Andy.'

Her arm falls.

Andy is talking. 'We let more of the animals go so we can keep the critically endangered ones going. Seems stupid, but everywhere else has gone to fuck anyway, I heard. Even Glen has gone. Don't know what Blondie said to him, but he's taken her cage and gone east, back home. So it's just me, Ange, and a couple of the rangers. Keith came back — left me again, of course.'

My stupid heart shifts in my chest. 'You'll be looking forward to seeing me, then.'

'Jean.'

'What?'

'Just stay there, would you? You can't come back now. Ange won't have you here. Not after Lee —'

I hang up, rip open the car door. Kim hurls herself toward me, too hot, gluey with tears. She's warm after the cold air, warm against my cold flesh, stinks like panicky sweat. Her hot sticky hand in my cold one is like a lotto ticket, a magic ring, a whole life I could live out my days around and never need more. She seems taller, even thinner: a grown girl.

'Granny,' she says. 'Granny. Granny,' she muffles into my face. Her cheeks drenched. Tears icy in the wind coming off the bay. She's shaking. She's given me all her warmth. I'm flushed with the love of her. 'Granny, he said close my eyes and count to a hundred.'

I try not to crush her. Lose myself in that mop of hair. Find a grandma voice resting under my tongue. 'Your daddy was never good at counting.'

'Is my dad drowned?'

'No.' I shake my head so hard. 'No. He's down with the whales. Talking to them.'

Neither of us believes me.

'Did you hear what the whales said?'

I swallow. Lie again. 'No.'

She settles against my shoulder. Mouth breathing. 'Could you do the voice? What whales said before they could talk?'

I squeeze my eyes shut. The memory of them,

Home.

Come home.

'Helloo. Helloo, I'm Mr Whale.' Open my eyes. Kim tries again.

'Helloo. I'm Mr Whale. I look like a big blue ... fish.'

'That's a good voice.'

'You do it, Granny.'

'You're doing fine.'

'You do it.'

I take my voice to the bottom of the sea. 'Hellooo. Do you know what whales eat? Young lady?' She shakes her head. 'Fish and ships. Don't blubber, that's my job!'

That makes her smile a bit. One of her teeth is missing. I think of it out there, lying on the seabed like a pearl. 'We going home now, Granny?'

Home

come home.

Hold her tighter. 'No. No, we're never going there. You're never to swim in that water. Understand?'

'To the Park. I want to go with you to the Park.'

I check over my shoulder. The policeman frowns. He's never changed his mind in his life.

'You have to go back first because —' She starts crying. Tears beading pink in her brilliant eyes. I lower my voice to a whisper. 'In this car, I mean, because they don't like Sue. No one does.' The dingo is still down there guarding Lee like it will do any good in the world. *Here, Yesterday, here.*

'You'll come in the campervan?'

'Yep.'

'With Sue?'

'Sue —'

'And Dad?'

I look at her hands in mine. Small and new and pink with heat. Alive. 'Yes.'

Outside, the policeman makes a movement. I can feel him just outside the car. My breathing goes crooked. I give her the soggy lump that is Hello Bear.

'I'm going to be right behind you, darling.' Kimberly starts crying again, but as I watch she sucks back the tears and snot until her face matches her eyes. Waves goodbye with the bravest hand that ever waved. She's stronger than me. When I get out of the car my legs buckle. I grab on to the cop.

'Can you tell her I'm just behind? Can you do that?'

He looks away from me, but I feel like he'll do it. I have to believe he'll do that as the car swings away with Kimberly inside it, pressed to the rear windshield. I wave gaily, happy as you please. The harder I wave, the harder I cry, and she waves back — maybe she's crying too, I can't tell. She's too far away. The car is getting small. They round a corner. She's gone.

FIFTEEN

They're burying people in pits. Whole armies of red-eyed do-gooders come in with their crosses dragging around their necks. My body like the end of a stick that was used to poke fire. I smell charred. Crouch here with a plastic bag of Lee's things, stinking of grief. The revolver pushed between my boobs — if it goes off, me and the tiger will join him. Until then I stand guard over my boy, until the sun goes down and the Christians come with their shovels and weird smiles, and tell me they need to put him in the ground.

'He wants to be on a mountain or by a lake,' I tell them. 'Something like that.'

Sue's got enough sense to keep her distance, resting her sandy arse on a small rise, but I can still read her body. Grass or wind, just the smallest whisper,

Smells like
guts. (Wait
for it.)

'He'll be with Jesus now,' says one of the Christians. She's got a hairy face and growing-out grey roots.

(Sad
meat.)

'It's your right to do a ceremony,' says another, eyeing Sue and her muttering. 'But we have to bury him tonight.' This one looks like an actual priest. His black clothes stick under his arms, between his soft legs. A black woollen jumper tied around his face. Proper ear plugs poking from the big holes of his ears and out his nose. He shields his eyes, as though the dim evening is filled with a great light. Sue has stopped whispering. Stares, body still again, while great wads of words pour out my gob.

'My Lee will smile his way into a fancy restaurant with no shoes on,' I tell that priest. 'Can't add up for anything, but he was really good at geography at school. When he was little his dad wanted to cut his hair all the time, and Lee staged a protest. Can you imagine? A little kid. With this beautiful hair and a little … poster thing. On a stick. And he climbed a big gum tree — biggest I've ever seen, stuck out in a paddock by itself. Graham let him. Lee said he could see the whole world. No, I remember what he said. He said, "I can see my whole life", so we got up there too. It's true: from up there it's like the world goes on and on —' The priest nods at the wrong moment. 'Anyway. That's my Lee. I just —'

'You shouldn't blame yourself.'

'Why not? I'm the mum. I'm the grandma. I'm supposed to —'

'*There's no condemnation for those who are in union with Jesus.*' He says it without feeling, but I lean toward him anyway. These god-men: cheap magicians with psychobabble wands. They used to come to our town and speak at the hall. My mum bent forward, drinking them in through her eyeballs. Every word. Now, it's me after a bit of that fairy dust. Anything to blur the edges of Lee's body, the ocean beyond, the whales humming *home*.

'How could he do it?' The words hurt my throat. 'How could he do it? Does he think the animals are better than us? Is that it?' I spit this. Glare over at Sue. She peers back at me through watery eyes. The slow, irregular wagging of her tail, like a dying clock.

Never

There.

Stay with its pack. But its pack isn't here. No Kimberly. No Lee.

'Animals' souls are ... different.' That priest finds a pair of plastic sunglasses hiding in his thick grey hair and sets them on his nose. 'A material soul can't go beyond its body. They can't sin, they can't face judgement —'

'My boy was an idiot, but he was no one's fool. He heard what they were saying under the water, Father. I did too. What do they mean about home?'

'I don't ... I haven't looked. Or listened.'

'Are they talking about heaven? Is that it? The final home?'

The priest turns to the water. The whales.

Long

awaited.

He tightens the jumper around his face. 'My job is people. And right now we need to bury these people fast. Before —'

The

rot,

says Sue.

The sad (old)

flesh.

'Anyway, I'm sorry for your loss,' the priest calls over the dingo, but he's far away. Shouting at me from outside a window or inside a car or from the afterlife. All I can hear are the animals. Sue, the night birds, the whales calling from the deep pit of the bay.

The Christians choose a spot on the rise by the sailing club. The ground scorched black and dry by pine needles. Flying foxes hang from the branches and throw down their plans. They thought they knew everything, but this is new.

A troubled

earth. Make this the intention.

It's what we know now.

The flying foxes shoot out overhead. Their sonars land — I'm a moving object. I open my mouth to tell them what happened and release the shrieking tongue of grief. The bats veer higher, then return to the pines that border the sailing club and settle there, hung like plush orange coats. The priest bows his head over a grave I never thought I'd see. Lee with twenty others — all young, faces up. It's only me and one other guy turned out to see them. Lee looks like he'll reach a hand and ask for help out of the pit.

'*Be gracious to me, O Lord, for I am in distress*,' the priest begins. Sue stands, sniffs the wind.

If the insides are

famished

the outside

can eat.

(Take it.)

'It's Psalm 31,' the priest says over her. I nod like I can remember what that is. He's encouraged, starts again. '*Be gracious to me, O Lord, for I am in distress; my eye is wasted from grief; my soul and my body also. For my life is spent with sorrow, and my years with sighing; my strength fails because of my iniquity, and my bones waste away.*'

And my bones waste away, my bones waste away. Be gracious to me, O Lord, for I wish I was dead too. One of the Christians comes over. 'Can you get that dog out of here? It's making us crazy.'

The best plan (don't do it) is

to let the meat

stew —

Wipe the tears off my face to reveal Sue, healthy as ever.

It's ready

now —

'Piss off, Sue.'

— there's space in the

ground.

'Go on. Fuck off.' She edges closer, head down, paws talking.

No one likes a
Bad
Dog. Bad dogs get
the bones —
I kick the dingo in her side. And again. Pull out that gun in front of everyone, and the whole place starts screaming except for Sue, still as sand. The whispers shift on her pelt but her gaze is steady on me. I don't wait for the lyrics. Her skull in my sight. Close my eyes on pulling the trigger because I've got half a heart and don't want to see what it does. It doesn't do anything. Graham used up the bullets shooting at Sue and those poor fucking cows. Sue takes her moment. Peels off across the rec ground and over to the oval at the back of the surf club, tail curling nothing words can describe.

I drop the revolver on the grass. One person grabs it, another leads me away from Lee in the pit and across the park. Taking me to the cop station and I don't blame them. A scrub and a lie-down for the rest of my life, away from those two-faced animal stories, is exactly what I need. It's an '80s brick place down a side street. A black-and-white sign squatting on the lawn, missing an 's': 'God Provide'.

'This is where Jesus lives,' says the woman on my arm. Something hisses,

Lover,

from the squat tree on the lawn. The woman flinches from it. She's done some botch-job head drilling by the looks of it — bored away the bits she needs and forgot to take the parts that let those shivering, shaking, flapping, leaping animal voices in. Something about the half-dead look in her eyes has me clutching her like she's a buoy in the bay. Only good because it floats. She's mangled, but she gets me up that God path and through the glass doors to where the air is sugary with bug spray, and the birds and cats and whatevers fade past the tinted glass.

—

The shadowy interior becomes a carpeted reception with padded white chairs stacked against the wall and open doors leading into other, darker, rooms. No animals I can see. The entrance clicks and slides — the air-conditioned chill on my sweaty face. I gulp shallow, desperate breaths of sprayed air. In the dim, a few bodies move. A little girl not much older than Kimberly has her arms wrapped around a woman's leg. That priest is there. Gives me a hug, but his eyes stay on the doors until they slide safely closed and lock themselves.

'I'm sorry to say we've no food.' An internal door is shut. People edge forward. They're frightened, I can see that, but they've been eating something. 'Before I can welcome you into the church, we need to disinfect you. Matthew?'

Matthew is the man from the foreshore who was dishing out soup. I blink at him, but he just comes on forward, bearing cans of insect killer like wine, and starts spraying. It rains down on me, cool on the skin. I open my mouth in case any of the little buggers got in. Another of the wardens, a wonky-looking young woman, puts her arms out, showing that I should copy, and pats me down with hands that have done this before.

'Nothing,' the soup man says.

'Righto,' says the priest. 'Welcome to the flock.' People flinch at that. The priest grins. Something stuck in his teeth.

No little voices whispering from the corners, no bodies betraying messages meant for their own kind. I'm shown into the church, the same beige carpet as all of them, murals instead of glass and more stacked white chairs. Bedding shoved up around the walls, each person or family with their own little nest. I'm unsteady on my legs. Balance on a stack of three chairs. A woman brings me water and a few communion wafers, her rash-raw hands red as her eyes. Sees me staring at her skin while I stuff some of the wafers in my mouth.

'It's the insect repellent,' she says. 'Or the disinfectant. We have to go around setting traps and poison and wiping everything down. Every day. In case an animal has crawled on it.'

I let another wafer glue itself to my tongue. The wall opposite us is filled with an enormous mural of Jesus at a country wedding, turning water into wine.

'Funny thing to do as your first miracle. I mean, wouldn't you heal the sick? Bring back the dead ...' My voice trails away to the pit on the rise, Lee inside it. 'I suppose you think he made the animals talk?'

'Not Jesus. Not God.'

'The devil, then?'

'Some of us are sent out to hunt, you know, with masks and everything. It's a bit dangerous. I don't have to do it because I've got my girl over there.' There's a kid off in the corner nicking wafers off the holy stand. 'But I disinfect the hunters and see what they bring in. It's pets.'

'Pets?'

'People's pets.'

The kid in the corner points, glances at her mum with a nervous giggle. A small fluffy dog has pelted out a kitchen door, thin bit of twine tangled around its legs, body blonde fire, screaming,

Hello. Please.

Please bite its soft.

Quick.

Help

me.

I jump up, calling the poor little bugger, but the parishioners shriek louder, climbing on their chairs like that dog is the snake from the garden of Eden. The woman rushes for her daughter and hauls her by an arm out of the room. It's funny, for a second, until the laugh dies in my throat. The little dog, too tangled in the twine to move, slumps panting in the aisle.

It's not just

me. Where's other

me. She's

still —

The god-botherers are faster than me. They grab that dog with WWF wrestling passion, using real lumps of wood, real knives. The little dog has enough time to issue a thick whiff of terror from its undercarriage,

Help

her,

before they've slit it ear to ear right there in the pulpit. There was no blood with Lee. He didn't even look that drowned. He might have come alive any moment. He might be alive right now in his grave. This little dog, though, is bleeding out on the beige carpet. The door to the kitchen is open. Matthew the soup cook leans on the jamb, then turns back. A fluffy tail on a chopping board. The steaming pots. Pain like a stab to my guts — he stirs a soup very much like the one he was serving up in the park.

SIXTEEN

More dead people wash in on the fresh tide. I watch from the grassy verge down to where the whales breach the bay.

Now it
is home we can spend
some
time together.

I'm cold with rushing water, breathing through my ears. Hold them shut, but it doesn't do much to block out the songs of the giant watery hosts to the worst Christmas ever.

It came
back.
Welcome home.

An engine starts out on the bay — police finally getting their shit together to get a boat out there. At the sound of it, the whales splinter like someone has thrown a rock at a song,

Was that the
window. Why
is the bed
unmade.
Where

has my life

gone.

Their giant confusion sends shock waves over the bay that has people crawling out of the water. Gasping up the bank.

Where. Are

you there.

Calling, not for us now, but for each other. A breach further out. The phone ringing and ringing. News you never want to hear. Then just the *slosh slosh* of the waves.

Drunken laughter from the pub on the corner. They're celebrating the whole world up there. And here I've lost my babies, with no one to say don't shoot yourself, Jeanie. Don't chuck yourself back in the ocean. Don't take a drill to your skull and forget to stop. The only other person who was at the funeral sidles up the bank.

'Drink?' He's not a trepan zombie, and no church that was worried about their donation box would have him, so I find myself following his skinny arse further up the bank to where people spew out of the pub and onto the pavement. Quieter inside. The guy pulls up a seat for me at the bar.

'I buried my brother today,' he tells me.

Can't find it in myself to care about his brother. The bartender has pink lipstick the exact colour of her eyes. Pours me a shot of vodka for free because my wallet seems to have gone the way of everything else. I take the shot. Wipe my mouth. My blood buzzes.

'Have you seen my son?' I ask the bartender. 'Lovely looking. He was here. Now he's gone.' I almost expect Lee to walk through the door there.

'How about your old man?' the guy suggests.

I take him in. He's either in his forties or hard living has sent him there. That washed-out face. I know this guy. Met him a million times before. 'Old man's long gone too.'

He takes this as an invitation to sit. 'The zooflu is nuts. Supposed to be finding a cure but where is it? I'm from out west. Thought I'd seen everything. Why aren't you in there, anyway?' His head flicks toward the bay.

'Why aren't *you*?'

We fiddle with our empty shot glasses. My bloody heart washed clean, resting on a bed promised by whales.

'It's the fish.'

Feel for my face. It's there. Sticking out like normal. I'm alive.

'The fish,' he goes on. 'The internet reckons they were poisoned, way back, from that nuclear stuff over in Fuck You Sumo or whatever.'

'Fukushima.' The bartender's eyes glint. Pours me another. The man holds up a finger. She rolls her eyes but pours him one too.

'Yeah, maybe they got poisoned and then the cows ate them, and then we ate *them* —'

'Cows don't eat fish,' the bartender tells him. 'Cats do. My old cat. Tizzy Puss. She was a nice cat. Now she says fucked-up shit.' The tender leans on the bar. Some spilt drink bleeds up her singlet. She whispers, 'You know how they bring chewed-up mice and birds? Everyone always said it's a gift or they're trying to feed us. It's bullshit.' That cat back at the house. Her invisible kittens.

'What is it, then?'

'They're catching time.'

'Pardon?'

'Some fucked-up clock. Like, if they stop the mouse they control time.'

I lean away from the bar. 'Animals don't have time.'

'You come over to my place and wait a couple of days until Tizzy Puss kills something and knocks it around the house. All she talks about is the passing and the movement and on and on. If I lock her out, she screams at the window until I go fucking nuts. Wanted to drill my skull, but I chickened out.' She pours me another shot. Points with a pink polished nail at my ranger shirt, the bit that Sue ripped out of it.

'Dog. In the water. If it wasn't for her, my son would still be —'

'I had a dog who would always try to save me too,' the fella chimes in. 'Yeah. "Rio". Lovely boy. But he never let me swim. If I could talk to him now.'

The bartender sets the bottle behind the bar and goes off to serve a couple of girls who look like they should be in after-school care.

'Doesn't make any difference,' I say to myself. The guy's right there. His eyes shine red. He reaches an impossibly long arm over the bar and nabs the vodka bottle, tucks it between his knees before that bartender can even turn around.

'How about you help me with this?'

We take off down to the bay, but there's still people climbing over police tape to peer at the empty water — no songs, nothing homely about it now. Lee buried with the others on the rise. Behind the sailing-club sheds is the line of Norfolk pines and beyond that, the oval with a cricket pitch. It's cold and dark. The vodka warms me. Night birds over in the trees won't go to sleep, voices float over the oval,

Fold it.

Tuck it back like *that.*

I'll *eat* your face. I'll *tie*

it together, *stranger.*

The way their voices tickle my skin, I half think it's Kimberly calling.

Like that.

'You hear them?' I ask the guy. He sits so close to me his leg touches mine. Can't remember if his name's Shane or Shawn. Leans in for a kiss. I pull back. 'What's your name again?'

'Shay,' he says and tries to stick his hand down the front of my pants.

I lie back on the spongy grass to help him. 'I thought that was a girl's name.'

He's wriggling around down there, but he doesn't know his business. I point him in the right direction. Think of that bartender from the pub. She probably knows her way around a vagina. Shove him off me and grab the vodka bottle for a swig. He looks so sad there on the ground. Fingers splayed like he's touched something yucky. I yank his pants down to show him how it's done. His ding-a-ling white and floppy in the moonlight. Pop it in my mouth, cold and soft on my tongue. A dead slug. Doesn't come to life no matter how hard I try. I sit back.

'Of all the luck.'

He looks like he's about to cry. 'I drank too much.'

I pat his bare leg. 'Don't worry about it, mate. I need a good sleep anyway. Taking my family up north in the morning.' I blink. Let out a sound.

'We could have a cuddle,' he suggests. 'We could just, you know, go back to your place.'

Something moves through the shadows under the pines.

Yesterday.

'What happened to that dog?'

Shay looks around. 'What dog?'

'Wouldn't let you swim.'

'Oh, Rio.' He lies back, hands behind his head. 'I stopped taking him to the reservoir because he wouldn't let me go out like I wanted to. Kept trying to save me. Grabbing at my shirt or my hand. I yelled at him until he stayed at home. I guess he wandered off to do something else and the neighbour got him. Ran him over.'

Look for the shape under the pines, but it's gone.

'I've got to —'

'Okay.'

He walks with me back over the oval and gives me a peck on the cheek at the pines. Sweet, like I'm his auntie.

—

All around this town, people are pulling doors shut and turning keys. Locking themselves in for the night. In the pub, in the grave. Sue and her cages — home and prison all at once. Well, I've got a van, and Sue's beside it: body quiet. Lee would be as real to me.

'I see what you were trying to do out there with those whales, Sue,' I call out. She watches me stagger down the road until I reach her. 'You were really trying to save me. I wish you'd gone for Lee, but, anyway, I understand. I *forgive* you.' Stretch out my bad hand. She bites it. Sinks a tooth right into the rotting cut. I feel the pain in my own teeth. The world stiffens, goes soft, and a vomitus tide of colour sweeps over my face. Sue says something. I buckle down and cover my ear with my good hand. Sue, sick of waiting, nips my fingers, my hair.

Get up, Bad

Dog.

Sit

up. Now.

I don't. She bites my ear so hard I feel for blood.

Get up, Little

Bitch.

There's half a packet of bread on the ground by the car. Tooth marks in the plastic and crusts. I didn't think I'd ever want to eat again, but I go for it.

Lickspittle, get

back.

I stare at Sue. 'I *said* I forgive you.'

She puts one paw on the packet and starts ripping into it. Jaws singing,

I'm the

Queen Mum. It eats

later.

'I don't think so.' Thunder from her wolf throat that rumbles my bones.

It eats after

me.

Sue's yellow teeth glow when she slashes through the bread. I tuck my hand under my breast to keep it warm. Wait. After a while, Sue jumps into the camper and curls up on the bed. I can make out the white tip of her tail.

Go on then

arse

sniffer.

I should kick her again. Refuse to eat the food and starve to death here. The thought that she might eat my remains forces me to move. Hunched over like the old woman I'm going to be, not the underling she keeps calling me. Grab the crusts and chew them down, slumped over the little table by the carpeted couch.

Bad Dog

who eats.

'You can stop calling me a Bad Dog for starters.'

I'm the

Queen. It's

the baby.

'No.'

The plan is to

follow.

Watch. Eat what I give it. Lower

than me.

Fight when I

bite. (Get

started. Be fresh.)

'Why are you being like this? We need to go back to the way we —'

It's not here, it's

gone.

It was here.

Now it's gone.

I swallow. 'Gone?'

It's gone.

'Sue —'

Stop barking.

'S—'

Shut

it. Listen.

I listen. To dogs and cats muttering at each other in the dark. To the rain scattering over the campervan roof like sand. Once I've listened for what seems like forever — time doesn't know me anymore — Sue gets closer. Jumps up on the couch seat beside me. I cringe from her mouth but inside it is a tender tongue. Nuzzles into my bad hand and begins to lick. It hurts. I start to blubber. She's more gentle, licking the green pus. When she finishes, it's cleaner. Even feels a bit better. Put my face in her furry side, which smells like grime and warmth and beach, and cry my guts out.

SEVENTEEN

Sue sleeps. I don't. For one hour and then another I stare at the square of light the moon makes through the window. Listen to footsteps clump down toward the camper. Bargain with God. If it's Lee, I'll die instead of him; if it's Kim, I'll dump the dingo; if it's Angela, I won't know whether to slap her or fall down and say *sorrysorrysorry, I fucked up, girl. What can I do? Tell me what I can do?* The footsteps pass. Insects buzz hopefully at the screen. Lee's things in the plastic bag. Long pair of sodden black jeans. I fold them. Hold them to my face, breathe in the fishy water. Sue wakes and puts her nose to the denim.

'Can you smell ...?' I can't say his name out loud, but I'm speaking her language.

If you smell down
(deep)
the
long day ends.

'The long day?'

Ends.

The jeans fall in a soggy clump. I turn away. Start to gather up the cups and plastic containers and shit strewn around the van, and then wash it all with some detergent from a squeezy sauce bottle by the little metal sink. Tears leave holes like bullets through the bubbles.

Time swills around me. It's all I can do: stagger to the mattress that's stuck to the sheet with I don't even know what now. The dawn through the ripped curtain — insects straight shooting. My living, breathless body on the bed. The thoughts alive in my head. The idea that Lee has nothing to eat takes root in my brain. What do you eat in the afterlife? They never thought to teach us that. Glance desperately around the kitchenette. Nothing there, for me or for Lee.

Only just close my eyes when they're open again, to bright sunlight. The mattress wet. Warm, long as you don't move. Soon as you move when you've pissed yourself, you're cold and you can't get warm again. Stay still as metal. Think of all the still things I'll tell Kim about. Quiet water. The turned-off TV. Milk in the fridge. Carpet. Death. Don't think about still things anymore. The van gets bright, dark again. Sue shouts into the air.

I'm big. I'm
a pack.
No one is the size of
me.

All that. I'd tell her to calm the hell down, but my lips have stuck together. Fall asleep with her call in my ears. In my dreams the words drop out and it's just noise again. The world is just noises, and I don't understand any of them. The whales moan. The dogs bark. The birds tweet-tweet.

'Lee?'

'Yeah?'

'Lee?'

'Yeah, Mum.'

One side of my body warmed by him. He's had a dream and he's crawled into bed with me and Graham. There's breath in his little ribs, a heartbeat through his chest, hair. Lee has all this hair. He lets out a sound, his deformed shape a lump in the dark.

'Lee-Lee?' I call, soft at first and then loud, 'Lee?' The dingo moves away from me and thumps down from the campervan bed. I go back to a sleep with no dreams. Awake again, my mum in my ear.

'Matthew, Mark, Luke, and John,' she chants, the cloying smell of her lipstick in my nose. 'Bless the bed that I lie on. Four the corners to my bed, four the angels round my head. One to watch and one to pray, and two to bear my soul away.'

'How many angels?'

'Matthew, Mark, Luke, and John. Bless the bed —'

'How many?'

'Four angels round my head.'

'Four.' I've got to remember four.

'And two to bear my soul away.'

Two. Four. By 5.02 pm on the camper clock, both Lee and Mum are gone. No Kimberly either. I reach over the empty bed and sit up with the horror of losing them. Sue paws at my chest, her fur whispering sadly. Confused eyes and uncertain tail.

Good

Cat.

'Shit. Sue.'

Where is

it.

'Come on, Sue, get up here.'

Is

it Queen or is it

Mother.

Is it Yesterday.

'I'm here, Sue.'

Where has

Queen gone.

—

I dream about that guy from the pub. Shane. Shay. Dream he's here in the van, cleaning it up for me. Sue nudges me, cold nose whispering,

It was a sharp

stick.

Feels like the middle of the night. Probably more like pre-dawn. I'm awake, but can't move. I tell Sue all about it. The words don't come out of my face. They just roll around in my head and they hurt. Mouth jammed shut with metal rods or something. A rough, ice-edged wind hooks in the open door of the van and prises me open. I find my tongue.

'Sue?'

A sharp stick

in a bad

wind.

My eyes dip shut. Sue nudges me again. Moonlight fires in through the windows. Sue's mouth wet with what looks like blood. The van has been ripped apart, everything tipped that can be tipped; everything else gone. Messy, empty.

Poke it in

the picture

place.

A cough rattles my chest, gets me up to sitting, choking, then sucking in that freezing air and looking around. My stuff gone. Handbag. Food. Nothing chewed, just taken.

Nasty

cut.

'Was it that little bastard Shay? Come in here and left me for dead?'

Poking,

Sue confirms.

I feel myself — nothing sore or broken. If it was him, the limp-dick bastard didn't touch me, or the blanket. The car keys are still in my pocket. Me and Sue get up the front to start the camper. We need the heater in our faces and the road at our feet. Smell of petrol burning the air.

'Don't we, Sue?'

What.

The van doesn't even chug. He siphoned it, of course he did. I start laughing. A sick sound — a horse dying on my tongue. Sue perched on the couch behind the passenger seat, head cocked, listening. I suck my sound in and swallow so it sits, a queasy lump in my gut. Crank the window open to see if he found the petrol stash tucked into the side of the camper. He found it alright. That laugh burbles up again, but the air outside is making noises worse than mine.

'Shh. What's that?'

It.

Barking.

'No. *That.*' Cock my head alongside Sue's. The hair on my legs and arms prickles. Meaning whizzes past the van then shouts inside. The whole place fills with signals: moving, gleeful words.

ME AND HE AND SHE AND WE AND ME.

EDIBLE,

the air says.

DRINKABLE.

I get down by Sue. She flicks a warning with her ear,

Don't.

'What is it?' I whisper. 'Little bats?'

The air screeches, screams. There are bodies all over the windows. The roof.

THE EYES ARE NICE.

THE NOSE IS NICE.

THE LIPS ARE NICE.

Sue snaps the air. Claws her snout.

Don't.

Don't.

Wrap the pink blanket around me and push past the dingo. Outside, something crawls in my nostril. I swat at it, passing through a cloud that screams,

HAS BLOOD.

THE WALL IS MOVING.

Bugs. Talking. Making words.

DRINK 'TIL DEAD.

THE EYES ARE NICE.

AND FULL.

I yell, but my words, my thoughts, my everything is sucked into the fog of meaning that buzzes, crawls, twists, and burrows. They're all over me. In my mouth, my nose, my ears, like they said they would be. Black, twisting bodies. Legs over my skin. Biblical. A plague of tongues. Casey up there at the Park following them to her end. That little girl at the hospital pawing at the ground. Me flinging my hair about my face to get the fuckers off me. Slap and kill a few. They scream themselves to death.

NO. NO.

DONE.

They fall on the ground like black balls of rain. The rest of them crowd around me like my killing hand isn't anything. Even when I break away there's millions, billions of them. They make up the whole world. Kimberly told me the number once. It was more than I've ever heard of anything being.

I start running, shaking my head around like the mad woman they'll turn me into. It works. Fewer bodies. The few left are so loud in my ear they take every thought I've got.

INSIDE IT'S

NICE.

I slap and shake, get the last few off me, send them flying to their next nice thing. Crazy through my hair for any left. Sink down on the pavement, blanket around me, legs over the gutter. Leave me here.

'Leave me here, Sue.'

She circles, calls,

Cat

Dog.

'I'm too weak.' My legs, my bones waste away. Sue gives me a sniff, considers me with her endless eyes, then turns away. I watch her tail sweeping,

Now

to find the

music.

A moment longer, and I'll lose sight of her forever. The thing that's been sitting in my chest gives an almighty scream, pushes me, fighting, to a stand. That brushy tail. The best plan is to follow it and Sue to wherever. When we're up the top of the street and I can see all the way down to where the camper sits, Sue says,

Keep

going.

Bugs through the air.

FIRE AND LIGHT.

EAT IT.

Some night birds high in the black sky throw down,

It's *old*.

Gone.

Or,

Wrong.

'You hear that too?'

Keep going.

Stink and

sour.

'What can you smell?'

Smell what

died

on it.

'Wait.' I sniff my bad hand. It smells of rotting.

There are no more black bugs, but I strain my eyes through the dark streets until I can barely move to save myself. Sue moves for me. Even with her friendly ears she looks stronger than she did before. Bigger. A roll to her shoulders, her back mature. Weight of the world on her neck. I've got an inkling to keep my arms still, avoid her eyes, approach her careful. She's sucking all the might out of me with that thick, gingery fur. Those big yellow teeth. Strong paws and a heavy tail. A great nose that fizzes with meaning. I want to touch it, see if it will buzz, but I need to be careful about touching Sue. Even while her body is bursting with messages, there are still things in her head. Dingo things I don't know about. I've got human things she doesn't know about either, even though I can't remember any of them right now. Every now and then an insect shoots,

HAVE IT

ALL,

past my head. I flop a hand at it.

MURDER.

There's cloud cover and the night is a bit warmer. Things have dried to damp. On the edge of town, by a thick patch of scrub, we find a shed in a sheep paddock filled with bales of mouldering hay, rodents chattering to each other underneath. Strained messages of something trying to parent too many kids.

See it

little. Where. There. Where. She

bit he

bit I bit ...

I'll bite all of

you.

'We're just going to stay the night,' I tell them. They don't hear me or don't care. Carry on their lives without me. Sue, on the other hand, is paused — waiting for me to follow her up some bales to a little platform near the rafters. The hay up there cleaner. I pull at the baling twine with my good hand, fluff some of the straw for the both of us, and spread the damp pink blanket over it. Pat the bed all cosy, but Sue doesn't want a bar of it. Body all rigid and quiet at the edge of the platform. A spider clinging to a beam tells the world,

IT'S MY
TIME. THE
EYES ARE INSIDE.

'Yeah, come on, Sue.'

Sue doesn't heed us. Her every muscle straining, muzzle pursed. Then she starts bloody howling.

Good to hear
your voice. I'm a new
bone with
an old nest.
I'm with
you.

Long calls. Designed to carry to distant packs, but those hot-weather wild dogs won't hear her.

'We're too far south.'

Her tail flicks, minds me. The rest of her, though, is thrown out to the fields.

I'm (don't call back)
here. I'm not
a road. I'm the
world.

Sound of it gets me in my valves. A commotion in my throat. Before I know it, I'm crawling from the hay bed with my gob open, and I'm calling too. The sound that comes out of me is strong as decay. I grieve for everything dead and alive. Sue is calling for a family — well, so am I. For a home — where is it? And my Lee, buried down in the beach. Kimberly taken up north in a cop car — as much my blood as this dingo. Old mum speaking full crow in the home. I even call for bloody Graham. I'm really getting into it when Sue stops me with a glance. Silence, then a siren-like howl from a long way away,

Sorry we
didn't get your
call. We're
here.
We're millions of
stars in
the
sky.

Scares the everything out of me to hear them respond like that. Whole bloody dog pack howling like an approaching cyclone around the shed. Has me diving for the blanket. Expect Sue to crawl in beside me, but fuck me if she doesn't prepare her body, paws muttering,

(Keep
it) together.

Purses her dingo lips and, with a high-tilted, vulnerable throat, answers,

I'll be your
sister. Your
mother (whatever).
I'll make you
more.

A bad time for howling across damp paddocks. We don't want wild dogs here. Stealing our food and messing with Sue. I duck down in the straw, shivering. Expect they'll reject her — a northern dingo used to her meals chopped and her territory small — but she catches something in their return call. A whiff that says,

Hello
(stranger). Come
closer. Let's see all
your faces.

Sue doesn't look at me when she rises, shakes herself down, and turns to leave. My whole life turns to leave. This time, I catch it with my good hand and don't let go. Her body stinks like calling. I muzzle her with my palm, and think about her biting me again. Think it's worth it.

Get

off it.

'Stay still.' She fights to face me. I pin her between my legs like a pig, grab hold of a bit of that baling twine and get it around her neck. Tether her to a post. She knows how to be on a lead, at least.

The

common ground.

'Good dog.'

This

is forever.

'Just need you here tonight, okay? I just need you to stay.'

Brave a pat on her face. She twitches her ear from me. Mutters,

Never

eat again.

'I'll find some food. I'll do the hunting. How about that?'

I don't do any hunting. I curl around the hot pain in my hand. The infection creeping under my skin as bugs that don't talk, just travel. Body aching with it. All night I listen to Sue huff a song about captivity, the fence, the moat, the dusty home.

Again there's

no

answer. I

can't swallow this.

'It's alright, Sue. You're with me.'

If

they've gone, if

they left without me I

won't

stop. Did they

call.
(Stay quiet, stay
still.) Listen.
Is it
them.

I listen. The long calls grow distant, disappear, and she doesn't try to find them again.

The rope has rubbed away a bit of her gingery fur by morning. Black skin beneath.

'Sorry, Sue. But you see why I had to do it.'

Unpick the knot watching for whispers on her pelt. She has her wolf on — her whole body focused on the clumsy fingers of my good hand getting her loose. When I do, she bounds away from me, body thrilling with disbelief.

I'm on
the other side.

'Just come back here. Sue. Come here and —'

She takes off. I knew she would. She'll come back, and she does. Plants her legs and purses her lips and starts howling long and loud so anyone or anything could find us. I grab at her again. Miss. Her white socks flick past me, and the morning closes around the spot where she was.

I wait all day and into the night. The mice are here, but Sue's gone. A short rain fills the air with pinpoints of light. Everywhere on the ground is black, sticky-looking where it shines in the wet. The mice deep in the hay.

Follow the
tracks
little. Where.

Here. Everywhere. Where.

The spider stretches one brown leg:

I SEE

IT.

I call too, but my voice is gone, gunk in my throat. Spit it out, not knowing what I'm spitting on.

'Where are you? Sue? Sue? Sue.'

That fucking dog. That bitch. Kick the tin shed wall so it cracks like thunder. The rodents shut up, whisper their horror. I'll beat the crap out of the miserable mutt if I see her again. I'll kick her teeth in. I'll rip that stupid fucking scruff off her neck. Mash her paws into a rock. She doesn't come back. The night ticks over in damp lumps that send me to the blanket but not to sleeping. A big dump of rain on dawn digs ditches in the soft ground, channelling water under the tin. Even the mice have moved off to deeper pasture. The solitary spider sings and spins against the beam,

ASK ME JUST

ASK. I

SEE IT. I SEE. IT

CAN'T TAKE ANYTHING.

I pull the blanket over my head again. The pain has reached my shoulders, an ache like need, like want, like grief. Finally knocks me into sleep. Wake snivelling. The snot runs over my lips. I suck at it. Have to eat something. The world outside the shelter is bare and badly lit. Without Sue, my body is septic and stiff with cold, and I can't get warm.

When I'm hungry enough, I shuffle to the edge of the platform to stare at the opening of the hayshed. My head like a burrow — I've got to dig myself out. Think through every step before I do it. The groan and pop of my hips when I roll up, protecting my hand, shuffle out of the blanket to my knees. The air outside the shed slices my skin as I count one hundred steps out, turn back. One hundred out, then back again. At forty-two I teeter into a shrub. A few big larvae, white, like the biggest maggots you ever saw, calling,

INSIDE, INSIDE.

My stomach groans. What do witchetty grubs even look like? Pick one of the grubs up.

ACID,

it screams.

MY FLESH. MY

SKIN.

'I'm so sorry.' I crack it in half with my teeth and it goes quiet. Milky, crunchy. Eat another without killing it first. Its body shouting down my throat.

INSIDE.

WE'RE INSIDE.

Straighten and swerve away, grinning with fright. A branch reaches out and claws my face. *Run. You go. The body. Run.* Across a paddock and another. A swampy bit of marshland that fills my sneakers with rank-smelling mud, bits of plastic, and rotting labels. Sue's tail in every bit of brush. My pulse bounces at a rush of wings, startled birds calling,

What is

it.

Another paddock surrounded by rusted and barbed wire that catches my shoulder and scraps down my back.

SUCK THE DAY

Its *insides*

are *old.*

Neck stiff from craning. A willie wagtail coaxes a mate,

Turn *around.*

Turn *around.*

It's *me* you're after.

MOISTURE AND STINK.

'Don't listen to them, Jeanie. This, now this.' Clump of trees where it's midnight, no moon. A smell like a solid wall of cigar, rhubarb, and rotting meat. If outside was quiet, this place is filled with voices. Struggle to get my bearings. Instead I wander deeper into the little forest. A bolthole of light, a glow at the edge where a smashed tree limb looks like the way out. Fools me. I take a step toward it. A bunch of voices start up at once.

This. Keep it. Don't
touch me.
'Who's there?'
Bring
it to mother. You
ate my sweetie. Bring
it.
'That you, Sue?
Don't touch
me.

Thing that looks like a rat, a monkey, and a fox got run over together beats in front of my face. Wings that thump so fast I can't make out their shape. And also: that smell. Smoky shit, sweet rot. The place filled with flying foxes. They shriek, they've been shrieking for a while. I have too. They fling themselves to the safest part, away from me, warning each other.

You want to have a bat
animals.
And it will eat
you.

I stretch out my hands like some guy doing a dodgy deal. 'I won't hurt you. I'm just trying to find the ...' Touch some plant that feels like it's breathing. 'The motherfucking way out of here.' The gap in the trees has let the rain in to make a small pond, and bugs circle the dry edges.

OH.

OH MOON.

I ONLY HAVE THIS ONE DAY.

The bats dive through, snapping up the insects and throwing out titbits of advice about me.

And it

will eat you,

they gossip.

Wrap-around

skirts.

It will

mash your face.

'I can bloody well understand you. I'm right here.' I feel blindly for the path I came along. The insects keep flinging themselves around the pond light.

OH MOON.

DON'T LET MY LIFE PASS.

Other whispers. Goggling in the dim. Wherever I stand, little bodies scream out. Where I run, they die beneath me.

HARD.

FUCK-HARD.

'Sorry. I'm sorry. I'm sorry.'

I sink down onto a pile of tree muck. The flying fox closest to me bounces her mind to the limits of the trunks and maps everything in it. I'm the only thing she can't map. She lays out her plans and shows me how they all looked the same until I stumbled in. What is me? Flings her sonar again but I'm too big for it, too new. For her, the map of the little forest is the whole world. She uses air like fish use water, a solid to push against, dig through. Her crumpled monkey face, her wings, the sonar she flops out,

How far

does

it

go.

She flings out sonar in a net. It bounces off me. Interest blooms in her like a mushroom.

Still, it's

alive.

She wants me to die like you want a big spider to die, but would never get close enough to kill it. A noise comes out of me. She hears it. Understands. She knows I'm a killer who makes scared noises. When I spread my arms, she spreads her wings. The air tick-tocks with beating wings. Her eyes catch light and shine. That tiny face. She glides down through the trees, revealing the path. I stagger after her, out of the forest, to gasp at the sweet empty air.

This is new.

And what is it

on a map.

Duck just in time to feel her friends pour out of the gap in the trees above me on their dinosaur wings, one, two, four of them. Calling,

Draw

it. Mapless.

I don't walk for long, but when I see the ruin of an old farmhouse lopsided in a field, my heart giddies. Sue will be there scabbing food. The sun breaks up misty sky. I pause, swaying on the worn wooden step. The occasional fly braves the currents of cold air to cling to the bits of my body that face the morning, crying,

MOISTURE.

'You can stay there, but —'

MOISTURE AND STINK.

'Please. Please. Please.'

The sharp bell of a magpie's beak hits the edge of a metal planter pot outside and they start carolling.

I'm a *female*!

I'm a *star*.

The loneliness crawls like flies over my face. I wave weary arms, trying to get them all to bugger off. The birds stare down, unmoved. One of them looks scraggly, on death, with a messed-up beak and patchy feathers. But she's the Star.

From *before*.

It's from before.

A predator *from* before.

'I was the Queen too,' I tell her. They don't listen to me. Keep talking like I'm not there.

At *least*

it would be a *familiar* death.

Feel silly knocking on the broken door — no people in the smoky depths. Soot licks up the walls. The scorched pressed-tin ceiling a sick brown. At the lounge room, exhaustion punches me in the guts. I crawl across the crunchy burnt carpet. Open a door connecting to a cold kitchen. The fridge is gone and the oven ripped from the wall, dragged into the centre of the room. A charred paisley rug is warm, pulls me face down. Body starts to heat up again and makes my hand hurt. I can travel the tracks of infection now, from the palm up the wrist to the shoulder and my head. Legs too. Aching. Twist and wrestle with that ache until it's only my heart punching me with blood. Stamping me down. Any other bodies come in or out of the house, I don't know about them.

When I wake, it's still day. A rat stares from the grimy white square of the chequered kitchen floor, longing for the open cupboard. I wait, give it a chance to run away, but it stays sitting there, throwing alarm calls over its shoulder to whatever else is hiding in the walls.

'Sue?'

This is unique. This is

special.

A chance for
all of us.

There are other messages too, coming from the rat's fur, and on and on, about storage, energy, coil. The fleas ping over the rat's back and belly,

BLOOD!

Crawling like the messages that form on the animal hides.

BLOOD! BLOOD!

It's a healthy-looking rat, brown and fine featured. Whole face focused on its nose. Eyes steady as doorknobs, watching me in the room.

Over the
open there is a
gap.
The gap is dark but we
can see.
The
round is hard but inside it's
sweet. The teeth
are sharp but
not sharp enough. The
beast is big but has no
teeth.
BLOOD! BLOOD!
Still, the beast
eats.

That awful naked tail. Behind the rat, the pantry has been cleaned out completely — any dropped grains eaten by the animals. The rodent lifts its face and sniffs.

Sweet
metal.

I get myself to a stand, edge around the rat and into the kitchen. Deep in the cupboard, there's a tin.

Sweet

sweet metal.

It's a giant can of peaches that someone would have served with cream not so long ago. Cutlery still in the drawer, a can opener, wedge of a blade to puncture the lid. The peaches were picked and packed in the time before disease, when I still had a family. I pull out a piece from the jagged tin and place it in front of the rat.

'Here.'

He sniffs and eats it squatting, quite neatly, using two small paws.

It gives me

some,

I want more.

'Yes, sir.' I pinch out another slice. The rat's body reaches for other warm bodies — the same but smaller.

Loved

that I love.

Provided that I

provide.

I reach out for Sue. For Kimberly. For Lee. The rat eyes the room, sees there isn't anyone else. Knows my want is in the past. There's only me.

The bringer and the

taker.

Too big to eat, too

big to

fight.

BLOOD!

DIG DEEP.

The rat lays out a plan. I shut my eyes, see it like I see its smell — through the cupboard to a hole to a ledge in the wooden support beam where there's a bed.

The tracks, the

tracks,

the railroad tracks.

Open my eyes to an empty kitchen, smear of peach juice on the floor.

There's no more human food. The rats want more human food, and there isn't any. I can hear them talking all about it in the rafters, gently egging each other on. Another one appears regularly in the kitchen and stares at me. He sings.

My balls are
big. I lick my
friends.

'Sorry, mate, but I don't have anything.' Mate.

It's
not just
me.

The fleas on his body coil and spring, coil and spring.

DIG DEEP.

On dusk, four more rats gather on the kitchen floor. Their presence is like one body — bigger than me. Family. Their hot sacrifice.

I would lie
down for
you.

The male goes past the lounge room door. His thick, pointy whiskers giggle back to his nest mates,

The mouth
can't
lie to the meat.

I'm not the competition anymore. I'm food. 'Sue,' I call into the hallway and out into the frigid air. 'Sue!'

The sun slumps further, and, outside, the moths stretch their long legs out of their holes, pushing against the ground, faces to the sky.

MOON. MOON.

DON'T LET MY LIFE GO.

The rats carry a fug of loyalty low and strong in their fat haunches. Even with the rug over my head, their body mutterings seep through the walls. I fall into a dream where Sue comes back, but she has human teeth and talks in a high, squeaky voice, moving her mouth. Her voice like Kimberly's voice when she's pretending to be the animals at the Park. Her voice the blood in my heart, punching my hand. Her voice singing, she has a singing type of sound. I wriggle closer to hear the words.

'What are you saying, Sue?' When I open my eyes she's really there, the door to the kitchen nudged open, her warmth in the crook of my body. A bit of rope tied around her neck, the end chewed. Someone else got her, tied her up. That's my dog to tie up, thank you very much. Her tongue on my sore eyes shows me big southern dogs with smells like farting mud.

'Hey. Hey,' I hiss. 'What were you were doing with that pack?'

Wet

meat.

'Tell me.'

The slow, irregular wagging of her tail, like a dying clock. It says, my pack.

Mating (mad

dog).

'You're with them now, is that it?' The words spit out of me. The rats scatter in the next room — history or mystery.

The season has

turned.

What they

want is

bending.

She whines this.

The inside (rip it)

tells the

outside

a story.

'You're supposed to mate with those fellas we brought in up north. Proper, pure dingoes. Not some mongrel like ...'

Her nether regions whisper pain, even while her teeth and jowls call their delight at whatever dog-stallion she found for herself. The intergalactic chemistry that happens when King meets Queen. Still. The rope. Sue nuzzles my face and licks it again, then my arms and hands. I push her away but she gets at me. A paw to hold my neck in place while she cleans my cheeks.

Good

Cat.

The fleas from the rats find us too. Their bodies burst, thrilling at the air.

NEW BLOOD.

Pain comes in the night. My life leaps away from me. My bad hand wet, and the agony comes in a wave that knocks me back to a time before all this. Sue reminds me where I am and where it hurts, dancing around my head with hungry breaths.

Rip it the

hell

away.

'You bit me again, you fucking bitch.'

She keeps dancing.

Gone.

Gone.

There's an old scented candle that the rats have hardly chewed. A long gaslighter by the stove and a rolling pin in the kitchen drawer. I scramble for these things with a mind like heavy footsteps, candle in my mouth tasting of vanilla, lighter cracking at the end. It shows Sue, sunset in the flame light, still dancing and looking guilty as hell. The rolling pin a weight in my good hand.

The

family
album.

'Hold still,' I tell her. She does. Even sits on her delicate haunches. Don't they know when you're about to bash their brains out? The cows lining up day after day to have things put in them and taken out. The mice calling, *run*, but staying in their cages. Whole thing goes to my fingers and makes the candle dance.

Eat
your
love.

The candlelight catches blood, slick as oil, over the white squares of the kitchen floor and onto the dark carpet where we slept. A sound from the cupboard. The big male's rodent eyes soft and brown. Sits on his haunches, lovingly chewing on a chunk of my hand.

I
feel it now.

Sue barrels into my leg. The motion bowls me over and pins me half in, half out of the kitchen. Sue lopes over me on sure paws and bounds into the cupboard. All the little voices — a radio not quite tuned with important news. I reach for Sue, but it's just my fingers twitching. Watch through the door as she plucks one of the rats. It falls into her mouth like it's made of nothing. Should have known: a wild dog can't stop at one. I have to bury my face in that filthy lino so as not to hear the noises — the terrified murmurs of the ones locked in the walls facing a slower death.

Where is my heart. Why
can't I see
it.

By the time she's done, she's murder itself. Fur and blood and gore all over. One shrivelled, untouched baby rat in her mouth.

Cold.

Quiet everywhere else. The little rat dies, and its ruined body goes still. Sue places it at my feet.

**This one is
for
it.**

EIGHTEEN

Sue is a few paces ahead on the highway when I trip over a collection of fine bones. She turns back to sniff. Chicken, I think, some kind of bird. A few hardened feathers stuck to a frame. The flesh has been picked over already by the sun or other animals. I stay by the carcass a moment, give my hand a stretch. The light over the paddocks shows how much blood is seeping out of my palm. Wriggle out of my yellowed singlet. Weak sun on my cold white skin. Get my teeth into the stinking cotton and rip it to crooked strips. The wound sings. Sue sings along with it. Notes of pain. Of sweat. Phrases of fear. Blood soaks the fabric. I tighten it until it stops. Shrug back into my ranger shirt and we stumble on.

Sue can tell if water is cleanish, and how long things have been dead. She can hear the heartbeats of the mice and rabbits hiding underground. She knows if there are other dogs nearby, where the eggs are, how to root around for things buried in the cold dirt, how to sleep curled around each other. She just needs her warm dog body, shade from the sun and rain, and company. I'd sleep all day if Sue would let me. My bones feel like they don't have any skin covering them anymore, even the muscle worn away. My sneakers are filled with my swollen feet. Clothes paste to my skin. Sweat rolls between my breasts even though it's getting colder. I'm off my tucker too. Sue wants us to eat dingo food.

Dinner

is ready.

It's another putrid mouse. 'Jesus, Sue.'

Time for

it.

My lips crack when I smile. Sue's tail sweeps the air.

Good

Cat.

'I'm not a cat.'

A Bad

Dog.

'I'm a shit dog.'

It

shits.

I go behind a tree. Have to tell Sue not to follow. She goes and sniffs it anyway.

Old

potato.

Not sick but too

hungry.

'You're eating my poo.'

Useless.

'Yeah?'

Sue finds water and starts bringing me a few different things to eat, so I can choose. Wind-fallen apples, yes. Half a dead bird, no. The end of a loaf of homemade bread.

'Where'd you get this?'

People.

'What people? There a town somewhere around? Take me to it. Hey, Sue?'

Shut its face
to
the end
of barking.

'I need some people food, Sue. You don't fucking know —'

She sets off down the highway. I follow, quickly, so as not to lose sight of her thick tail and my sanity with it.

Sue wants to be near me, and she wants to be as far away from me as the road will let her be. Biting distance is too close. But she comes back in the night stinking of carrion and wants to rub her chin over my face. It feels almost sexy, her hard bristled chin all over me like that, but when I try to push her away she pins me with her paw and whispers,

Good Cat. It is
ready to want my
shit.

'I've had enough of your shit.' Choke a laugh. That paw on my windpipe. She eases up only to rake my face with her sharp claws, the pads on her feet rough as road.

Has it pissed after
the
rain.

'Sue, that ...' Again with the raking. 'That fucking hurts.'

Has
it —

'Yes, I did. I pissed, okay?'

She takes a sniff at my pants, and I'm not keen on that paw again, so I let her.

Has
it eaten sky
meat.

'Ate some of those apples you got.' I point. She gnaws at one of my knuckles.

Good

Puss.

I laugh properly — her tongue. When she takes it away, it's cold and wet, and she's off up the road again, muttering to the nuclear codes charting her womb. Heaven could fall down on me, and I'd still be looking through the debris for Sue. Try to remember, as I trot up the road after her, how long dingoes gestate for. And they'll talk, those dingo pups. Sue will be their mother.

She won't let me sleep. She's got energy for the both of us. Her tail flicks one way, her paws tell stories to the ground. For Sue, the hunger aches like love, and lives in the little gap between free and captive. For her, it's a gruff sort of being. Time is laid out like some sort of whacko tarot reading, a rule to every moment. Sue's rules are full on, but they're real. She throws them down her tail at me while we walk along. I have to watch for them, careful.

Unless others aren't as
good, succumb to
others.
The other can get
better quickly so
watch, in case it needs to
bow.
Don't take other's foods, others
can't take from it.
If it eats dogs, be
secretive.
Encourage each other.
Let each other feel all the
time.

(Carry)
a message with its
anus.
Pay particular
attention to dirt and wind.
(Enjoy
everything.)

For Sue, smell is like the internet — shooting stars of info that explode from letterboxes, trees, paddocks. She adds to them with her leg half cocked. She responds, she deletes, she reads for news. She knows how long and how far and how sick and what sex and in heat and in hunger and half dead.

End
words.

She goes on about it all in her bloody sleep. When she wakes up, I'll ask her what dingoes dream about.

I try to walk in a straight line, but I can feel the angle of the world. Sue was in front, now behind, herding me. I stop to unpeel the bandage. Lick my flesh and taste the rot. Swollen twice its size, but it smells less now that Sue has been taking care of it. Nearby, up a graded dirt drive, a grey metal shed with mud sprayed up its side. The driveway scattered with white leaves like snow, so light they spin around on winds that stir the dirt and gravel into whirligigs. Feathers. Thicker by the gate then spread out again, littered up the highway ahead. The whole place neat but for the down, silent as a graveyard. A sign says, Sunny Girl Local Barn-Laid Eggs. A dancing chicken-woman on the front. Boxes of eggs stacked up by the door. Further in, a grimy filing cabinet. I find the key in exactly the same place Graham kept his — under the inner sole of an old leather shoe. Fucking farmers. Inside the cabinet is a plastic bag filled with all the coins this fella ever had rattling around in his pocket, and a few notes too. Take the bag, and on the way out I scoop an egg and tap it on the edge of the shed. It explodes. The gassy, putrid rot of it. A heavy blowfly comes hunting, bombing the shells, my festy hand, and Sue's nose and eyes.

SUCK.

SUCK AND FUCK.

Sue rubs a pissed-off paw down her face. For her, this fly will be here forever and it's worse than hunger or death. The blowfly weaves off, droning its thirsty song. Wipe my hands on a stiff rag by the door and trot after Sue, who's already halfway down the drive. Seemed like it would never stop raining, and now it seems like it will never start. A little church with a padlock on its door. I check for God. Nothing. Check for Sue — everything. Sleep at intervals about a hundred times a day. Seems like every time I drop off, Sue is pushing at me with her cold nose, calling,

Now

Cat Dog

beat it,

and we have to run around. I nearly trip over myself, trying to keep up with her.

The fields turn to stock feed and tractor lots, and then houses start bursting up like mushrooms in the nearby. That rat-infested farmhouse back there was the start of another little town, only ten or so kilometres inland from where I buried Lee. People crammed here too. Cars. Army snoozing, playing cards on the flat hoods of their jeeps and utes, holding their phones up for signal. A bank of charcoal clouds are piled up on the horizon, but here it's bright. I can't see an animal, but there's normal, red-eyed people inside a shop. No zombies here. Sliding automatic door jammed shut. I bash on the glass, leave bloody prints. People crane their necks, look past me at Sue standing there like the statue of a dingo. Her neck ruffed up and ears cocked, muttering,

That one is all
fleshy. (Don't
eat it.)

A man edges out the sliding door. I smooth my mangled hair with my good hand, try to smile. Go to move past, but he bars my way. He *is* fleshy.

'I need bandages and antiseptic and things such as that.' Lady of the manor. Throat filled with muck. Clear it.

'You know you can't come in here,' he says.

Good under
the tough
bits.

Take a look at myself. Fucked-up hand draining blood, clothes covered in filth, legs all cut up.

'You can't be here in this town. With that.' The guy points at Sue. She's not covered in muck. Healthy as ever. Caramel gleaming in the sun's glow. White blaze spotless. Only a few flecks of blood around her lips and on her matching white socks. 'This is a people town.'

'What's a people town?'

A
bony
place.

I touch Sue. The whole town like the inside of a skeleton. The guy strains his face with trying to ignore her. 'You're lucky you didn't come here when the Land Patrol was here and shooting,' he tells me. 'They've gone now. Kid got in the crossfire. Bit of a tragedy. Army had to intervene. But there's other ways. You won't see a bird around here.' We look at the bald streets. No birds. Insects, though. A fly barrels through the air between us.

SOME LOVE.

Man stares at it like he's insulted.

'I'll just get my supplies.' I shake my bag of coins. 'Come on, mate, I'm not in a good way here. My hand —'

'You'll get out of here before there's a problem.' He glances at the army. Calls out to them. Points at Sue, at me. Waiting for new instructions, they tell him. Sit tight. It'll all be over. Nothing's over for the people in that minimart. They've stopped their shopping and they're gathered around the glass doors and windows like we're the worst show on earth.

LOVE STARTS
HERE HERE HERE.

Realise I'm crying. Crying and bloody, and they won't let me in, even when I bash on the doors and scream blue murder. Sue butts me away down the street.

Shift
it Cat Dog. Good
Cat. Salty.

Those army guys with their phones up, filming the damned parade of two. Watch us the whole way down the long paved road out of town. The houses aren't empty, either. I struggle past their quivering curtains and blinds, still bawling, holding on to a bit of Sue's fur like I can't see. I do see, though. See a dead Persian cat that hangs by its tail from a basketball hoop in a driveway — bell collar sparkling in the sun.

The clouds start rumbling, and when it's raining again I put my hand to use and drag a bit of tin up against a fence post for us to rest under. Winter sun half-mast in the sky, and me and Sue looking at each other with hunger — a cave that you might shout into and never have your voice return. Deep, anyway. When it's dark, she leaves. Comes back with a rabbit. She hasn't killed it — I can hear it singing out of her mouth.

The day, the
old day.
'Sue.'

The day was new, why
is it
old.

I put my arm over my eyes. 'Sue, for Christ —'

She bites down. The rabbit doesn't have any more day or any-thing. I don't think about that when I'm skinning it, pulling on the warm meat, like licking iron and an old goat at the same time. Only after, with a full stomach, does that rabbit's song get stuck in my brain, *The day, the old day, the end of all my days.* I hum along with it, my belly full and warm again. My old mum and her shitty stews thickened with flour and game, but on a cold night: guts warm and faithful. I'd eat those stews again. I'd eat them every night and for breakfast too.

'The carrot, the potatoes, the onion, the bunny, no garlic at all or spices, but salt. So much salt.'

Shut
it.

'She had these home-made bowls that fitted in your hand. She had —'

Shut
it
Bitch.

'What's that about, Sue?'

She bolts straight at the entrance. A growing tension that bounces off the tin. Her growls shake my blood.

Get up. Get
out.

'What is it?'

Run, Dog.
Run.

I grab up everything I can find. My damp sneakers, the empty plas-tic bag. Sue sniffed out Lee and Kimberly for thousands of kilometres. Sue found me in the rat house. She says go, I follow. We run across the black field, my bare feet stabbed, ankles rolling on the pockmarked ground. Sue's white-tipped tail flashes like a rabbit's arse in the dark: *warning, warning*. Nothing. Stumble in the direction I think she's gone, but it's pitch. The blackness sucks the light from my eyes. Makes dancing alien shapes. There's Sue. Where? There. Tail flashing,

Run.

Run.

I jog toward her. Fingers outstretched. We run up the empty highway toward the morning. When the whole place has become dingo-coloured, she pauses. Her body crackling. Whispering about gold or something.

Fill us forever

with warm, beating

wealth.

I'll say

it with a bad smell.

'See something?'

I'll say warnings

or love.

To starvation.

'Sue, what is it?'

She flicks an ear.

Quieter.

'I can't see anything —' I'm too slow. Sue lunges, teeth bared, then ducks her head and nips my heels and my calf. Small smiling bruises all over the back of my legs and feet.

We stumble and walk all day. Don't make it anywhere. My body in clicks and creaks.

'Got an idea of heading north, Sue.' Sun so weak in the sky, but it's morning and that's east. North is the other way from where we're headed. 'My old mum up there, remember, Sue —'

Play.

'No, Sue, I'm saying —'

Play.

'It hurts.'

Stop

yapping.

Sue wants me to not talk, just move. I squat on the road edge, put my hands up over my face to protect it from the onslaught of little nips. She dances around me. I have to turn to wherever she is or she bites harder. My forearms get bitten up. She scrapes at me with her paws. It's just her playing. I'm crouched, trying to remember it's just her playing. I feel like a kid too. Slumping along after a dingo. Trying to focus on the messages from her rear, but a whole flock of birds have come up overhead to throw down their stories. The big ones training the little ones. Makes me smile.

Follow, follow, *follow*.

***Wait*.**

Wait for *position*.

Now *lead*.

Lead. *Lead*.

When I look back at the road again, it is a ball of dust and at its middle, a fast-moving square. Another army jeep. We edge to one side. A hairy hand chucks a small white package from the window. Lands on the gravel. I stoop to pick it up. Sue sniffs it, turns her head away in disgust.

Nothing to

eat.

The packet is so clean and square in my filthy, blood-caked fingers. One foil blister with a pill inside. The jeep slows to a stop. The hairy hand drums against the side of the car. Another young soldier in fatigues and a tightly wrapped face gets out and jogs toward us, pauses a few metres away.

'Can you speak?' she calls.

What is

it.

I grunt. My mouth so dry.

'Do you still have language?'

I move my tongue to work some thick saliva through my mouth. 'Yeah.'

Watch

it (Cat Dog).

The woman's shoulders relax. 'Great. You know what to do?'

I look down at the packet. 'NoZo one dose.'

'The instructions are on it but we're supposed to ...' She turns to glare through her sunglasses at the idling jeep. 'We're supposed to tell people how to use them. So it's just one dose. Take it now. You got some water?'

Careful.

I hold the packet up. 'This is some sort of ... painkiller ...?'

The soldier laughs. Her uniform is new. She's so clean. 'It's the cure.'

My lips move around the words. *The cure.*

'You didn't know?' she asks. 'It's amazing how many people don't know. Heaps have gone animal, I guess. Whole town back there. Army and everyone. Completely clueless.' I squint against the glare of her voice. 'That's why we're supposed to go around and hand them out, not just chuck them at people. It doesn't take long — fifteen minutes you'll notice a difference, a few hours and you'll be fixed. It's compulsory to take it. We're allowed to use force. If we have to.' She touches a black box at her hip.

I shake the packet to hear it rattle.

What is

it.

'It's medicine, Sue.' I peer at the soldier. Black glasses covering her eyes. Doesn't even seem to notice the dingo. 'Have you taken it?'

The soldier looks uncertain. 'We're not supposed to until the last.

So we can communicate with the animals if we have to. Some people couldn't wait, though.' She glares again toward the jeep. 'It totally works.' She pulls a square bottle of water from the pocket in the leg of her pants and unclicks the lid. 'We've had one hundred per cent success rate in a case study involving sixty people aged between eighteen and eighty-three.' I recognise the water from aeroplane meals. Sue's interest blooms again.

I

can drink to

water.

'Think I'll wait until —'

The soldier puts her hand to her hip again. I've forgotten the word for that black box. 'You need to take it now, madam. I have the authority to use force.'

(Take

its face.)

The soldier tightens her grip on the box, and the word comes back to me: taser. I reach down to touch Sue's spiky ruff with my bad hand, mauve and rosy against the tan. Sue looks up at me, swallows.

Is this its

friend.

'She's helping us, Sue. I think. I mean,' I turn back to the woman, 'what will happen to me and —'

'You'll be well,' the woman tells me firmly. 'You'll go back to your normal life. You can get that hand seen to before it falls off. Tie up your pet. It'll be over. You got a family somewhere?'

My old mum with her crow talk. Room full of dears with their stockpiles of wishes and an in-house cook. They'll be dead. They'll be having a sherry party. They'll have flown off with the crows. Another blowfly screams past, gagging at my face.

SUCK IT AND FUCK IT.

It lands near my eye and there's a release:

SUCH JOY.

I swat at it. From the sky, the birds note,

Piss.

Piss lights the ground.

I can see it.

SUCK IT.

Is this its

friend.

Its friend can

fuck off.

The soldier gives a brisk wave at the jeep. The door opens and a massive leg and a stun gun appear. The woman reaches into her pocket and pulls out another white box. This one has a needle inside.

Poison

anus.

The soldier flicks the needle with a practised nail. 'Easier if you just take the pill, but anyway.'

Sue's got her wolf teeth ready:

Prick its friend

in the eye

hole.

The man at the jeep readies his stun gun.

'Hold up. Wait a second. Here.' I kneel and pour some of the water over Sue's mouth. She tilts her muzzle, licks it from the air. Haunches calling,

Forever.

Sue first, then me. The white pill the size of a flattened pea. I put it on my tongue, then fill my mouth with the water and let it wash like first rains down my throat. The soldier waves the man in the jeep away. Moves closer.

'Show me. And under your tongue. Good. Keep an ear out for more instructions. From the government. You'll be able to hear them properly now without all —'

A horn blast from the jeep makes the woman and Sue jump.

Dick

dancer.

'Dickhead.' The soldier backs away. Flashes a smile that shows how recently she was in high school. I watch her spin, jog. The jeep skids, and the dust rushes up again. The pale red of the side of the road and the bitumen.

Sue and me. My hand in her fur. We keep walking. What else is there to do?

Stay

quiet. Stay

still.

I could throw up that pill. I could vomit it up like the fly and talk with Sue, until.

SUCK.

Piss.

Is that its

friend.

'Sue.'

Follow

me.

'Sue.'

I'm the

Shiny One.

Come

on Cat

Dog.

'I just —'

Bad. Do

it.

I do, I follow.

There,

says Sue.

'Where?'

I look behind me but don't know what I'm supposed to see. My stomach hurts. Sue's nose is pointed at me, her tail sweeps the air, whispering. I can't quite make out the words.

'What's that, Sue?'

There.

I look down at myself. Same ripped, stinking ranger shirt. 'Something on me?' I can't see or hear anything.

Where has it

gone.

'Well, whatever it was, can't have been important.' My mum used to say that when I couldn't remember what I was talking about. The birds are still flapping around above us, but it's hard to see whether their wings are saying,

Follow

or

Lead.

Then, they fall quiet.

'Hey, Sue. Sue. We should find something to eat. Where should we sleep? What do you think, Sue?'

Her ear moves. She glances up but doesn't say, *shut up* or *stop barking.* I squint at her. Body quiet but not in her wolf way. I can see her tail move, her ears twitch, her eyes on me, but I can't quite make out the words.

There

or

Here.

My guts churn. The quiet drills into my ear canals until quiet is all I can hear. Nothing from the birds. The bugs gone to ground. The rabbits stunned in their burrows. The sheep hushed in their field. Roos struck mid-bounce. I move my face around, trying to catch something. A whisper here. A squawk and a buzz.

'You hear that, Sue? You hear that nothingness?'

She shivers, and her paw presses the ground.

I'm the

kin,

she whispers. Stares at me with amber eyes. Flecks of gold on gold leaf on solid rounds of gold. Not wolf. Half-breed dingo show dog trying to say something. Telling me to go somewhere with her, about the food, or the flies. The highway. I grab her. She doesn't say whether that's okay or not so I grab her. The need to hold on to her gets me in the heart. Seems that one of those rats got inside and is trying to gnaw his way out. I pick through Sue's fur, searching for whispers. Hairs yellow at the end, fading to white, and then pocked black skin. A flea — so quiet now, contained — clings to that flesh. I cling too. A whine in Sue's throat.

'What is it, Sue? What do you want to say?'

She starts panting. I wait for the meanings to dribble off her tongue. Sit there on the road edge holding her like that for I don't know how long. Then I put my face to her side and try to hear if there are babies in there, curled like the bean she once was. Dingo dog babies. Some Sue. Some other. Does she want them? Does she know?

'I always told Kimberly that I'd ask you something,' I mumble into her fur. 'Now is as good a time as any, right, Sue?' The silence roars. 'I said I'd ask what you want. What do you want the most out of anything? You'd want a pack, wouldn't you? A pack of your own to run with. Or all the food you could eat so you wouldn't have to hunt for it. All the food I could eat too. If we had that, you wouldn't have to look after me. Would that be better, Sue? If you didn't have to, you know, mind your Jean? I'm your good Cat Dog, aren't I.' A bug scoots past, buzzing, mysterious. I let go Sue's face and jam my fingers down my throat. Retch and retch but nothing comes out. Not even a rat. Sue watches, head cocked. When I was pregnant with Lee, I felt full, like the universe was coming together right in my belly. Then he was out, and real, and I loved his separate little body like I'd go mad with it. But

Graham had to tell me to stop clawing at the empty space he left. I rip, now, at my face. The universe gone. My empty ears, my empty nose, and my eyes. Can't taste what Sue's talking about, or feel it in my pores. Imagine her saying,

Where is

it.

Where.

But I can't be sure. 'I'm here,' I tell her, in case she did say it. Case she's listening. 'I'm right here —'

The dingo licks her lips, looks away.

ACKNOWLEDGEMENTS

My eternal thanks to my spectacularly supportive partner, my heart: Tom Doig. Thank you for playing the long game, in life and love.

Thank you to my family, Anne Whisken, Hayden Whisken, Gavin McKay, Rachel Greaves, Granny Judy, Jenny Gill, Harry Doig, Alice Doig, Luke Mcannalley-Shaw, Jack Doig, and Jeanne Marie Colé. As well as my aunts, uncles, and cuzzies from the Hodgson, McKay, Gill, and Doig clans.

And the children! Thank you for being your spectacular selves, my nieces and nephews. Your brilliant minds and humour give me the courage to keep writing. Thank you, Sae, Erryn, Asha, Finn, and Lana. Thank you, Kenai, Lyra, Kyrie, and Celeste.

Thank you, my dear friends and your extraordinary children and animals: Brea Acton, Peter Arena, Emilie Zoey Baker, Kelly Chandler, Tom Dunstan, Michelle Ferris, Sam Gifford, Robert Harding, Pete Haydon, Bella Li, Michael Nolan, Phil Smith, Amy Spiers, and Sean M. Whelan.

I was so lucky to find a home for this book with the Scribe family. To be on the same page, every page, with Marika Webb-Pullman has been a wonderful dream. And I can't give enough hugs to the rest of the Scribe Aus and UK teams, especially Henry Rosenbloom, Cora Roberts, Chris Grierson, Sarina Gale, Laura Thomas, Chris Black, Adam Howard, and Colin Midson.

Thank you to the early and late readers and advisors, especially Luke Anderson, Clare Archer-Lean, Philip Armstrong, Romy Ash, Collin Bjork, Kelly Chandler, Tom Doig, Henry Feltham, Victoria Feltham, Anna Krien, Lisa Lang, Evelyn Meisell, Max Milne, Anne Whisken, Hayden Whisken, Charlotte Wood, and Selena the dog.

This book wouldn't have been possible without the support of the writerly geniuses in the University of Melbourne Creative Writing Department. Kevin Brophy and Amanda Johnson, my supervisors: thank you! Thanks also to Barbara Creed, Elizabeth MacFarlane, Radha O'Meara, and Eddie Patterson, and the Knowing Animals Reading Group, especially Hayley Singer, Lynn Mowson, and Susan Pyke. Thank you also to my wonderful colleagues at Massey University; your warmth and creativity means the world.

When I was in a rather deep hole of illness and despair, a number of people and organisations shone some bright lights down. Thank you to Women of Letters, The Boon Companions, Melbourne Writers Festival, The Emerging Writers Festival, Writers Victoria, and The Wheeler Centre, along with The Readings Foundation and Wheeler Centre Hotdesk Fellowship.

I am indebted to many authors and their words, especially *Dog Boy* by Eva Hornung, *Bear* by Marion Engle, *The Conversations of Cow* by Suniti Namjoshi, *Diary of a Steak* by Deborah Levy; the short stories 'Water' by Ellen van Neerven and 'The Author of the Acacia Seeds' by Ursula K. Le Guin; and Val Plumwood's essays on 'Being Prey' and 'Babe: the tale of the Speaking Meat'.

Thank you so much to the staff and Traditional Owners at The Northern Territory Wildlife Park as part of the Artist-in-Residence program, especially Natalie Hill, Shael Martin, and Jasmine Jan, as well as Matt Robbie; and thank you to The Centre for Great Apes, and the captive and wild nonhuman animals in these sanctuaries and beyond for their generosity and expertise. A Marten Bequest Travelling Scholarship supported these creative research trips.

Extra special thanks to Bucket (magpie), Katie (wallaroo), The Mosquito, and Elsie (dingo).